Anchored Hearts Vol. 1

Letting Go

International Bestselling Author

J.M. WITT

Acknowledgments

Words will never be enough to express my gratitude to those who have supported me along the way.

To my husband: Your support is what gives me strength.

To my children: You remind me that it's ok to dream.

To Melanie, my friend and CP: Thank you for being there every step of the way; critiquing, laughing, and plotting with me. I look forward to doing it again.

To my friends: Your encouragement is more uplifting than you know.

To all the bloggers, fellow authors and my fans: Thank you, thank you, thank you! Without you I never would've made it this far.

Letting Go

one

Blackbird

~ CASSIDY ~
May

IT WAS A COOL, SPRING SATURDAY NIGHT. I had just been promoted to Junior Event Planner at Bea and Cecily, more commonly known as B & C, and I was out to celebrate. My 'boyfriend' was performing at the Blue Horse for the first time. My best friend, Holly, was dating the band's front man, Sam, and she was the happiest I remember seeing her in all the years we'd been friends. I wasn't sure it would last, but time would tell.

We got to the bar, which was an unfamiliar one to us, and took our seats. Holly was crooning about Sam and I was *trying* to listen. After our drinks arrived, she mentioned that the bar was just purchased by a friend of Dan's. I simply shrugged my shoulders and smiled, vaguely remembering her saying that Dan and the new owner went to high school together. If she mentioned a name, I didn't catch it.

Holly was also celebrating. She had recently gotten a job at an art gallery. She was a free spirit, which tended to get her in trouble from time to time. It was probably what drew me to her like a moth to the flame. She was out-going, artistic, and had mountains of confidence— knew how to love and live fast and hard. The fact that she was also an orphan had made her super independent; she'd been supporting herself since she was seventeen.

My upbringing was the opposite of Holly's. I grew up in a middle-class family, with an older brother, a mom and a dad. We had our share of drama just like every other family. I went to school with the same kids from elementary school all the way through high school. *That wasn't necessarily a good thing.*

I was with Dan, the bassist, for a few weeks by the time that night rolled around. Meeting Dan had been a setup, which I normally hated, but there we were. I remembered Holly asking me, "What's the worst that could happen?" a few weeks prior to meeting Dan.

What a loaded question. I over analyzed anything and everything. Holly was one of those people who could just let go; I truly envied that quality. She was always telling me, "Just let go, Cass! Have some fun."

Currently I was preoccupied, staring at the tall drink of water that had just walked out of the back room. *God, he was hot!* He was on his cell, clearly in a heated conversation. He had me completely captivated and I couldn't take my eyes off him. Close to six and a half feet tall, his face was *clearly* chiseled by the hand of God. Great nose, cheekbones and a jaw line covered in a dusting of hair. It was obvious that he worked out; he was built like a linebacker with broad shoulders and that perfect V shape that many athletes are able to maintain.

"Hey, I'm talking to you! What are you looking at?" Holly pulled me from my trance just as the object of my desire turned his back. *The view was almost as nice as his front—if that damn shirt wasn't hiding his ass from my hungry eyes.*

Holly followed the nod of my head. "Damn! He's got to be close to seven feet tall. I wonder who that is." She seemed just as intrigued as I was.

I rolled my eyes at her exaggeration of his height. "Just because you're a dwarf doesn't make him a giant. He's perfect!" I could hear Foo Fighters playing overhead, though I don't recall what song. Holly continued to admire him until Sam walked over with Dan following close behind. The night proceeded like any other. The band performed three sets while I drank too much and danced too little. I couldn't stop my eyes from searching for *him* all night.

A WEEK LATER we were at the Blue Horse again. Dan walked over to Holly and me, in between sets, with Sam and the object of my lust behind him. *Oh shit!*

"Guys, this is James, he's the owner. We go way back." Dan smacked James on the shoulder, which was a feat considering the height difference. James didn't look amused and only took his eyes off mine long enough to introduce himself to Holly. He then held his hand out to me.

"And you are?" Is there such a thing as eye-fucking? 'Cause if there was he was doing it. I felt myself blush when I took his hand. Electricity ran up my arm and down to my core.

"This is my girl, Cassidy." I wanted to shout at Dan *'I'm not your girl just because we're sleeping together.'*

James held onto my hand a little longer than necessary, running his thumb back and forth across the back of it. He looked down at our joined hands and I followed his gaze. He was trailing a finger over the blackbird tattoo on my wrist, studying it intently.

"Blackbird, it suits you."

I was speechless, mesmerized by the green of his eyes and envious of his long dark lashes. His touch sent goose bumps up my arm and no one seemed to notice except the two of us.

Similar encounters happened several more times over the following weeks. James and I had various run-ins at the bar, in the back lot, and at the front door. Each time he would shake my hand and call me 'Blackbird' and I would remind him of my name, to which he would simply smile. I welcomed the contact each and every time, sometimes seeking him out purposely, and he always left me wanting more.

June

MY WHOLE 'RELATIONSHIP' with Dan was a blur of late nights and early mornings—mostly spent with him, Holly, and Sam. The three of them were a great and horrible influence on me all at once. Every morning that damn alarm clock went off I regretted my late night shenanigans, but at least I was in my own bed. One thing I insisted on with Dan was that I stay at home on work nights. Soft Rockets (yes, that was the name of the band) had gigs every Friday and Saturday. I looked forward to Saturday every week; the day I could finally sleep in.

On that muggy Friday night I walked up the steps after a long day at work. When I walked inside the apartment that Holly and I shared, I could hear my iPod blaring _White Houses_ by Vanessa Carlton, _again_.

Holly played it constantly and I was getting sick of listening to it. I could hear Vanessa shrieking all the way down the hall.

Our apartment was a dump and not in the best part of town, but it was ours. I met Holly at The Diner almost five years ago. I was looking for a job while taking classes when I met her. We got to talking one night while I was in my usual booth studying and she mentioned they were looking for another waitress. I needed the money and took the job. We hit it off immediately and we had been inseparable ever since.

Dropping my purse on the table, I headed to Holly's room after turning down the music. I threw myself on her bed as she poked her head out of her closet, "How long do you need? They go on at 9!"

I let out an exaggerated sigh. "You sure Sara can't go? I'm wiped out."

Sara introduced Holly and Sam. She was a friend of Holly's from the art gallery. I slept poorly the night before—another case of insomnia—as images of James raced through my head. Besides being tired, I wasn't up to seeing Dan. Our arrangement was completely casual and I'd already seen him three times that week. I wasn't even sure how much longer I wanted it to last. However, I *didn't* mind the thought of seeing James. We eye-fucked each other every chance we got. I was always in a better mood after laying eyes on him. *I'm a horrible person.*

"Cassidy Charles! You are not backing out on me now! Get your ass in your room and put on something nice and sexy!"

Nice I could do. Sexy? Had she met me? I obeyed on a chuckle. I really shouldn't have been so opposed to the whole thing. One of my favorite things to do was go to a bar and listen to local bands. I dragged myself off her bed and headed to my room.

I strolled to my closet and proceeded to try on half a dozen different shirts. I went 'bold' and settled on my khaki dress shorts, a nude cami and a low cut sheer lavender tank with a sequined hem. I pulled my hair up in a loose bun, with a few strays circling my face, and put on my dangly silver earrings. I touched up my makeup, darkening it around my eyes. Now what shoes to wear? That was always the worst part. I was a clumsy fool and decided to play it safe with some silver ballet flats.

"You are *not* wearing those shoes!" Holly snuck into my room and caught me off guard. The girl was a pro in heels. She could walk down the beach in stilettos and not wobble at all. Me? I wobbled in my tennis shoes.

"Holly, you can't be serious. I hate heels and heels hate me. You know this!" And I certainly didn't feel the need to add any inches to my height that night. Dan wasn't much taller than me and I was uncomfortable towering over him. What I wouldn't give for a *tall* guy, like James.

I heard Holly, 'eh-hem' so I looked up and my jaw dropped, no longer oblivious to what she was wearing, as she did a spin for me. It *must* be love. I had never seen her go to so much trouble for a guy; she had pulled out all the stops. She was wearing a short green backless dress and six inch heels, her blonde hair, with highlights the color of the rainbow, sat just below her shoulders with a section pulled up on top. She looked great.

"Is that new? How serious are you about Sam? Or are you just serious about his doggy style?!"

"Ha-ha, you're killing me! Yes, it's new. Don't you have a dress you can wear? And maybe it *is* serious, and not just about his doggy style," she winked.

I blushed and responded, "You know I hate wearing dresses, especially to the bar! And I don't want to hear any more about Sam's doggy style!" I wasn't naïve, but not that experienced either. Dan had proven to be just another 'okay' lover on a short list. I was beginning to think 'great' lovers didn't exist.

"Hasn't Dan shown you his doggy style yet? At least put on some heels."

"Holly Martin, I'm not some cheap and easy girl like you! Easy, yes; cheap, NO! You know I don't kiss and tell."

We both laughed, knowing my statement was false. I rifled through my shoes and found my most comfortable heels; closed-toe nude wedges. They would have to do. I double checked myself in the mirror and smiled at myself in approval. I threw the ballet slippers into my purse, just in case.

That night the city was buzzing and the breeze coming in off the lake was a welcome one. Summer seemed to arrive early with record highs. We took a cab to get to the Blue Horse early. On the ride to the club I couldn't help but wonder if James would be there. I remembered the first night I saw him and all the subsequent nights after.

"Cassidy, come on. We're here." I had spent the entire cab ride daydreaming. We headed into the bar and snagged our usual high-top table beside the stage. Holly set off looking for Sam while I ordered our usual—Corona for Holly and a fuzzy navel for me.

I rubbed my tired eyes and put my glasses back on. They were sexy, sleek and easier to deal with than contacts in a smoky bar. I couldn't handle these smoky bars for long without wanting to rip my eyes out. Who was I kidding? I was a complete hypocrite. I always ended up stealing cigs from Holly when out at the bar. My dad would kill me if he knew.

Gazing around, I listened to the drone of the sound system playing *Shelf in the Room* by Days of the New. That had to be close to a dozen times, if not more, in the past six weeks the band had played there. The place could certainly use a face lift. Peanut shells scattered the tattered floor and several of the tables and chairs needed replacing or at least refinishing. The restrooms were on the other side of the bar directly across from us at the front of a long hallway. Further down the hall there was a side door leading to an office and then a door leading to the back lot.

I heard some cursing and loud bangs and looked to the back door. The guys were lugging in the final pieces of music equipment. Holly came strolling in on Sam's heels. He was carrying a guitar case and Holly was carrying his bag. Sam was about my height, a little too thin, with dark hair that could use a wash and a cut.

I couldn't help but look around for James. I immediately felt guilty because of Dan, but then reminded myself that Dan and I were keeping it casual, he had said so himself the previous night. Sam and Holly were back at the table making out like horny teenagers. It was embarrassing and at the same time I was feeling a little envious.

I peered over Sam's shoulder when James suddenly appeared. He was on his cell, like usual. As if he knew I was there, he looked up and right at me. His eyes bore into mine before he winked. I clenched my legs together trying to subdue my body's response to him. He pulled his free hand through his hair and tucked a loose strand behind his ear. His hair was long, the color of dark chocolate, wavy and falling down around his face. It was usually pulled back and my hands were immediately itching to run through it. I liked 'hair down' James.

He was wearing dark denim jeans that hugged him just right. His green and blue plaid shirt was unbuttoned just enough to expose a smattering of chest hair. It was un-tucked and the sleeves were rolled halfway up his arms, exposing a tattoo on his left forearm.

My heart stopped as he smiled that smile that made my heart dance between stopping and starting. *What I wouldn't give for a real fuck instead of those outrageous eye-fucks.* I remembered thinking if he wasn't careful, I might lose all sense and tackle him in front of everyone; Dan be damned. That smile completely transformed him from a large, brooding, scary male into a teddy bear. His smile immediately creased into a frown and his attention went back to his cell conversation. He walked toward the back room, clearly frustrated.

"Earth to Cassidy!"

I was startled out of my trance and knocked my water all over the table. I barely missed soaking Sam and Holly with it.

"Dammit! I'm sorry." *Typical.* I cursed my innate ability to terrorize people with my nerves.

Sam and Holly said in unison, "No harm, no foul." They were both used to my klutziness by this point in our friendship.

The waitress came over with a stack of napkins and helped me clean up my mess. "I'm so sorry!"

"Don't fret, girl. It happens all the time." She dropped her voice. "Besides, he is quite something to look at!" Holly and Sam were oblivious to her comments as they were nose to nose *again.* I was mortified that my gawking was recognized by the waitress. *Get it together, Cassidy!*

Blushing, I acknowledged her with a soft laugh and smiled. "Holy hell he's so hot!" The waitress nodded in agreement. The object of our affection came out of the back room, no cell phone in his hand and stormed out the back door. He was gone. The waitress and I sighed in harmony. I wanted to pick her brain about him—maybe she knew more about him—but the band was welcomed to the stage and hearing anything below a scream was impossible.

Soft Rockets was pretty good and I thoroughly enjoyed watching them play. Most of their stuff was covers with some originals added in here and there. When the first set was over, there was still no James in sight. It was never going to happen! He was way out of my league. I should've just ended things with Dan, knowing he wasn't the one for me.

The remainder of the night proceeded like any other. In his usual fashion, Sam dedicated the last song of the second set to Holly. A joke between the two of them that I didn't quite get, but I laughed as Holly pulled me on the dance floor as the first guitar riff started. They were covering *Bad Girlfriend* by Theory of a Deadman.

Holly and I headed to the bathroom after the song ended. She stole the first available stall as I shouted at her, "Hey, I was first!" We both laughed as I waited my turn.

"I'll meet you out back, Cass!" She smiled as I took over her stall once she exited.

"Sure thing, Hoe!" She laughed as she left the bathroom.

I finished up, washed my hands and retouched my lip gloss. I recognized the song playing over the loud speakers; Our Lady Peace was blaring *Somewhere Out There*.

I was fixing my shirt while walking out of the bathroom and rammed face first into somebody's shoulder and upper chest. I would've crashed back into the bathroom if it wasn't for his hands on my upper arm and around my back; they were the only things that kept me steady.

"Shit! Sorry about that!" I said it before I even bothered looking up. Whoever the guy was, he was tall and built. My eyes were level with his throat.

"You should watch where you're going, Blackbird." That deep resonating voice, with a slight hint of gravel teased my ears and his sweet breath feathered down my face. I inhaled deeply before looking up, breathless. It was James with that smile on his face. *I'm clay, please mold me.*

My heart started thrumming a million miles a minute. My skin felt on fire where his hands were. His beard was a little thicker than it was six weeks ago, but not overgrown at all. He smelled delicious; I just wanted to bury my face in his neck and take a big whiff.

"Are you alright?" Now he looked concerned at my lack of speaking.

"You smell divine!" *I couldn't believe I just said that.* I briefly rested my forehead on his shoulder, humiliated. *What the hell is wrong with me?* I quickly raised my head, remembering I didn't know the guy. I mean, we'd been eye-fucking each other for weeks, said 'hi' a few times, but I didn't *know* him. "Yes, I'm fine, thank you." I gently pushed my hands against his chest as I tried to regain my composure.

He chuckled and for the first time, I noticed that he had a scar above his left eye that slashed through his eyebrow. I loved his eyes; the vibrant green sucked me in every time. He slowly removed his hand from my back while the other remained on my upper arm. The loss of his hand on my back was almost unbearable, like someone detached a piece of me.

"So, you and Dan, is it serious?" He was shameless—and maybe interested?!

The question caught me a little off guard. I responded with, "I d-don't know? You have a better offer?" My stomach was fluttering so viciously and I couldn't believe how brazen I was being.

He removed his lingering hand from my upper arm and smirked. He took my right hand in his and caressed my tattoo. That electricity was there again, zapping our hands and sending shivers up my arm and down my spine, "Maybe I do. Cassidy, in all seriousness there's something I've been meaning to talk to you about."

I grinned uncontrollably when I said, "Oh yeah, what's that?" He stilled, continued to hold my hand in his and then looked somber. Maybe he *was* serious.

He took a deep breath and then let out a loud sigh. God, he looked nervous. Suddenly, all that could be heard was the *POP, POP, POP* of a gun followed by screams.

two

Salvage

~ CASSIDY ~

Everything instantly became a blur. After several moments, I was aware of James covering me as we hunched on the floor. One hand held my face to his chest and the other circled around my back. His masculine, clean scent assaulted my nostrils while my hands covered my ears. When I removed them I realized it was eerily quiet except the music blaring from above. The next few seconds felt like hours.

"Are you ok?" He ran his hands over my body out of concern. He returned his hands to my face, seeking acknowledgment in my eyes that I was ok.

"Yes, yes I'm ok." We started looking around trying to gauge where the gunfire had come from.

At the same time the back door opened and the drummer, Mike, came running in. He was screaming for someone to call an ambulance.

James looked at me, startled, and pulled his cell out of his pocket and started dialing. Mike's face was white, an utter contrast to the red that covered his hands. As realization hit me, I pushed away from the man protecting me and ran toward Mike.

James was right behind me yelling into his cell. "Yes, the Blue Horse on 7th street! Shots fired! Yes, people are hit! NO, I don't know how many!"

Mike was in shock when I reached him, barely coherent. He mentioned that he was on his way inside when he heard the shots. He confirmed my fears when he said that Dan, Sam and Holly were all hit. I ran past him and made my way out the back door.

I froze in my tracks; everything seemed to move in slow motion as I took in the chaos surrounding me. Dan was lying in the street and Holly and Sam were on the sidewalk. Sam was the only one moving, doing an army crawl over to Holly and leaving a trail of blood in his wake. Several bystanders made their way around the building and were shaking their heads in disbelief.

I sensed a hand on my shoulder right before I made my move toward Holly and it fell away. I was holding Holly's head in my lap, willing her to wake up, when the police and ambulances arrived. Suddenly there was an arm around my waist, pulling me away from Sam, Holly, and Dan as the paramedics got to work. I started batting at the unwanted arm around my waist, realizing immediately my attempt to get free was futile. I turned into my captor's chest and realized it was James.

SEVERAL HOURS LATER, Calvin walked me up the steps to his townhouse, dragging my suitcase behind him. Having a cop for a big brother was a blessing and a curse. I was feeling broken and humiliated all at the same time. How did I get into this mess? How did I end up in the back lot of a bar covered in blood? I started recounting every moment I had spent with Dan and Holly both. Calvin interrupted my thoughts.

"You can take my room. I'll take the couch." I knew better than to disagree with him. We already had a brief argument, which I clearly had no energy for, about me staying at his place. He walked me to the bathroom and turned on the shower. "You got it from here?" His hand was rubbing my upper arm out of concern.

"James," I whispered.

"Who?"

"Calvin, where's the guy from the bar that was with me? He brought me to the hospital."

"Cass, when I got to the hospital, I found you huddled in a corner all alone. What guy?" He stared down at me with a puzzled look on his face, clearly thinking I had lost it. He wasn't very attractive with his face all screwed up in concern.

Holly always raved about his preppy good looks. Cal was six foot two, with dirty blond hair, usually very clean cut, tan and probably not an ounce of fat on him. He worked out religiously. The only feature we shared was Dad's blue eyes.

"Never mind, it's not important. I got it from here." My voice was barely above a whisper. *He'd left me all alone?* Calvin gave me another hug, kissed the top of my head and left me to tend to my shower.

Looking in the mirror, I barely recognized the broken woman staring back at me. My face was tear stained, streaked with mascara and a couple drops of blood on my cheek. My clothes were ruined so I tossed them in the waste basket. Then I noticed my hands were stained with blood, which caused me to start shaking again.

Several minutes later I was still sitting on the floor of the tub, willing the water to wash that night away. I checked my hands again to make sure every drop of blood was gone. I stared at the blackbird on my wrist and couldn't help but think of James. I didn't understand where he had gone. I reached to crank the hot water up realizing the cold dial was almost off entirely. I didn't normally like HOT showers, but that night, I just couldn't get it hot enough. There was a knock on the door.

"Cass, I have some clothes for you. Is it safe to come in?"

Is it safe? I didn't know if I'd ever feel safe again. "Yes, Cal. Just put them on the sink. Thanks."

The door creaked open. "I'll be in the living room if you need anything." I grunted my approval and the door closed again.

I wasn't sure how Cal got me back to his place in one piece. I didn't remember him finding me huddled in a corner at the hospital, just him carrying me out. I *did* remember turning into my captor's chest and realizing it was James. I broke apart in his arms; he left to get coffee and never returned. Cal and his partner Frank arrived shortly after and then I recalled Cal lifting me and taking me to my apartment. Cal walked me in and helped me pack a bag; I was no help at all. I could barely form the words to say 'yes' and 'no' when he asked what to pack for me.

After several more minutes in the shower the heat started to fade away. It was a lost cause; I had drained the water heater. I turned off the water, opened the curtain and began shivering the minute the cool air hit me. I grabbed the robe hanging on the wall and pulled a spare towel from under the sink for my hair. Thank God Cal didn't live like the bachelor cop that he was. He had all the necessities and he was tidy.

I broke into half a smile when I saw that Cal placed an old Army tee and a pair of his sleep pants on the sink for me. I knew he packed pajamas from my place, but he knew me too well. I used to steal his sleep pants and shirts all the time in high school. It made him crazy, which is why I did it.

I didn't even bother running the comb through my hair before coming out of the bathroom. The only thing I wanted was sleep. I went straight to Cal's room and crawled into bed. Hearing what sounded like reruns of *Cops* coming from the living room, I wasn't surprised. Cal had been a cop for a few years. He was also an Army vet, had a degree in Criminal Justice, but had decided to be a cop. His plan was to be part of the undercover narcotics squad. In an effort to earn his place on the squad, he was currently pulling double duty and working midnights. Listening to him tip-toe around the house while I lay in bed was a welcomed distraction.

I looked at the clock to see it was close to five in the morning. The rays of dawn were nowhere in sight through Cal's blacked out windows. I closed my eyes, but even with them closed, all I saw was the ambulance lights whirling round and round and Holly, Sam, and Dan. *Holly, Sam, and Dan.* I never got to thank James. Eventually I fell asleep with my tears saturating the pillow as I listened to the drone of the TV.

THE DAYS AND weeks that followed the shooting were some of the darkest days of my life. Calvin was taken off the case because of his personal connection, but that didn't stop him from nosing around. He came home a couple days after the shooting to let me know that they had made an arrest, finally.

"They arrested the son of a bitch owner; they found drugs stashed in his office. He was in lock-up when I left today. They think it might've been some retaliation thing with his dealer. We got him, Cassidy." I gazed at him over my cup of coffee, complete and utter shock evident in my expression.

"The owner!?" I felt sick to my stomach and my throat began constricting. James—the hunk I was eye-fucking for weeks on end, who was also the owner—was a druggie? A dealer? *Oh God.* My taste in men was atrocious. Of course he would be bad news; I was attracted to him. Why did I have an affinity for guys that were no good?

"He's some privileged rich boy from the upper west side." He stopped talking after seeing the distress in my eyes. "Don't worry, Cassidy. We'll get him to talk and we'll find out who did this."

A FEW DAYS later, Calvin came home on a tear. He was cursing as he stormed in. "The fucking charges have been dropped. His lawyer got the charges thrown out. It's complete bullshit."

I knew without question to what and to whom he was referring. The tears welled up in my eyes. "Cal, I can't do this. Holly is gone, Sam too, and I can't change it. I know it's your job to find out who did this, but I can't hear about it. It's just too much."

"Shit, Cass. I'm sorry." He walked over to me and pulled me to his chest. "I'm an idiot. I won't bring it, or him, up again." I nodded into his chest.

End of October

I<small>T WAS A</small> F<small>RIDAY</small> and life was back to 'normal'. Of course, normal now had a whole new meaning. Monotony had become my middle name; all work and no play. My life revolved around my job. My favorite time of year was in full throttle. I had the masquerade ball that night and the Children's Hospital auction was the following Friday night, a week from today. Dad's wedding was about a month away and then we had the holidays coming up. I was wholly dedicated to my job and my hard work had paid off. I was several weeks into my third promotion, in as many years, at B & C.

I was running around my apartment like a chicken with my head cut off. Moving before the masquerade and the auction was a huge mistake, but I couldn't pass up the place. I owed my client, Mrs. Whitford, a million thanks; I was indebted to her.

B & C planned Mrs. Whitford's masquerade every year and I was given the lead this year, at her insistence. She sang my praises to my boss, Cecily, more than once and had insisted she'd only work with me from that point forward. She also knew I wanted to get out on my own after I mentioned that I was apartment hunting. While I loved the time with Cal, it was time for me to spread my wings again. And living with my brother would kill any chance of me having a love life, if I ever *tried* to have one again. And staying in the apartment I'd shared with Holly was out of the question. There were too many memories there.

The Whitford's owned several properties, so she said, and insured me she had just the place for me. After a few tours of the place, along with some input from Dad and Cal, I took the leap. It was all just too good to pass up considering the price, location, and amenities.

The townhouse was an end unit similar to Cal's, but bigger, and it was in a safer part of the city. It had two bedrooms, two and a half baths, an office, and three parking spaces including the attached garage! They recently had it completely gutted and remodeled. I had hardly unpacked a single thing in the previous two weeks because I was so busy at work. The only things I had put away were most of my clothes and a few kitchen essentials.

Dad and Cal brought boxes upon boxes from my storage unit and from home. I couldn't wait to really dig in and start settling the place. Chessa, on the other hand, loved all the boxes and new hiding spaces. She jumped off one box and into another scaring the crap out of me. I splashed my coffee and cursed the three month old tortoise hair kitten. She had been a house warming gift from Cal and Dad.

"Where did I set my blasted wall charger, Chessa?" Having my wall charger for my laptop and phone were imperative if I was going to make it through that day. I eventually found it in a box with my dishes. *Seriously, Cassidy, with the dishes?*

I looked at the clock on the microwave. "Shit, shit, shit!" It was already a quarter to nine. I told Lena to be at The Benedict hotel no later than nine and here I was, her boss, running late. It would take me fifteen minutes just to get downtown, if I was lucky. I had a quick meeting with J.J. Benedict to finalize a few things for the masquerade and the auction next week. All eyes were on me.

Last year, Cecily and I did that event together and the year before that I was her personal assistant. I didn't know why I was so nervous. The auction was the one I should've been worried about. *Cassidy Charles, you got this!* I texted Lena to let her know I was on my way and to stall Cecily if she decided to show her face for the meeting. Cecily liked to show up to client meetings with no warning. Lena responded with a wink, symbolizing that we were in the clear. *Love that girl!*

I grabbed my laptop bag, my purse, a garment bag holding my dress, and my overnight bag. "Good Lord, what am I forgetting?" Keys and phone were in my jacket pocket, Chessa had been fed. "Well, it's too late now. Wish me luck, Chessa." She responded with a purr and dove back onto the pile of boxes consuming my living room.

I MADE IT downtown in record time, listening to news radio. I took a mental note to find my iPod that weekend. Pulling into valet, Andy greeted me with a smile. He helped me out of my car while a bellboy rushed over to help with my bags.

"Miss Charles is with B & C; she's in charge of the masquerade tonight and the auction next week." The bellboy acknowledged Andy, who was the head valet, before he drove off with my car. Andy was a good kid and had been extremely helpful over the previous few weeks. I insisted to the bellboy that I would carry my laptop and purse; I couldn't afford to have them out of my sight.

I rushed inside and hurried over to the desk to get my key. Mrs. Whitford had graciously provided me with a room for the night. I thanked the desk clerk, Sabrina, and turned away from the desk with my purse and laptop bag in hand. Lena was there with a smile on her face and she had a coffee in each hand.

"Dammit, I forgot my coffee at home. You're a life saver, Lena!" I took a swig of my peppermint mocha cappuccino as we headed toward the elevator.

Lena responded with her usual, "No problem, boss!"

"What floor, Miss Charles?" The bellboy had been patiently waiting for me to finish my business at the desk.

I looked at the envelope holding my key card, "Looks like the twelfth floor, room 1204."

"Right away, ma'am." I inwardly cringed at his use of ma'am and Lena and I shared a chuckle. I was *not* a ma'am, not yet! He pushed several buttons, more than normal, on the panel before the elevator began its climb.

Lena and I started hammering out texts as the elevator made its ascent. No Cecily yet. As the elevator door opened, I rushed out without looking where I was going, as usual, and walked right into a buff business suit. *Klutzy Cassidy at her best.* I really *was* a walking calamity. My cell and purse dropped to the floor with my purse contents scattering back on the elevator floor. I managed to save the business suit from my cappuccino.

"Dammit. I'm so sorry, sir." I dropped down and I saw large, tanned hands helping me pick up the contents of my purse. I was absolutely mortified as my birth control pills were handed back to me, along with some gloss and other miscellaneous items. *Cheese and rice, Cassidy!*

"No worries, you should watch where you're going, Cassidy." That deep voice stirred my insides, but I couldn't even look at him because I was so embarrassed. I was certain I was probably as red as my cranberry blouse.

"I'm fine, again, I'm *so* sorry. Thank you for your help." I gathered my items and rushed into the hall without even looking to see who it was I collided with and ran down the hall. *Wait, he said my name. Oh God, he must have thought me the rudest person.* I turned to see who it was, but I was too far away and he was safely inside the elevator. Lena was staring into the elevator, gawking. What had I missed?

The bellboy hurried out, stuffing something in his pocket and stuttering, "S-Sir, absolutely sir, will d-do, sir."

Lena pranced over to me with a huge grin on her face. She asked me, "Don't you know who that was? He's a dream." She was over the moon.

My cell started buzzing again and I rolled my eyes at her. "Come on, Lena, we have work to do." I was sure the caterer, Francis, would be in touch any moment with the most recent catering disaster. I continued walking toward my room and began to wonder if I was on the wrong floor. Not seeing any other entry doors on my side and end of the hall had me confused.

"Are you sure we're on the right floor?" I asked the bellboy.

"Down on the left, ma'am. May I?" He asked for my key and hurried ahead of us, opening a door at the end of the hall.

Lena strolled in after the bellboy and I followed. "Holy hell, Cassidy!"

I walked into the room and couldn't believe my eyes. It *couldn't* be the right room. I looked to the bellboy and he nodded, confirming we were in the right room. I stepped back in the hall, and sure enough it had a plaque with 1-2-0-4 engraved on it hanging by the door.

"Holy hell is right! This can't be right." The bellboy assured me again we were in the correct room. I wasn't sure what was going on, but I didn't have time to investigate. Mrs. Whitford was *way* too generous. I rummaged through my purse for some bills for the bellboy.

"Already taken care of, ma'am." He finished placing my items on the couch and pranced out the door with a smirk on his face before I could object.

Shrugging my shoulders, I let out a squeal as the door closed. Placing my purse on the entry table along with my hotel key, I did a slow spin and took in my surroundings. The suite was decorated impeccably; granite and marble greeted me everywhere. *This was unbelievable.* I'd never stayed anywhere so fancy. There was a fully functioning kitchen with black cabinets, stainless steel appliances and white granite countertops. I ran my hand along the counter, admiring the glints of silver in it. It was a small kitchen, but no expense had been spared. A Keurig coffee maker was on the counter and next to it was a stand full of every flavor of coffee imaginable along with a bowl of apples, bananas, and oranges. I grabbed a banana, knowing I probably wouldn't eat again until later that night. The living room had a deep blue suede couch and two matching oversized chairs facing each other, separated by a very ornate coffee table. The entire right side of the room was glass from ceiling to floor, overlooking the river; the view was breathtaking.

"HOLY SHIT, Cass, come here!"

I heard Lena yelling from what I assumed to be the master suite. I walked in chewing on my banana and gasped in awe. The bedroom was incredible. The king size bed was covered in a silver satin quilt and pillows to match. The headboard was black wrought iron designed like a trellis; it was stunning to look at. I was afraid to even touch it. I walked toward the bathroom to discover a large walk-in closet separating the bathroom from the bedroom.

The bathroom itself was a dream. There was a double headed shower with at least four body sprayers and a rainfall showerhead on the ceiling. You could fit half a dozen people in there! Next to it was a huge sunken tub for two. There was a huge vanity, at least six feet long, spanning the opposite wall with a toilet and bidet at the end.

"Cassidy, I think we're in one of the junior penthouse suites." I nodded my head in agreement. No detail had been missed. Hopefully that was the same with the decorations in the ballroom.

The Benedict hotel had been all over the news in the previous weeks. The hotel had its grand opening the night before last. Unfortunately, I was too busy to make it, swamped with final prep for the masquerade. We were both startled back to reality when our cells started chirping and vibrating in unison.

"Alright, let's get to it! I have a meeting with J.J. Benedict about tonight and next week's auction and then I'll meet you in the ballroom. Please finalize the auction menu and then confirm everything with Francis for tonight." I threw my peel away and we headed down to the main floor, responding to texts as we went.

I MADE MY way across the street and checked in with the security desk. After they confirmed my appointment I headed to the elevators and made my way up. I entered the reception area through the glass double doors and realized the office was eerily empty. I rang the bell that had been left on the counter, noticing hallways leading to my left and right and I looked around hesitantly.

"Hello?"

"I'm in the office, Miss Charles."

I followed the sound of the voice coming from my right and made my way toward French doors. As I walked into the office, I noticed a credenza on the back wall with bookcases on each end and a desk in front. There was a large man standing with his back to me as he shuffled through some papers.

I was instantly aware that the man couldn't be J.J. Benedict. J.J. was older, and this man was, well, not old. He was tall and I noticed dark hair, not grey hair, pulled back and he wore a tailored grey suit.

"I'm supposed to be meeting Mr. J.J. Benedict. I apologize for my tardiness. Did I miss him?"

He turned around with a killer smile on his face and recognition slammed into me like a freight train. "Hello, Blackbird."

three

Redemption

~ CASSIDY ~

I TENSED UP AS MEMORIES flooded through me like a dam had broken. I suddenly felt transported to another time. I was with Holly and we were laughing and getting ready for another night out. We were walking through the bar to find someplace to sit. Then we were chatting before I was distracted by the image of a beast of a man. He had his back to me before he turned and smiled. Those eyes, that smile…the bathroom, Holly, Dan, Sam; it all came back. *You should watch where you're going*…POP, POP, POP…screams, blood, black bags, lights and sirens.

The wind was knocked right out of me. It was him, James. *Why was he here?* He looked completely transformed in that suit. His hair was pulled back and he was sporting several days of growth on his jaw. I felt like a cornered animal looking for a way out. The room began to spin and I couldn't make heads or tails of where the exit was.

It was too much all at once. I couldn't breathe and I quickly felt overheated. He glided to me, cupped my face and tilted my eyes up to his. *God, I'd missed looking at him.* His eyes somehow breathed life back into my lungs. "James?" Tears filled my eyes as a barrage of emotions flowed through me. Love, loss, fear, regret, anger, relief; the list went on and on.

He whispered, "Please don't cry. I saw enough tears fall from your eyes that night to last me a lifetime." He attempted to pull me into an embrace. It then dawned on me that James was arrested for the events that happened that night and I pulled away. "Don't run." I was in complete panic mode, not knowing what to do. He hesitated before letting go.

Get it together, Cassidy. "There must be some kind of mistake. I'm supposed to be meeting Mr. Benedict." My words were barely audible.

The smile returned to his face. "You've found him. I'm Jackson James Benedict III, J.J.'s son."

I took a deep breath as I put some distance between us and smoothed my hands down the front of my black pin stripe pants. I had to get it together. I felt like someone just threw me off a carousel at warp speed. *J.J.'s son?* I looked at him in disbelief.

"Cassidy, I have so much to tell you."

"It's Miss Charles. I think it would be best if I finalize the details of the auction with Mr. Benedict, *your father.* I can wait for him to return or reschedule." Ugh, I was never going to be able to look at J.J. the same way again. His son was the devastatingly handsome bar owning drug user? This just didn't seem right.

"I apologize, Miss Charles. Actually, the auction is my baby this year since it's being held in my hotel. Father met with you previously because I was busy with other business affairs. You'll be dealing with me from now on."

Smug bastard. "I apologize, I was unaware." I was feeling thrilled and worried all at once.

"Please, sit down. Have you had breakfast? I'll make it quick." He motioned me toward a small table as he pulled a chair out for me. There was a tray of bagels, fresh fruit, and a carafe of orange juice with some dishes and cups.

I took my seat, not quite knowing what to do, and he sat in the seat across from me. I could feel his eyes devouring me. I started rattling off details concerning the auction and some items that needed refining. He poured himself some orange juice and was chewing on a bagel. I tried to avoid looking at him as I shuffled through my stack of notes.

"How are you doing?" The question was one full of concern and I wasn't sure how to answer.

"I'm fine. How are you?" I tried to answer with as little emotion in my voice as possible. I had to keep this professional. I picked up my cappuccino and took a sip. He leaned back in his chair with his legs crossed. I couldn't help but take in his physique from the tips of his toes, up his outstretched legs to his groin. I was vaguely aware that I was biting my lip.

"I'm better now that you're here." That got my attention and my eyes removed themselves from his crotch and found his eyes. That smile was my undoing.

The same flutters from months ago were there and I was getting nervous. I decided to pick up a bagel and started grinding on a piece. We sat there for several minutes exchanging glances. He just watched me intently and I pretended to be oblivious to it, to him. When I finished half of my bagel I set the remainder down, "If that's all you need, I think I'll be going." I stood abruptly.

He was at my side immediately as I tried to place the chair back. "Let me help you." He placed his hand on top of mine and I was instantly aware of the warmth moving through my hand and up my arm. I wanted to run away and jump his bones all at the same time. I yanked it away, repositioned my bag and rushed past him.

Before I knew it, I was face first on the floor, nose to nose with the plush cream carpet. *Please tell me I hadn't just fallen to the floor in front of him!* The tears were welling in my eyes from pure embarrassment. I didn't even know what I'd tripped on, probably my own feet. I felt his hand on my elbow trying to help me up.

"Are you ok? You should watch where you're going, Blackbird." His words, his voice, traveled through me and I realized he was the one I barreled into coming out of the elevator earlier that morning and it was also what he had said when I ran into him after leaving the bathroom that night at the bar.

"Stop calling me that. I'm fine." I bit out as I swatted his hand away. I felt a tear roll down my cheek as I stood.

"Cassidy." He held my shoulders and shook me gently to get my attention. I looked up at him and then placed my face in my hands. He pulled me to him and the flood gates opened. Attempting to calm me, he shushed me and stroked my back.

I could've stayed in those arms forever. "This is so messed up. I should go." I tried to push out of his arms, but he refused to release me. His hands were circling my upper arms and he just looked at me utterly disappointed. "Let me go!"

"I WILL NOT!" I jumped in alarm. He looked like he was ready to spit nails. "I apologize, I didn't mean to yell. Cassidy, I don't know what you think of me, but clearly you have the wrong idea. I need to explain."

"Explain what? That your drug habit got my best friend killed and your daddy's money got you off?" I shrieked at him as I shoved against his chest.

He was clearly baffled at my retaliation. His voice dropped to a whisper and he started rubbing my arms. "Cassidy, I swear to you, I had nothing to do with what happened that night. The charges were dropped and not because of my money. The only connection is the fact that I own the Blue Horse. I despise drugs and the havoc they wreak." He released my arms, visibly shaken. He headed to the couch and dropped down, looking defeated.

I didn't know why I hadn't rushed out the door. My intuition was telling me he was honest. I owed it to him to hear him out. Cal had said the charges were dropped. I set my purse and laptop bag down on the couch across from him and placed my coffee and cell on the table separating us. "Mr. Benedict, I'm sorry. Talking about that night is still very hard for me. Can we start this meeting over?"

He looked up with a glimmer of a smile. "Are you okay? That was quite a tumble."

I started laughing. "I'm the worst klutz, ever. It's a serious problem." We were both laughing then. He smiled at me as we sat in silence for several moments. I had to keep this professional; he seemed to read my thoughts.

"So, the auction?"

He pulled me back to reality as I grabbed my notes back out of my bag. "Lena is at the hotel finalizing the time frame and food selections. Everything seems to be in order except one thing that Cecily wanted me to check on." His brow furrowed in question. "The check that we submitted for the ballroom rental was never processed. We can issue a new check if need be..."

"There's no need to issue a new check, Miss Charles."

"Okay, great. I'll let Cecily know it will be processed any day then?"

"Let Cecily know that the ballroom rental fee has been waived. Cecily can give the money to the charity if she likes."

"I'm sorry?"

"We won't be accepting the room rental fee. Consider it our contribution."

I was shocked. "Mr. Benedict, this isn't necessary."

"Please, call me James."

"James, this isn't necessary."

"I know it's not necessary and I don't want to discuss it further."

Well, I wasn't one to look a gift horse in the mouth. "Thank you very much, it's very generous. Unless there's anything else, I should get back to the hotel. The florist will be there soon."

"Cassidy, I'd like to take you to dinner." I choked on my cappuccino and started coughing uncontrollably. He stood up and came back with a bottle of water. He handed me the water as I was getting my bearings back. "Is it that shocking that I'd ask you to dinner?"

I was a little dumbstruck. "Um, well, I just, I…"

He sat down next to me and placed the bottle of water he had just given me on the table and took my hands in his. "Cassidy, I know you felt it all those months ago. I felt it, too, and I still do. A day hasn't passed that you haven't crossed my mind. There's something here," he motioned between our bodies.

I was looking at our hands and it was there, that electricity. I looked to him and a shudder caused me to roll my shoulders. My heart started racing and I clenched my thighs together, trying to subdue the throb between them. Before I could say a word, he leaned in and tucked a loose piece of hair behind my ear. He cupped my face and gently touched my lips with his own.

How many times had I fantasized about that very moment? I accepted his kiss, knowing that if Cecily found out I'd probably get canned. Both of his hands were on my face, lightly caressing. His lips were gentle and felt better than I had ever dreamed. I molded my lips to his and inhaled his sweet breath. His tongue gently ran across my upper lip. I slid closer to him and placed my hands on his lapels. Our tongues began a torrid dance that had my entire body standing at attention. It was a kiss I would never forget and one I never wanted to end.

I worked my hands up to his neck and to the tie holding his hair and couldn't resist removing it. I'd been dying to run my fingers through his hair since that first night I saw him. He encouraged me with a groan and started kissing my jaw while working his way back to my ear.

"James...we should stop," but my actions betrayed my words as I dragged his mouth back to mine.

"Shut up, Cassidy."

Before I knew it he pulled me onto his lap, not sure how he managed it. His hand was on my hip and I could feel his erection straining against my thigh. I felt my own hair fall from its tie as he tugged on it gently. It felt wonderful and I whimpered into his mouth, barely aware of my phone ringing. I slowly pulled my face away from his. "Shit. I have to get that."

"Cassidy, let it ring."

"It could be Cecily," I pled as I tried to slide off his lap, echoing his groan of disapproval. I gave up trying and remained on his lap, straining to grab my phone. I looked at the number, not recognizing it so I sent it to voicemail. "I don't know the number. If it's important they'll leave a message."

I tossed the phone down on the couch beside us as he tightened his arms around me. I needed to be closer to him so I repositioned myself. I straddled his lap as his mouth assaulted mine. I helped him out of his jacket as he started fumbling with the buttons on my blouse. He rolled his hips and hit my core just right and made my stomach drop. I moaned into his mouth and pulled his shirt out of his pants.

"You like that," he whispered in my mouth as he continued rolling and grinding his hips into me. I clung to him and began sucking his ear. "You're making me wild, Cassidy."

"Oh God, I've dreamed of this, of you, for so long."

"Holy hell, I'm so sorry." We'd been caught in the act.

Red handed.

I jumped off his lap and he was up almost as quick, shielding me with his body. I peeked around his shoulder and saw Lena and a security guard standing in the doorway.

The security guard took in the scene and offered his apologies to Mr. Benedict before heading back to the lobby. Lena on the other hand turned her back to us, but not before I noticed she was fifteen shades of red.

"Don't you people knock?" James was furious. "Ray, get back in here." Oh no, he was going to annihilate the poor security guard. Ray made his way back in and was apologizing profusely. "I expect utter discretion, not a word."

"Yes sir, of course, sir." James nodded to him and Ray headed back out. Lena was now facing us and she mouthed '*sorry*' to me and I just shook my head. This was bad and completely unethical.

"Lena, what do you need?" I asked her while tucking my shirt back into my pants.

"I'm sorry to interrupt, I didn't know."

"LENA! It's alright. What do you *need*?"

"Right. Francis is throwing a fit; something about the choice of appetizers."

I released an exasperated sigh. "This man is going to put me in an early grave if I don't put him there first."

"Who's Francis?" I sensed the tension in James' voice. I looked to him seeing he'd already fixed his hair and was putting his jacket back on.

"Just the caterer, nothing I can't handle." I pulled my purse off the table along with my bag, shoved my phone inside and started to leave.

"Cassidy?" James placed his hand on my arm. "Dinner?"

I dropped my voice so Lena couldn't hear. "James, I can't do this. This is unprofessional, I'll get canned. I have a lot to get done for tonight and the auction next week."

"Cassidy, this isn't over. Not by a long shot. You won't get rid of me so easily." He released my arm as I headed out the door with Lena.

"Not a *word* Lena." She nodded as I left James staring after me.

THE BALLROOM WAS spectacular. The hotel sat on the north end of town, lakeside. The ballroom opened up to a beautiful garden that overlooked the river. There were over two dozen gold and crystal chandeliers that hung from the twenty foot ceiling. The center pieces were in their resting spots and thirty tables formed a circle around the enormous dance floor. It was going to be an amazing night for my first masquerade. Last year I hadn't attended the event after coming down with a bug during the final preparations. I was giddy just at the thought of my dress and all the other patrons in their costumes that night.

Cecily was originally against the location choice when I told her we booked The Benedict for the masquerade this year. She was convinced they wouldn't be done with the remodel in time and even booking the auction there was cutting it close. J.J. Benedict had assured me for months that everything would be ready. He was right.

THE REST OF the day was a flurry of double and triple checking all the arrangements. I had to keep Francis in line, secure the floral arrangements, and finalize the seating chart per Mrs. Whitford's specifications. Before I knew it, my time was up. It was just after five and the doors opened at six-thirty with dinner being served at seven. I had to go get ready.

I found Lena to let her know I was headed up to my room. I hated her; she didn't even look like she'd broken a sweat. Me, however, I could feel my blouse clinging to my back. She assured me she'd be up soon to do my hair and makeup. I grabbed my pile of notes, extra brochures, purse and jacket and rushed toward the main elevators.

I tried to organize my pile of crap when the elevator door dinged open. I walked in, still looking down, unaware of my elevator companion.

"Twelfth floor?" I simply nodded because I was so preoccupied with my notes.

I rushed out as Godsmack echoed down the long hallway. I almost dropped the phone trying to answer Cecily's call and cursed Lena at the same time. The girl had great taste in music, but she had to stop changing my ring tones. "Yes, Cecily…"

~ JAMES ~

I ENTERED MY room laughing. Godsmack? Interesting. She didn't look up once to see it was me with her in the elevator and I didn't have the heart to cause her more stress before the masquerade. I threw my briefcase on the couch and dropped down on the other end as I loosened my tie. I knew this day would come, I just hadn't predicted it taking so long.

I was caught off guard in the elevator that morning when she barreled into me and I had to stop myself from calling her 'Blackbird'. She was making this harder than I had anticipated. My head was pounding as I pulled the tie from my hair. Resting my elbows on my knees, I placed my head in my hands and sighed. Even stressed out, she was breathtaking.

I had left her alone twice that night; once when the cops were questioning her and again to grab us some coffee from the vending machine. The last time we were in the same room together she was cradled in the arms of a cop. It was evident I was long forgotten as she was carried out of my life, or so I thought. I later discovered that the cop was her brother and set my plan in motion. Though, I hadn't planned to be kept away from her for so long. She'd haunted my dreams, especially her unforgettable eyes, almost every night since I first laid eyes on her. Now she was just down the hall. This had my father and Aunt Bev written all over it. I remembered my conversation from that morning with Dad.

As the bellboy hurried out I told him to refuse any tip she may offer. He acknowledged and hurried out with her bags.

"That boy is terrified of you, James. What did you do to him?

I ignored his question and sighed.

"When are you going to talk to her? After all this time, James, what are you waiting for? You've avoided her long enough. She's staying in 1204 for the night. Your Aunt Bev assures me she's single on top of being an excellent event planner. Nothing is standing in your way."

I glared at him and decided to ignore him. I knew it was a mistake to confide in him. "I assume Aunt Bev is paying for the suite? Whatever you're up to, DON'T! Besides, I have a meeting with her in thirty minutes." He just chuckled. The man was worse than Mother when it came to meddling. He started to ask me again when I was going to tell her. "Leave it be, Dad."

I hadn't attended the masquerade ball in years. She had to be good if Cecily had given her the reins. I should've stayed away from her, for her sake, but I couldn't, not anymore. And given her response to me at our meeting, she couldn't either. Just thinking about her had me hard as a rock.

I checked my watch. The masquerade began in less than an hour. I finished removing my suit, cranked up the sound system and got in the shower. Still rock hard, I obliged my aching cock and was rewarded with a quick and meaningless release.

I made hasty business of getting ready. GNR was humming through the surround sound system. I shaved off my thickening beard, leaving the goatee, hoping it would help disguise me. I scoffed as Axl started singing about having *patience* while I put my suit on. I pulled my hair back, put on my mask and checked my watch again. I made my way to the elevator and tugged at my tie. I normally hated these functions, but I was hopeful tonight would be different. It was a quarter after six and I thought that maybe she had already headed down when I heard the click of her door.

I immediately went stiff as the ache in my pants was renewed. The shower had done nothing to cool me down. She looked fabulous with her flaming red hair pinned up with a few pieces framing her face. The dress was strapless, black and olive green taffeta. The floor-length gown hugged her curves perfectly and puddled just below her feet. As she approached, I could see that she was feigning bravery as she smiled hesitantly. I was mesmerized in the blue lagoons that were her eyes; her black filigree mask just pronouncing them more.

~ CASSIDY ~

I HAD TO GET down stairs. Lena had left several minutes ago and I had assured her I'd be right behind her. She hadn't inquired about James and I was thankful. I checked myself in the floor-length mirror for the tenth time and recalled dress shopping, which was an absolute nightmare.

After a long day of dress shopping with Lena a few weeks back, she told me about a shop across town that rented designer dresses for all occasions. It was in the posh part of town so I took her word for it. She was an absolute life saver. I needed a masquerade dress and one for the auction. We headed to the shop, and after trying on dozens of gowns, I settled on a one shoulder blue number for the auction and a black strapless gothic ball gown for the masquerade. Both dresses fit like a glove. I had never worn anything so elegant and I was nervous as hell. Lena assured me that I would knock them dead both nights.

I checked my hair and makeup, again thanks to Lena, miracle worker that she was. I was tying my mask when my phone started buzzing again. "Shit." I looked to see it was just a text from Calvin.

Knock them dead, sis!

I smiled at his text while grabbing my evening bag and double checked that my key was in it. "You got this, Cassidy." I made my way out the door.

I froze when I saw a masked man standing by the elevator. "Shit." I tried to catch my door before it locked. *Click.* Too late, I couldn't turn back. The masked man lifted his head and smiled. *Good Lord. Now that was a smile to make hearts melt.* I returned the smile as I walked his way. *Please don't trip, please don't trip…*

I made it to the elevator, without tripping. Whoever he was, he was sex on legs. His dark hair was slicked back and I noticed he was clean shaven except for a goatee. His mask looked like solid steel and did nothing to give away his identity since it covered most of his face. The suit hugged him in all the right places I could see, and was all black except for the green tie that almost perfectly matched my dress. His hands were in his pockets and he flashed an incredible, familiar smile at me. I struggled to keep eye contact and to keep my breathing even.

"Good evening, Miss Charles. You're a vision."

The minute I heard his voice I knew it was him. *Shit!* What was he playing at? "Thank you." I took a deep breath. "I didn't realize you'd be attending the masquerade tonight."

He pushed the down button to the elevator and outstretched his hand toward me. I don't know why I offered my hand to him, but I did. He raised it to his lips and kissed my wrist. His touch sent a thrill through me. His lips lingered a little longer than necessary and I blushed before pulling my hand away. He released my hand as the elevator doors opened. "Shall we?" I stepped in and he followed, pushed the button for the lobby and the doors closed.

He still hadn't answered my question and I wasn't going to press the issue. I turned to him as he closed the distance between us. "You look ravishing."

I tried to maneuver around him and got tangled in my dress. I was instantly aware of his hands on me, one on my upper arm and the other around my back. The hand on my back began caressing my skin leaving me short of breath. We were against the wall when I looked up at him. He wasn't smiling anymore.

"Pardon me." I looked into those green eyes at the same time his masculine scent traveled through my senses. I couldn't help but close my eyes and inhale deeply. I was instantly turned on and scared as hell. *What was wrong with me?*

"You should watch where you're going, Blackbird."

Why did he always call me that? I mean, it was endearing and I kind of liked it. I started mumbling, but before I knew it, that sweet breath of his mingled with mine. I closed the last inch between us as his lips softly pressed to mine. I had lost all sense, kissing a man I barely knew, again. I reached my hands up to his head and freed his hair without thought and started running my fingers through the damp strands. He responded with a groan and deepened the kiss as his hands ran across my back. His hands were like hot stones, velvety hard. His tongue ran across my upper lip which caused me to shudder.

"I've imagined this moment for ages, Cassidy. I've tried staying away." I opened my eyes to see that his eyes were now a vibrant green. I moaned as he rubbed his arousal against my hip. His cologne was intoxicating and I felt like I was in a fog. I ran my fingertips over his smooth cheek.

The elevator bounced to a stop and chimed that we had reached the lobby. He growled, pushing away from me just as the doors opened.

"Cassidy, come on. Cecily is here!" Lena grabbed my hand, oblivious to what and who had just happened to me and pulled me toward the ballroom. I gazed back at James, breathless, and the smile was back on his face. *What the hell just happened?*

four

Masquerade

~ CASSIDY ~

I DIDN'T HAVE TIME TO CONTEMPLATE it further. Cecily was there and she didn't have much to say. I had worked for her long enough to know that when she was quiet, she was pleased. Shortly after the doors opened the guests started piling in. Lena and I were busy welcoming guests when Mrs. Whitford walked in. I made my way over to her, happy to see a familiar face. She was beaming!

"Well done, my girl. Everything looks fabulous. And you look stunning. I almost didn't recognize you with the mask. Why are you still single? I have a feeling that you won't be for long." I blushed as she kissed my cheek and I thanked her for the many compliments. "I just love Halloween. It's my favorite time of year." I chuckled at her enthusiasm. "You remember my daughter Jane."

"Yes, of course."

I shook Jane's hand and we began catching up from the last time we'd seen one another. She was an attractive brunette with brown eyes and stood a few inches shorter than me. She was single, recently moved back home and, I was guessing, around my age. I knew I would love to get to know her better. Something told me we could be great friends.

Everything ran smoothly through dinner. I was seated with Mrs. Whitford, at her request, though I didn't have time to enjoy my meal. James was seated next to Jane and it was apparent to me that they knew one another. I couldn't help but wonder if they were more than friends, or were at one time.

I was still turned on and humiliated all at once. He made me lose self-control too easily. I avoided eye contact, but anytime I tried to sneak a peek at him I would discover him already drilling his eyes into mine.

The wait staff began to remove all evidence of dinner as couples made their way to the dance floor. The music fell right in with a masquerade ball theme; dark and haunting classical melodies filled the air with the occasional gothic rock ballad. Mrs. Whitford was very serious when it came to her annual masquerade.

I had just returned from the powder room and was admiring my handiwork from my spot in the corner; everyone seemed to be having a great time. I was suddenly startled when someone spoke in my ear from behind.

"May I have this dance, Cassidy?"

Startled, I turned to him. His hand was outstretched and he was holding out a blood red peony for me, which he had clearly pulled from one of the floral arrangements. I took it cautiously. Knowing I should refuse him, especially if he was attending with Jane, I carefully placed my hand in his and allowed him to lead me to the dance floor.

I instantly recognized the song that began to play. Phantom of the Opera was my favorite musical. It didn't matter how many times

I saw the musical, I always hoped for a different ending; I'd always felt sorry for the Phantom. I thought if it were me, I'd pick the Phantom every time. *Music of the Night* played its dark seductive notes as James pulled me into a strong embrace and glided us across the dance floor with ease.

The lights were low, his head bent and I could feel his steamy breath grazing my ear. "You look lovely, Cassidy."

The flutters rose up again and my senses were in overdrive. His gravelly voice raked over my being. I could listen to him read the phone book. I felt like a girl who just had her first kiss with a giddy ball of nerves and a flock of butterflies flitting about in my stomach. I rested my cheek on his shoulder and enjoyed the moment; a moment I wanted to last forever, knowing it couldn't.

Gazing around the floor, I saw Mrs. Whitford and Jane looking at us while they exchanged some words. I raised my head and stared into his eyes. He simply gazed back as I abruptly tried to pull away from him.

"I'm sorry, I'm being terribly rude. You should be dancing with Jane, your date, Mr. Benedict."

His hold on me was unbreakable. He would not let go. "Jane is fine. I assure you, she's not my date, Cassidy, you are. And I asked that you call me James."

His voice was meant to give orders, but that didn't mean I'd obey them. "James, this can't happen."

He pulled me tight against him again, whispering into my ear, "It already has, Cassidy."

I was lost in the music and in the warmth of his arms. His cologne had intoxicated me, again. I felt like we were alone in the room, that night only meant for us. The hand between my shoulder blades slowly traced its way to my lower back. He was on the verge of being inappropriate, but I didn't dare stop him. It was beyond intimate what was going on between us.

I whispered, "James, I apologize for the incident in the elevator and your office. I've given you the wrong impression. It won't happen again."

"Cassidy, what are you worried about? We're grown adults indulging in our attraction." The song began its demise. I searched his eyes as the song completed its haunting melody. He pulled me outside to the terrace, dragging me to a corner not yet occupied by other couples. "Cassidy, I know you feel it, too." He pulled his mask off.

"Cassidy! Cassidy Charles."

I turned to see my boss headed my way. There was no avoiding her. I put on my best game face, flashing her a smile. "Yes, Cecily?"

"I knew you had it in you. You did a marvelous job. I didn't realize you were acquainted with James." She smiled at James and he nodded in return. "We have a few things to discuss, but they can wait. I expect to see you first thing Monday." She turned away before I even had a chance to respond. I still couldn't figure that woman out even after working for her for three years.

I was then bombarded by other guests and staff with compliments, questions, and other tasks regarding the entire evening. Getting time alone with James to digest all of what had happened would have to wait. Reluctantly, he left me to my work.

The evening finally wrapped up and I looked for him in the diminishing crowd, but he was nowhere to be seen. Jane came over with a glass of champagne and a huge smile on her face. I happily took the drink and swallowed its contents whole.

"James isn't your date is he?"

She smiled and said, "No, Cassidy, he's yours."

"What is *wrong* with you people?!" I removed my mask and placed it in my purse.

"He knows what he wants and that's you!"

She kissed me on the cheek and congratulated me on a successful night before leaving. I was speechless and didn't have a chance to ask her meaning. I proceeded with some cleanup duties for what felt like hours.

Long after midnight I made my way back to the terrace and the balcony. The lights of the city sparkled like diamonds on the water and it made me remember how Holly loved walking by the river at night. The tears snuck up on me, at the thought of her, and started rolling down my face. I missed her so much. I began to shake from pure exhaustion, or the cold, I wasn't sure which.

My feet were killing me, and before I had a chance to remove my heels, I felt his presence. I didn't need to turn to see his face, I knew it was him. I felt the weight of his jacket fall around my shoulders. The jacket was warm, like him and my shivering began to subside.

I let him pull me to his side as his arm wrapped around me. I didn't have the energy to fight him off and I couldn't explain the overwhelming tug at my heart that told me this was where I belonged. I didn't know this man and I had never expected to see him again. Call it fate, destiny, whatever you wanted. At that moment every trivial thing telling me to run from him seemed to fall away.

I was vaguely aware of the elevator doors opening and realized he was carrying me. *Did I fall asleep?* I reached up and touched his face as the elevator doors closed. He looked at me like the promise of a million stars was in his eyes. "How, what…?"

He gently whispered, "In due time, Cassidy." His response was to a question I wasn't asking. He punched a few buttons on the panel and the elevator started moving.

He leaned down and placed his forehead on mine. I closed my eyes and lifted my chin, welcoming his kiss. It was soft and tentative, almost seeking permission to possess me. I ran my hands over the stubble beginning to form on his cheeks and pulled him closer. He accepted my invitation and his tongue assaulted my mouth. A hint of liquor was on his breath and had me wanting to taste more of him. My entire being was vibrating with need. He released his hold on my legs and I slid ever so slowly down his body as he held me up against him, my feet barely touching the floor.

Our tongues continued dueling and exchanging blows. He traced my upper lip then greedily sucked on my tongue before pulling my lower lip between his teeth. Aphrodite herself must've taught him to kiss. He ruined me; no other kiss had ever compared and never would. I moaned my appreciation into his mouth. Before I was aware of it, he had pivoted and I was now up against the back wall of the elevator. I ran my hands up to the back of his head and wrapped his hair around and through my fingers. He growled in appreciation.

The elevator stopped and alerted us that we had reached our destination. With the speed of a bullet he pulled *Stop* on the panel and we were suspended in air. James pulled me to him and removed his jacket from my arms, throwing it aside. I noticed that his tie was already undone and hanging around his neck. The top few buttons of his shirt were open too and my hands were itching to touch his chest. I could see the muscles in his neck tensing before he lowered his mouth to my jaw and kissed a path to my ear. His hot breath on my earlobe had me reeling.

I grabbed his arms, desperate for something to hold onto. His mouth traveled along my exposed collar bone as my chest began heaving. His hands then encircled my waist. I wasn't used to a man making me feel small and being able to easily overpower me the way he did. I loved it. Even through the layers of my dress I could feel his arousal against my lower abdomen. I gently swiveled my hips which immediately caused him to curse.

"Cassidy?" He pulled back and gazed into my eyes, looking like a starving man in front of a buffet.

It was a question and I answered him. "Don't stop, please," I begged him.

"I don't want to do anything you're not prepared for. If you ask me to stop, I won't lay a hand on you."

I was panting but managed to breathe out, "But I want your hands all over me."

He smiled that devilish smile and pounced on his meal. We were nose to nose, winded like a couple of marathon runners.

"Those eyes have haunted me for months."

His hands cradled my face while his thumbs traced my cheekbones. I was shaking as he wrapped his hands around my neck and feathered them down my shoulders and to my arms. He intertwined his fingers with mine and slowly raised our joined arms above my head. "Don't move." He pulled away and stood to his full height. "That dress is exquisite, like it was made for you."

I couldn't help but chuckle and his eyes immediately questioned me. "It's a rental." He was amused and tilted his head at me. I really needed to learn how to keep my mouth shut.

Finally, he spoke, "We can fix that."

Before I had a second to question him he attacked my mouth once more. He then lowered himself so that he was kissing the top of my chest. He wedged his leg between mine and I shifted slightly, eager for the pressure of his thigh against my pussy. *Damn dress and all its layers.* He knew just what I needed. His hands pulled down on my shoulders so that I was rocking back and forth on his thigh as his groin pressed into my hip. I was humping his thigh like a horny teenager and it was miraculous.

Before I could object, he spun me around to face the elevator wall.

The cool steel against my cheek was a sharp contrast to how hot I was feeling. My hands lowered to my sides.

His hands were on mine again and he guided them up once more, "You make me want to lose control. I told you not to move." I had never been so turned on in my life. One more touch from him and I was likely to explode.

He buried his head in the back of my neck. I let my head fall back to him and his mouth was there, waiting for me. I felt his hand in my hair while the other traveled down my side. His hands were like liquid fire on ice and soon all that would be left of me was a puddle on the floor. He started pulling pins out of my hair while running the other hand along my side and under my breasts. I was trembling with a need I didn't know existed until then. Once he had all the pins out of my hair he circled my hair around his wrist and pulled back before massaging my scalp.

"Oh, God."

"You can call me James, though God is nice, too," he panted in my ear.

I let out a chuckle that was immediately silenced when he bit the curve of my neck. He was still massaging my scalp while his other hand moved down my stomach to my hips. He hit along the inner curve of my hip and I bucked against his arousal. His hand abandoned my scalp and joined the other on my hips as they started trailing down to my thighs. I pressed my thighs tightly together seeking some form of relief as he pressed harder against me. There was nowhere for me to go—pinned between him and the elevator wall—and I was grateful.

His left hand spanned across the space between my hips while his right hand vanished under my dress gaining access to my body. My pussy was a pool of want in my satin panties. Ever so slowly, he trailed his hand back up my leg to my panties. I felt his knee behind me, nudging my legs apart, and I happily obliged. His thumb brushed against my mound while his fingers dug into my thigh. I could already feel the inevitable spiral of my release looming and I took in a sharp breath. He continued massaging my mound, causing my womb to tremble, while running his hand back down my quivering thigh to my knee. He left a sizzling trail of desire behind his fingers. He then skimmed across the back of my knee and it took all of my being not to break out into giggles. My breathing quickened and he instantly heard my body's confession.

"Ticklish are we? Just here or are there other places?"

I simply nodded, unable to form words, and I could feel his smile on my neck. His hand continued to travel the expanse of my leg. Before I knew it, my dress was hiked up around my waist and pulled to the side as he pressed his cock against my rear. *Why was he clothed? I wanted him naked!* Every muscle in my body was flexed. I was going to be sore tomorrow and it would be sweet misery.

His hand possessed my soaking center as he cupped my aching sex while his other hand spread across my breastbone. My entire being tensed even more and I ground into his fingers greedily.

"You're wearing satin, I love satin. You're so wet for me Cassidy. I'm wet for you, too. Do you feel that? My cock is so hungry for you."

His tongue glided across my exposed shoulder blades with the precision of a surgeon's blade. My head was tossing from side to side. I couldn't take much more of this, and the way he talked to me was making me lose control. I was immediately aware of what I had been missing all those years. His hand moved up to circle my neck.

"Don't hold out on me Cassidy. Just let go."

His fingers found their way inside my panties as a shiver ran up my spine. His long fingers ran over my lips to find me wide open and waiting for him. He slid his middle finger inside my trembling core while applying pressure to my pulsating nub, and so began his expert assault. I let out a scream and jolted back against him. I couldn't get close enough to him.

"James, oh God."

I threw my arms behind me desperate for him, grabbing the first thing I came into contact with; it was his hair and I pulled it. He continued biting, sucking and kissing my shoulder, neck and my ear. He was grinding into my behind vigorously and I was like a knotted rope ready to unravel. In and out, in and out, my hips met every thrust of his hand.

"More, James, give me more," I mewled, shocked at my own words.

He knew exactly what I needed without asking further and added a second finger. "Fuck, Cassidy, you're so tight. I can't wait to bury myself in you."

I didn't want this to end—ever—but my body was racing to the top of the hill so fast and I couldn't stop it. It was only a matter of seconds before I fell down and tumbled over the edge. My entire being fell apart panting his name.

five
Exposed

~ CASSIDY ~

H<small>E CARRIED ME OVER THE THRESHOLD</small> of the elevator and before I knew it we were at his hotel door. I vaguely recalled him scooping me into his arms and nuzzling my neck; I was way beyond spent. The day had caught up to me full force and I was still feeling the tremors of my previous orgasm reverberate through me.

"My key is in my breast pocket," he breathed into my ear.

His voice pulled me from my trance and the realization of what just happened hit me. He saw the alarm in my eyes as I took in my surroundings; I must have looked like a deer caught in headlights. He probably thought I was a complete tease since I was the only one who got off. Of course, he may have thought I was a slut for so easily succumbing to his advances.

He stroked my cheek as he said, "Pleasing you was all I wanted. I'm not that guy, Cassidy." He saw the question in my eyes and elaborated,

"I don't have to take every time I give. That's not how I work." I was well aware that things would likely never be the same again.

We walked into his suite which was almost entirely dark. Setting me down on a stool next to the kitchen island, he went to the fridge and took out two bottles of water, handing me one of them. I took the bottle and started drinking and couldn't help but feel awkward. I just 'kind of' had sex with a man I hardly knew. And the things he did to me in that elevator! No one had *ever* done that to me, not like *that* anyway. What must he think of me? I was a cheap, wanton hussy. Oh, God. I had to leave.

"I shouldn't be here…"

He moved like lightning. "Cassidy, don't be embarrassed…" How did he do that? He could read me like a book. "I know I have a lot of explaining to do, but you're exhausted and you need to rest." I started chewing my lip and gazed up at him questioningly. He closed the distance between us and placed his hands on my shoulders, gently rubbing up and down. "You can trust me, Cassidy; I'm not going to hurt you. We won't do anything that you don't want to do." His voice was low and breathy.

Wanting to believe him with every fiber of my being, I hoped beyond hope that my faith in him was well-founded. I wrapped my arms around his waist and rested my head on his chest just as he wrapped me up in his arms and kissed my temple. Several moments later he took my hand and led me to the staircase.

We reached the top of the stairs and a long hallway lay ahead of us. I was so exhausted I didn't notice how many rooms and doors there were. Walking us into his room, he turned the lights on low.

"I'll get you some more comfortable clothes." I stood awkwardly by the bed as he walked over to a chest of drawers. "Are you a t-shirt girl?"

"A t-shirt is fine." He pulled out a gray t-shirt and walked back to me. I looked up at him as he cupped my cheek and turned my face into his touch, savoring it.

He pulled away quickly and handed me the t-shirt, "Let me help you. Turn around."

I willingly obliged him. He expertly released the clasp on my dress and slowly pulled the zipper down. I heard him inhale sharply and a shudder ran through me.

"You're not going to make this easy on me, are you?" He was running his fingers over my back where the zipper had fallen open and laid a kiss on each shoulder blade. "Put the shirt over your head, Cassidy, before I go back on my word."

I understood his meaning and pulled the shirt over my head. I put my arms through the sleeves of the shirt and placed it down over the dress. The shirt practically hit my knees and I chuckled.

"It fits you well," he said sarcastically.

"Maybe if I was ten!" We both laughed.

I held on to the dress and turned to face him. He crouched down in front of me and gently pulled the dress down my legs. I lifted one leg, realizing I still had those wretched heels on. They were lovely, but even after over a week of practice I hated them and wanted to burn them.

I went to lift my other leg out of the dress and lost my balance. He was at a disadvantage, crouched down in front of me. I tumbled forward and took him with me. I found myself lying on top of him, nose to nose, cursing myself and I started to apologize.

He started laughing at me and I wasn't quite sure how to respond. At least he was lighthearted. "You really are a klutz, aren't ya? Are you ok?" His hands ran the expanse of my back while holding on to me.

I started laughing, too. "I'll be fine when these damn shoes are off my feet and out of my life!"

The electricity was building inside me like a dimmer switch being turned to max capacity. Being this close to him was dangerous and we both grew silent. He tucked my hair behind my ear as my heart began hammering against my chest. Just when I thought he would lean in to kiss me, he jumped to his feet, pulling me up with him.

He guided me to the end of the bed and sat me down. "Let's get these off of you." He knelt in front of me and removed my heels. Once both shoes were off he started rubbing my feet and I let out a deep sigh. "Feel good?"

"You have no idea."

His hands worked expertly over the soles of my feet and my Achilles. Abruptly, he jumped up again, walked to the head of the bed and pulled the covers down. He came back to me and held out his hand.

"Give me a minute." I excused myself to the bathroom, as my bladder was in desperate need of relief. Finishing up, I washed my hands and gazed in the mirror. Looking like I'd been hit by a train, I had raccoon eyes thanks to the mascara, eyeliner, and tears. I cleaned it up as best I could and opened the door.

I was breathless.

He had changed his clothes and I missed it. His feet were bare and he'd traded the tuxedo for pajama pants. As I continued to devour him with my eyes I noticed he wore a tank that clung to his well-muscled body. I spotted another tattoo on his upper arm that I couldn't quite focus on in the low light.

He pulled me toward the bed and had me lie down before turning out the light. I heard some rustling of clothes while I relaxed. Wondering if he was removing his shirt, I grew excited waiting to find out and tried to seek him out, but the darkness was blinding. It was by far the most comfortable bed I had ever slept in; I was sure being exhausted helped. The sheets felt wonderful against my naked legs. His scent blossoming around my head made me feel tipsy.

Sensing the weight of his body as he lay down next to me, I waited for his touch when he said, "Goodnight, Cassidy," but it never came. The man had mad skills when it came to self-control. If only I had the energy, I would've pounced on him, but sleep claimed me before I could.

I came to before the sun made its arrival. Slowly, everything from the night before came back to me. His arm was around me as he cradled me to his chest; the warmth was almost insufferable. I turned my head to find he was dead asleep. Suddenly overcome with panic, I decided I *had* to get out of there. I slipped out of the hold of his stellar body and got off the bed with ease. I didn't want to risk waking him so I just grabbed my dress and shoes and made my way out of his room and down the stairs. Finding my purse on the kitchen island, I headed for the door.

"Cassidy!"

I nearly screamed I was so startled. Still trying to remain quiet, I tip-toed to the door and slipped through as stealthily as I could, just to have it slam behind me. Wearing nothing but his t-shirt and carrying my dress, shoes and purse, I ran down the hall as fast as I could. It took me a second of fumbling with my keys, but I finally got into my room. My door closed and I swore I heard another, "Cassidy!" booming down the hall.

"Shit, shit, shit." Why was I running from him?

I threw my dress and shoes to the floor and sank down the door. My knees were pulled to my chest while I rested my head on them and I felt my door shake like there was a gorilla pounding on it. *Bang, bang, bang!* My entire body vibrated from the force of him hitting the door.

"Cassidy, I know you're in there. Please open up."

I pushed myself up the door and sighed. I didn't know what to say to him. "Go away!"

"Cassidy Charles, open this door! You can't run from me forever."

"Yes I can!" This was ridiculous. We were acting like twelve year olds.

"Don't *make* me call hotel security! You let me in or I'll let myself in."

He wouldn't dare, would he? I decided to face him. I opened the door yelling at him, "You wouldn't!"

He was on me instantly. I didn't even have a moment to take in his appearance. His arms were around my back as he lifted me off the floor. As I clung to him he walked us over to the kitchen before setting me on the island.

"Why did you leave? You scared me." He was holding my face in his hands. "Cassidy, look at me. You can't deny the attraction between us. It was there all those months ago and it's still here right now."

There was so much emotion surrounding my thoughts and feelings for him. I was drawn to him since the first time I saw him and still was. And then it all went to shit in one night. I looked into his eyes and they were full of concern.

"I'm scared of what I feel when I'm around you. You scare the hell out of me." He looked stricken and dropped his hands from my face. "Not afraid of you, afraid of this," I waved my hand between us. "I've never been so drawn to someone. And you left me that horrible night without a word. I didn't know what to think. And then you were arrested and I couldn't process it."

He pulled me to him and started talking into my hair. "Baby, I didn't leave you that night. I never wanted to leave you. I came back with our coffee and I saw you with a cop. He was holding you and I got the wrong impression."

"Wait, what?! Calvin…you thought I was with…." I was crying and laughing at the same time. "Calvin is my brother." I pushed away from him just enough to look at him.

He wiped my tears and said, "I know, I found out a few days later when they were questioning me." He must have felt me stiffen. "Cassidy, the charges were dropped. You know that, right?" I nodded my answer and he embraced me again. "I promise you I had nothing to do with what happened that night."

"I spent months trying to hate you so I could get over you, but I couldn't and I never even had you."

"Baby, you had me, you *still* have me. Last night was just confirmation, Cassidy."

"Confirmation? You took me to bed and let me sleep! I thought you had second thoughts after I clobbered you to the floor."

He looked at me like I'd sprouted a second head. Laughing softly he said, "Is that what this is about, you running out this morning? You think because you're clumsy I don't want you?"

"Yes?" I felt like a complete dolt once he said it out loud.

"You're more genuine than anyone I've ever met. You're a little clumsy, so what? Your feelings are written all over your face and have been since the first time we locked eyes. It took every ounce of control I had not to claim you as my own every time I saw you at the bar. Admittedly, I lost control in the elevator. I had planned to take it slower with you." He was all smiles and I felt myself melting again. I was transfixed on his face and ran my hands over the stubble on his face then back through his hair. "Besides, I'm fond of the shirt you're wearing and I need it back."

I laughed, "Shut up."

"I can't believe you ran down the hall in only my t-shirt."

"I don't know. I've grown attached to the shirt. You may have to fight me for it. And look at you. You ran down the hall in only your sleep pants."

Holy hell, he wasn't wearing a shirt. Why hadn't I noticed that before? I'd been itching for months to run my hands over his chest. I placed my hands on his chest and noticed him suck in his breath. I flashed my eyes to his face and realized his eyes were closed. He stood in front of me while I remained sitting on the counter. I took my eyes back to his chest and took in the tattoo covering his right shoulder. It was a dragon that spanned from the top of his shoulder down his whole upper arm. I traced it with my fingers, "This is beautiful."

"Thank you, Blackbird. You like it?" He was practically panting as my lips kissed his shoulder. I spread my legs and pulled him closer to me. "I'll take that as a yes." His hands trailed up and down the tops of my thighs.

"Why do you call me Blackbird?"

"Why do you think?"

I looked into his eyes, not sure what to think. I ignored his question and went back to admiring the dragon, "This must've taken hours?"

He chuckled, "Maybe." He increased the pressure on my thighs and moved a little closer. "Do you have any other tattoos, Cassidy?"

He tasted almost as good as he smelled. I kissed from his tattoo, across his collar bone and licked up his neck to his ear before pulling his lobe into my mouth and breathed heavily, causing him to shudder.

"Maybe."

He groaned. "Cassidy..."

"I know how you can find out," I whispered.

six

Phoenix

~ CASSIDY ~

I PULLED BACK TO LOOK AT HIM AND HE dove onto my mouth. I moaned out in surprise and wrapped my legs around him, with my heels resting against the curve of his ass. His hands held my face to his and I couldn't get enough of his tongue. He abandoned my mouth and continued his trek down my jaw to my neck.

I was kneading the massive expanse of his back feeling his arousal bounce on my thigh. I shifted myself, tucking him tightly against the center of my body. He let out a growl that caused my skin to tremble. My breasts were heavy and aching for his touch. Like he could read my mind, he conquered my right breast with his mouth while the other got relief from his hand. My head fell back as I relished his touch through *my* shirt.

The anticipation was killing me. I wanted him, needed him. I reached down between us and pulled the cord that kept his sleep pants in place. They loosened just enough to grant access to my hands. I seized his cock and he bucked into my hand.

"Dammit Cassidy. Be careful, you're playing with fire." He was large—larger than anyone I'd ever been with—but I was up to the task.

"I like fire. Burn me if you must." I loved how quickly we responded to each other's little quips. Before I was aware of it, he yanked the shirt off me and smothered me with the heat of his body.

James ran his hands over my ribcage while asking, "Is it finished? It's beautiful."

I raised my head to see what he was referring to. He found one. It was kind of hard to miss with my shirt off. "Only thing left to add is color."

"Are there any more?"

"Maybe." I smirked as he growled at my limited response.

His growl was the sexiest sound I'd ever heard. He pulled me back against him as the hard length of his manhood pressed against my panties. I rotated my hips and whimpered when a surge of passion ran through us simultaneously. His hands seized my hips as he thrust against me, causing my insides to churn.

"James, please don't make me beg." I was panting like a dog in heat as he licked his way down my abdomen. He circled my navel while his hands traveled down and under my ass and began squeezing. "Oh, God!"

"I thought I told you to call me James?" He lifted his head and I could see the smile in his eyes.

I breathed his name and he smiled, returning to his task. I couldn't take much more and felt his hand travel up the center of my body as he pushed me down on my back to the cold countertop and I jumped in surprise.

"You're cold."

"Only my back. It's a nice contrast to the heat of…" I didn't finish my statement because I was fighting off another convulsion.

"The heat of what, Cassidy?"

His tongue was running along the band of my panties. I couldn't even process coherent words. I'd never been tortured like that and didn't know how much more I could take. I cried out in expectation and frustration.

"Do you want me?" He asked the question as his teeth tugged on my panties and his hand helped slip them down my hips. I raised my ass to help him with his task. "Let's see if you're ready."

"God, yes I want you. I'm ready, James, please." I couldn't stop squirming under his gaze. I tried to pull him closer with my legs and heard him lightly chuckle.

"Patience, Cassidy."

Every time he said my name like that I swear my clit throbbed a little more. I felt his gaze, down there, examining and my instinct was to close my legs.

"Oh no you don't. I *want* to see you. You're open for me and so beautiful." He planted a chaste kiss in my well-manicured curls. Before I had a chance to object, his fire-hot tongue pierced my center and did one torturous lick upwards, ending at my clit.

"Ohhhhh!" It was half groan half scream.

"You're ready." He was panting as he abruptly stood and pulled me off the counter to meet his face. He threw my arms over his shoulders. "Hang on."

I bound my legs around his hips eager for him to thrust into me; he didn't oblige. I cried out in despair as he walked across the suite, toward the bedroom, with me wrapped tightly around him.

"Soon, baby. You deserve a proper fucking in a bed, not on a counter."

"The counter is fine for fucking." His hands dug into my ass and yanked me closer as I sucked on his ear. He picked up his pace and I could feel his shaft bounce against my rear with each step he took. "You're killing me, James."

"I'm not sure I'm the one doing the killing here, Cassidy."

Finally in the softly lit bedroom, he walked to the bed and pulled the folded quilt to the floor. Before I could stop him, he peeled me from his body and let me fall to the bed. The satin sheets beneath me were cool and felt wonderful. I stretched out and reveled in the feel of the sheets against my body.

He started a slow crawl up the bed. Kneeling between my legs, he reached down and grabbed my calf. He lifted it up until my foot was in his palm, smiled wickedly at me before sucking my big toe into his mouth.

I wasn't prepared for this foreign act, but threw my head back enjoying the odd sensation. "Oh God, that feels good."

His mouth worked up my leg as his hands made their way to my hips. Soon his mouth was kissing my ribcage and breasts while his hands moved to mold the muscles in my neck. His face was above mine and I could feel his steel erection on my thigh. I tried shifting under his weight but he had me pinned to the bed.

"James, if you don't fuck me soon, so help me!" I didn't even know what I meant by that statement.

His hands were on each side of my head as he pushed himself up on his arms. He positioned his shaft to lay at my opening, wiggled and then looked at me alarmed. "You cuss like a sailor, you know that?" He was grinding on my pelvis, causing spasms that reached all the way down to my toes. "What will you do if I don't fuck you, Cassidy?"

I was dying from anticipation and lost for words. "I don't know what I'll do. You're driving me mad."

"What did you mean then?" He placed tiny kisses all over my face.

"Please, James, I need you inside me, now!" I grabbed his ass and dug my nails in. I got the groan of approval that I was looking for.

He was beaming with pride now while I was blushing. I grabbed his face and pulled his lips to mine. He met my tongue and we were beyond hungry for each other.

He whispered into my mouth, "Do you have any condoms?"

I looked at him startled. "Shit." I just brought an overnight bag and didn't plan for that. "Let me check my purse." He jumped off me and I got up to find my purse. *Please let there be a condom in there.* I was digging through my purse and checked the concealed zipper. *SCORE!* I'd never been so thankful to find a condom in my life.

"Did you find one?" His arms went around me as he bit my neck. *Where the hell did he come from?* I didn't even hear him leave the bed.

I held the condom up in the air between us as he turned me to face him. He attacked my mouth only the way he could. Snatching the foil packet from me, he walked me backward to the bed. We fell back on the bed as he kissed me. Soon, he pulled back and we were both so out of breath we were damn near wheezing.

"James, please." He got up on his knees in an instant and ripped the condom from the wrapper. "Let me." I took the condom from him and he tensed in response. I pulled myself up far enough to attend to my duty. He was quite large and I couldn't wait for him to plummet into me.

I placed the condom on the tip of his damp arousal, wrapped my hand around his shaft and looked up into his eyes. His cheeks were puffing as I slid the condom down in place and then pulled him to me.

He steadied himself over me and I felt him at my entrance, closing my eyes to savor the moment.

"Cassidy, look at me. I want to see your eyes."

As my eyes opened and focused on his, he pushed the tip of his cock inside me. His eyes fluttered for a moment and I reached up to stroke his chest. He opened his eyes and they were that vibrant green again.

"James, fuck me, *now.*" He drove all the way into me and I let out a scream. It was both pleasure and a tiny bit of pain as I grew accustomed to his size. My nails gripped his arms, "You feel so good."

"Are you ok? I'm being careless." He looked at me concerned.

"I'm perfect. Please don't stop!"

He pulled out to the tip and slammed back in, barely giving me time to adjust. He did this over and over again; I was nearly in tears because it felt so good. I wrapped my legs around his back as he dropped to his elbows and plunged his tongue into my mouth with the same force his cock was hammering into me.

With his arms underneath me, I felt like I was floating above the bed. I was on a James fuck ride and I loved every second of it. His slick back forced me to tighten my hold. He showed no mercy and I began losing control as he started swiveling his hips. I gasped for breath as we were nose to nose.

"James, you feel incredible..."

"No baby, that's *you* who feels incredible."

I flashed a quick smile as I threw my head back on another thrust. He started sucking and licking down my neck.

"I'm so close, oh I never, oh God..."

He picked his head up and looked slightly concerned. "You never what?"

My head was spinning; I was so close. My whole body was a tensed up ball of sexual frustration. "I've. Never. Come. During. Intercourse. Not like this." Each word was a statement. Oh God, he was slowing down. I shrieked at him, "DON'T STOP!"

"Don't hold back, Cassidy. Hang on to me."

He pushed himself up slightly and the angle of his hips had his penis hitting my reclusive sweet spot. I didn't think it was possible, probably because no one had ever managed to find it. I'd never felt like this; so full and ready to implode. I couldn't reach around his back at that angle so I hooked my arms under and around his shoulders.

He growled out, "You hanging on?"

My barely audible voice whispered, "Yes."

He lost all abandon and started fucking me harder. I didn't think he had 'harder' in him. I tightened my hold as the spasms got more frequent. I tensed around his shaft even tighter, which solicited a groan from him.

"I'm so close…" Over and over again he pumped into me. I wouldn't be able to walk the next day and I didn't care. He swiveled and rocked and thrust. My body was ready, even though my soul wanted it to continue forever. "Don't stop, oh, I'm going to come. James, please don't stop."

"I'll never stop, Cassidy. Come for me, baby."

Warm sensations shot out from my womb to the tips of my toes and the top of my head. I was moaning as my release overtook me. My thighs were locked so tight around him while I milked him. He dropped back down on top of me and quickened his pace. I threaded my hands in his hair and jerked his mouth to mine.

"You're driving me crazy with that squeezing of yours," he panted into my mouth.

"That's the point." I smiled and tugged his hair, still coming down from my own high. "I want *you* to come." My words seemed to set him off. He ferociously drove into me a couple more times as the convulsions took him over.

"Fuck, oh God."

I ran my hands to his ass and squeezed as he shot his release. As the last few shudders left his body, he collapsed on me. I loved the weight of him on me. I kissed his shoulder as he moved to leave my body and I grabbed onto him in protest.

"I'll crush you, Cassidy."

"I want to be crushed." He snickered and rolled over while taking me with him keeping us joined. He caressed my back as I lay on top of him and listened to his heartbeat slow. "You're amazing," I stated as I circled my finger around his nipple.

"You're pretty amazing yourself. I didn't hurt you, did I?"

"I don't think so, but maybe you should examine me to find out." I milked him again and he flinched before he chuckled.

"Insatiable are we? What have I gotten myself into?" He was massaging my rear and ran his hands up to comb through my hair.

"If it's always like that, then yes. Insatiable." I trailed my hand up and down his side as his hands continued to do the same on my back.

"You've really never had an orgasm during intercourse?"

I couldn't hold back the yawn and whispered, "You're the first during intercourse." He went to pull me off of him. "Please don't go," I softly breathed in his neck. I was dozing off as he gently separated our bodies.

"I'm just getting the blanket. I'll never leave you again, Blackbird." He kissed the top of my head and pulled the satin comforter over my body. I saw him tie off and discard the condom before he crawled under the covers and pulled me back against him. I tangled my body with his and focused on his even breathing. It was the last thing I remember before sleep conquered me.

~ JAMES ~

STARING DOWN AT her, I reflected on the last eighteen—or so—hours.

It seemed like I lay next to her for hours, not minutes, just listening to her soft breaths, before sleep took me the night before. I replayed the entire evening in my head more than once; she was absolutely breathtaking. I didn't know how I managed to stay away from her for so long; I was an idiot to wait as long as I did. As the rays of dawn started peeking through the windows I'd rolled over to gaze at her, only to find her gone. *Dammit!*

Cassidy was going to drive mad, I just knew it. Jumping out of the bed, I'd called her name just before hearing the door to the suite close. Throwing on my sleep pants, I went after her. Upon finding her in her suite, I had never felt so frenzied before or been so filled with lust, want, and need. Once I had her I knew I would never be able to get enough. She was tempting and teasing as she met and responded to every touch.

'Burn me if you must.'

I'd pulled my shirt off her and captured her perfect breasts. Taking turns kneading one while I sucked and licked the other. Her hands gripped my hair and pulled me closer. Something had caught my eye and I lifted my head to see what it was.

Cassidy had a tattoo of a phoenix. It was a black outline and lacked color. The head of the phoenix was next to her breast, under her armpit. The body traveled down and under her breast, along her rib cage, with the tail wrapped under the same breast. It was beautiful.

SHE WAS HALF on her side and half on her back and sound asleep. The sheet was down around her waist and her hair was a mess all over the pillow. She was exquisite. Her right breast was covered by her right arm while her left arm rested over her head on the bed. Her tattoo was in full view. I sat down next to her and ran my index finger over the phoenix. I wondered why a phoenix, or birds in general, and remembered what she said when I asked if there were more. *'Maybe.'* I was tempted to start examining her from head to toe to see what I had missed, if anything.

It had been over four months since that night. I'd kept my distance from her as long as I could. Not a day went by that I hadn't thought about her. *My Blackbird.* Never before had a woman corrupted every day and every thought in my mind. When I found out she worked for Cecily Brighton and was planning Aunt Bev's masquerade, the rest of my plan was easily set in motion. Though, running into her on the street by *accident* may have been better.

Confiding in Dad was what almost blew my cover. If she had recognized me in the elevator with Dad, she may have never given me a second chance. But she wouldn't have been in that elevator if Dad hadn't told Aunt Bev. I hadn't planned on Aunt Bev renting the suite down the hall from mine for Cassidy either.

"Damn meddling," I said to myself as she rolled fully to her back and began to wake.

~ CASSIDY ~

I ROLLED OVER and sensed his eyes on me. Finding him devouring my naked body with his eyes was incredibly erotic. He was smiling and already dressed. I was momentarily embarrassed at my nudity and pulled the sheet up to cover my breasts.

He asked, "Sleep well?"

I stretched, let out a groan and sat up. He moved closer and placed his arm across my body to rest on the other side of my hip. We were face to face.

"You cheat." He looked at me confused. "You've showered and dressed." I ran my hand up his thigh and he smiled knowingly.

"I have some work to do."

"It's Saturday. Oh God. What time is it? I'm supposed to be checked out by noon." I was ready to freak out looking for the time.

He started laughing. "I own the hotel Cassidy. Take your time."

Now I was confused. "You own the hotel? I thought your father…"

"No, the hotel is mine, just like the auction."

"Oh, well maybe I'll stay all day and you can attend to some work here." I pointed to myself as I tried to persuade him.

He smirked and kissed me quickly before he got up off the bed. "Get dressed. It's after noon. Breakfast will be here soon."

I yelled after him. "I didn't order breakfast and how'd you get dressed anyway?" I remembered that we were in my suite, not his. "You only had pajama pants on this morning." He was already out of the room.

"I own the hotel, Cassidy. Now get dressed." I wasn't sure if that was an order or a request, but it sounded more like an order.

seven

Devious

~ CASSIDY ~

ALL THE SHOWER JETS WERE AN amazing luxury I had never experienced. I was thoroughly disappointed that he didn't join me in the shower. When I stepped out of the shower there was still no sign of him. Wrapping the bath sheet around me, I walked to the sink. I rummaged through my makeup bag to find my moisturizer, toothbrush, and toothpaste. When I'd finished with that, I dried my hair and was suddenly aware of the smell of bacon. My stomach growled in response.

I threw on my white jeans that had the rips down the legs, my grey camisole, my blue sweater, and my silver ballet flats. I tossed everything else back into my overnight bag, grabbed my garment bag holding my dress and headed for the living room. Dropping everything on the couch, I went into the small dining area where James was sitting. He was scrolling through his phone looking good enough to eat, wearing black suit pants, a white oxford that was unbuttoned on top and no tie. His hair was down and I noticed he hadn't shaved.

I sat down across from him and waited. "Have you already eaten?"

"Yes, I'm sorry. I was famished. Please, go ahead." I couldn't resist and I dug in.

He was being awfully quiet as he hammered away on his cell. Several minutes later there was a knock at the door. I looked to him, a little startled at who could be at the door.

"It's just the bellboy." He pushed himself away from the table and headed to the door. James gave him a few instructions before the boy loaded the cart with my belongings.

"Do you have everything, Cassidy?"

I got up from the table, having had more than my fill of bacon, eggs, and fresh fruit. "Yes, I'm certain." James hadn't said a word about where we went from there and I was trying not to get self-conscious.

Before the bellboy left James handed him some bills from his wallet. "Have Andy pull Miss Charles's car around front." The bellboy nodded and scurried off. James looked at me, all hard and serious, and I realized how intimidating he was.

"Come here." I hesitantly walked over to him, wondering what he was about to do. I shrieked as he picked me up like a child and pressed me to his chest. He wrapped his arms around my waist as I looked down at him. "I didn't give you a proper good morning kiss."

I laughed and leaned down to his lips. His kiss was at first soft but turned hot and steamy. His hands ran down to cup my ass and I groaned in response. "Good morning. Or should I say afternoon?" I smiled and kissed him again. "You seemed so far away a few minutes ago."

His brow furrowed as he set me back on my feet. "Just business stuff." He kissed my cheek and whispered in my ear, "You're perfect.

Now, out with you." James motioned me toward the door and smacked my ass when I got in front of him.

"Ow!" I slapped his hand away as he grabbed it, intertwining our fingers. I glanced down at our hands and for a moment my heart faltered.

When we reached the lobby he let go of my hand and led me out to the front of the hotel with his hand on the small of my back.

Andy, the valet, rushed over, panting, "Sir, I'm sorry, I couldn't get Miss Charles's car started. We tried everything."

"For the love... I'm sorry, Andy. I can have a tow truck sent to get it." James motioned against my offered solution.

"Andy, call Joe and have him come take care of it." He looked at his watch and sighed. "Please go get the Rover, Andy." Andy ran back toward the garage and James pulled out his cell, hitting a few numbers. "Hi, Jennifer. I need you to push my one-thirty appointment." He sighed and spread his hand across his temple. "Of course she's already there. Just deal with her, Jen, I'll be there as soon as I can." He pushed a few more buttons before placing his cell in the breast pocket of his jacket.

"James, I can call a cab to get me home. It's no trouble."

"Absolutely not." Just then Andy pulled up in a beast of a SUV. It was a Range Rover and probably had every possible upgrade available. James opened my door and I climbed in. I buckled myself in and noticed that the interior still smelled new. My bags were placed in the back and a moment later James climbed in.

James pulled away from the curb and headed south out of downtown. I sat for a few minutes just gazing at him. It dawned on me that he seemed to know where he was going. "Don't you need my address?" He looked surprised by the question.

"Er, uh, yes please."

"You rotten sneak. You know *exactly* where you're going. How do you know where I live?"

"I own the hotel, Cassidy." He smirked at me and moved his eyes back to the road.

I took him at his word, though I wasn't sure he was being truthful. I decided to power up the stereo. I pushed play and recognized the voice singing immediately.

"Is this the new Maroon 5?" He nodded yes. "Mr. Benedict, I wouldn't have taken you as a Maroon 5 fan." I giggled. He just glanced at me and gave nothing away. "I need to get the radio fixed in my car so I can listen to something other than news radio." I started quietly singing along.

When the song was over he reached over and pushed a few buttons. "I like this one more, especially the part about having my hands on a miracle." He placed his hand on my knee as I sat back and listened to Foo Fighter's *Miracle*. As I listened to the words it was a struggle for me to not choke up. When the song was over I smiled my approval.

A couple more songs played as he drove along. All too soon he was pulling into the drive of my townhouse. "Do you have plans for today?" I turned to him as he took my hand in his.

I let out an exaggerated breath. "No, just unpacking. I've been living out of boxes for weeks. I'm dreading it, but it has to be done."

He nodded, pulled my hand to his lips before he let go and got out of the SUV. I unbuckled and went to open the door, but he was already pulling it open. James walked to the back end and started pulling my bags out. I shut my door and made my way over to him.

"Shit!" He glared at me, silently asking me what the hell my problem was. "I'm supposed to have the dress back to Frida's today. My car..." I ran my hands through my hair. "Don't worry, I'll call Cal."

"Where's the shop, Cassidy?"

"NO, I'll figure it out; please don't go to the trouble."

"It's no trouble. Where's the shop?"

He looked utterly determined. "Umm, if you're sure…" He flashed me a 'don't mess with me' glare. "It's on 4th Street across from Duke's."

He put the gown back in his SUV before scooping up my other bags. I dug through my purse looking for my keys. I spotted my pills and took a mental note to take them when I got inside.

We walked up to my door, I unlocked it and stood there, not sure what to say or do. He set my bags down just inside my door and gathered me into a big bear hug. I sagged against him and inhaled deeply before he pulled me back and kissed me.

"I miss you already." My heart skipped a beat at his tender words.

"When will I see you again?"

"Soon."

Before I could question what that meant, James bounded down the porch stairs two at a time. He waved before hopping in the SUV and driving away. A few seconds later, I heard my phone alert me of a text message. I pulled it out of my purse and saw a text from an unknown number.

Go inside before you let the cat out.
XO ~J

I looked around and spotted Chessa making her way through the obstacle course of boxes and shut the door just before she reached it. "Sneaky." I wasn't sure if I was referring to James or to Chessa.

How'd you get my number!?

I wasn't waiting long for his reply.

I own the hotel, Miss Charles. Go unpack.
XO ~J

So you keep reminding me.
Yes, Sir!

I like when you call me Sir.
XO ~J

I bet you do! Come back and I'll call you sir all night.
XO ~C

Be careful what you wish for.
XO ~J
P.S. *I like your XO ~C*

I placed the phone back in my purse, ran upstairs with my bags and traded my jeans for some cut-off sweats. Once I got back downstairs I cranked the radio and dove head first into unpacking.

~ JAMES ~

I FOUND THE BOUTIQUE, parked and grabbed the garment bag out of the back. Rushing inside, I found a little old lady behind the counter. There were all sorts of dresses on a dozen or so different racks.

"Can I help you, sir?"

I looked to the little old lady who seemed to be almost half my height. "I'm returning this dress for Miss Charles."

"Oh!" She looked me up and down with hungry eyes which caused me to chuckle. "She caught herself quite a specimen did she?" She winked at me. "Would you like to look around?"

I looked at my watch. I really shouldn't have kept Melissa waiting any longer, but I was intrigued by the shop. "You wouldn't happen to have Miss Charles's measurements on file, would you?"

"*Now* you're talking. I do and her dress for this weekend is ready to be picked up, too."

"Is she renting that one as well?"

"Yes, sir. It's quite a stunning dress, especially on her with all that red hair and ivory skin. It's a shame she'll only wear it once."

"May I see it?"

"Now Mr…"

"You can call me James, James Benedict. It'll be our little secret." I winked at her.

"If you say so." She walked into the back room.

I still had the other dress with me and noticed some hooks by the front desk, so I walked over and hung it up. A few moments passed before she walked out from the back room with a large garment bag in tow. She hung it up next to the other dress and unzipped the bag.

"Lovely, isn't it?"

I was taken aback by the shade of blue. "It's almost the exact color of her eyes." She nodded in agreement.

"I might be willing to sell it James, James Benedict."

"What did you have in mind?" She perked up and we got down to business.

~ CASSIDY ~

I HAD MADE A LOT of progress after spending several hours unpacking. All my kitchen boxes were empty and I loaded the dishes into the dishwasher to give them a once over before use. Finding a note pad, I took note of some odds and ends that I needed from the store. There was a knock on the door; I wasn't expecting anyone.

I headed to the door and opened it up. "Cal!" I threw my arms around his neck and gave him a big squeeze. "What are you doing here?"

"I come bearing Chinese and helping hands." He smirked at me as he held up a plastic bag full of Chinese takeout.

"You rock! Come on in. Watch your step. No work tonight?" He nodded confirming it was his night off. "You have your tux for Friday?"

He screwed up his face in disgust. "Yes. You owe me!"

"I know!" I opened the bags and placed the food on the counter. "You got enough food for an army."

"You know me, I can never decide and you're always eating my sesame chicken." He winked at me.

There was another knock at the door. What the heck? Oh, shit. If it was James, this wasn't going to go over well. Cal never forgot a face. I was not ready to have this discussion with him.

"You going to get it or am I?" Cal looked to me.

"I'll get it; you just get the dishes out of the dishwasher." I rushed toward the door and took a deep breath before opening it. "Jane! What are you doing here?" I noticed a cab sitting at my curb.

"Sorry, Cassidy. I hope I'm not intruding. Mom and I wanted to give you this." She handed me a large wrapped box. "It's a thank you for the hard work with the masquerade."

"Oh wow, thank you. You didn't have to go to all that trouble." She stood there as I noticed a gift bag in her other hand. "Please, come in. The place is a wreck. I'm unpacking, but my brother is here with Chinese."

"Sorry, I didn't realize you had company..."

"Nonsense. I insist." I gently pulled her inside and waved the cab off.

"Ok, one second, I need to pay the cabby." She hurried down the stairs to the cab while I went back inside.

I remembered Mrs. Whitford mentioning that Jane had just moved back home a few months prior. She was living across the country with a real 'douchebag', or so her mom said. I liked Jane and thought maybe I could pick her brain about James. I moved a few boxes to clear space for the gift box. The front door closed and Jane made her way inside.

"Jane, this is my brother Calvin."

Calvin turned around to shake Jane's hand and instead he started checking her out. I walked behind him and nudged him. "Stop being rude, Cal," I whispered.

He stuttered, "Sorry. Jane is it? You can call me Cal." He shook her hand. "You like Chinese?"

Jane confirmed that Chinese sounded great. "Oh, here, this is for you, too." She gave me the gift bag which was clanking about.

"Jane, really, it's too much." I opened the bag and found three bottles of the champagne from the masquerade.

"Mother said that you really liked it." I was speechless knowing that they were over $300 per bottle. I didn't spend that much on, well, anything. "Open the box!"

"Yeah, Cass, open the box." Cal was almost as excited as I was.

"Holy sh... crap...Jane!" I was shocked at the generosity. "It's amazing."

Jane just shrugged it off. "Please, mom can afford it. It's nothing. Get good use out of it!"

"What the hell is it?" Cal looked at it and had no clue what it was. Jane and I shared a laugh. I explained to him that it was a top of the line coffee maker that came with several different flavors. "That's too fancy for me. I'll stick with my black coffee, 3 sugars."

I ran over to hug Jane and thanked her again. We served ourselves some Chinese and decided to pop one of the bottles of champagne. I poured each of us a glass before we headed to the living room. We chatted, ate and drank a little too much, except for Cal who always stopped after one drink. It was like we'd all been friends forever.

eight

Don't

~ CASSIDY ~

CAL HAD TAKEN AN IMMEDIATE and obvious interest in Jane and it seemed to be mutual. I decided to see just how interested and asked her, "Jane you'll be at the auction on Friday, right?" That immediately had Cal's attention.

"Oh yeah, can't get out of that one. What about you, Cal?"

"Yup, I'll be there. Looking forward to it." I giggled and Cal threw me a dirty look.

"Oh, how quickly we change our stripes!" I laughed and he tossed a pillow at me. Jane seemed to get what I was playing at and blushed.

The rest of the evening went off without a hitch. We were starting to wrap things up when *Crash into Me* by DMB started playing. The radio was off and I suddenly wondered if it was someone's ringtone. "Is that your phone?" They both shook their heads.

"Found it." I saw Cal pull my phone off the charger on the kitchen counter. "Who's James?" He was holding the phone out of my reach and waggling his eyebrows.

"Knock it off, Cal. Give me the phone." I wasn't asking nicely. He tried to hold the phone even higher. Two could play that game. I grabbed his nipple and twisted. He dropped his arm and I snatched my phone.

"Dammit, Cass, that hurt." Jane was in stitches.

"Good!" I rushed out the front door and stood on the steps for some privacy. "When did you change my ring tone?"

"Hello, Cassidy." He sounded somber and dark.

"You ok?"

"I'm fine. What are you wearing?"

His question caught me off guard. I decided to play along. "Nothing. What are you wearing?"

"Don't lie to me, Cassidy." I sensed that he was smiling on the other end of the phone.

"How do you know I'm lying, Mr. Benedict?" I was taunting him.

"Because you're standing on your front porch," *What the hell?* "And if you're naked on your front porch we're going to have a problem." I started looking up and down the street, but it was too dark to make out a thing. "Get rid of your company, Cassidy!" I wanted to respond but heard the call disconnect instead.

"Somebody's blushing." Jane stated the obvious as I walked back in the door.

I shrugged my shoulders and the smile on my face spoke volumes as I hiccupped. I may have overdone it on the champagne. "You're supposed to be on *my* side!" I scolded Jane.

"I should get going. It's getting late," Jane said to me with a wink.

"How are you going to get home?" I asked her.

"Oh yeah." She pulled her cell out, "I'll just call a cab. No biggie."

"I can take you."

"*Now* who's blushing?" I stuck my tongue out at Cal and Jane. I was giggly and had clearly had too much to drink.

"Who's James?" he asked me again.

"Ask Jane. I have a feeling she knows him better than I do." I faked a yawn and ushered them out the door as nicely as I could. I watched Cal escort Jane to his truck. As he walked to the driver's side he waved and threw me a wink. "Behave!"

"I could say the same to you, little sister!"

As they pulled away I walked back inside. I decided to clear the dishes and reload the dishwasher. There were probably twenty empty boxes of various sizes stacked in and beside each other on my living room floor, and although we'd made a lot of progress unpacking, I still hadn't found my iPod. Dammit. My phone started playing the same tune again and I rushed to answer it. "Yes, Mr. Benedict." I was attempting to give him my best sexy voice.

"You said you'd call me Sir all night. What are you wearing, Cassidy?"

My heart started racing. He sounded so sexy and brooding; I was instantly wet. "Nothing, Sir."

"Don't lie to me, Cassidy!" I jumped about a foot off the floor as I heard the front door slam shut and then he locked it. He came through the front door without me even knowing he was here.

"Yes, Sir." I was breathless and he was on me in a heartbeat.

~ JAMES ~

AFTER I LEFT FRIDA'S, I drove to the office where I knew Melissa was waiting. I should've known better than to keep her waiting. This was going to go one of two ways; bad or really bad.

I parked in the underground garage, in my designated spot, and took the elevator up. Taking a deep breath, I prepared myself as the elevator stopped and the doors opened. I could hear the screaming from where I stood and I rushed through the double glass doors and headed toward my office. Jennifer, our secretary, ducked just before a vase shattered above the wall behind her.

I stormed into my office and roared, "Melissa, enough! Sorry Jen, I can take it from here." Jen scuttled out and shut the door behind her while mumbling profanities. "God dammit, Melissa. What's the problem now?"

She slithered over like the snake she was, immediately smiling at my presence. "Hey, baby. I've been waiting a long time." She was pouting. She started running her hands up and down my arms before I grabbed her wrists and held her away from me. "I need an advance on my rent." Now she was batting her eyelashes at me.

"Stop the bullshit, Melissa. You live in your Dad's building." I escorted her to the couch and made my way to my desk, flopping down in my chair. "What's really going on? Are you using again?" She started fidgeting.

"Nothing, no, it's all good."

"You're sure? The deal is off if..." I glared at her. I really felt sorry for her. We'd known each other since we were kids. The biggest mistake I made was taking her to bed.

"No, no, I just got over extended and Daddy has cut me off, with the exception of a roof over my head. Please James."

My heart got the better of me and I just wanted her out of there. I told her I'd help her anyway I could, as long as she stayed clean. "How much do you need?" She jumped off the couch and threw herself on me. "Melissa, get off." I pushed her off me again and headed to my safe.

After Melissa left I got caught up on some business. I scrolled through my email and dealt with them accordingly. Once I'd checked in with all the contractors and confirmed all was good, I decided it was enough for one Saturday. I had struggled to get my mind off Cassidy ever since I left her on her doorstep.

Things had gone smoother than I had anticipated when I revealed myself to her. My instincts were correct about the attraction; it was mutual and intense. I did a quick run through the office and locked up before leaving.

When I pulled out of the garage I realized it was already dark. Looking at the dash, I saw that it was already close to eight p.m. I recalled the morning at the hotel and her responses to my touch, which was immediate every time. She had welcomed every advance, so why was I so nervous to show her my kinky side? She was the first woman in a *very* long time I had *wanted* to get kinky with. Bits and pieces at a time would have to do. I didn't want to scare her away by going too fast. I was getting hard just thinking about tying her up. I decided I had to see her, immediately.

I drove toward her townhouse and couldn't stop my blood from boiling when I saw the Ford pickup in her driveway. It took all my strength not to knock down her door. I parked down the street, after memorizing the plate, and called Smith. It felt like I waited for far too long for Smith to call back. Finally, my cell rang.

"Smith, what took so long? Oh, sorry Joe. Yes, whatever needs to be repaired just do it and send Jennifer the bill. Make sure everything is working, including the radio." My call waiting beeped. "I'll be in touch tomorrow." I switched lines. "Smith?"

I felt like an ass; it was just her brother. I growled, "Thanks, Smith." That was a meeting I was not quite prepared for. Calvin, no doubt, would not react kindly to my involvement with his sister. I decided to pick up my cell and called her.

She caused me to smile with her questioning the ring tone change I made to her phone. "Hello, Cassidy." I gave her the best somber tone I could muster.

"You ok?" It was working, she was sounding concerned.

"I'm fine. What are you wearing?"

I heard her sudden intake of breath and her quick response. "Nothing. What are *you* wearing?" Lying minx.

"Don't lie to me, Cassidy."

"How do you know I'm lying, Mr. Benedict?" She thought she had the upper hand. I liked playing this game with her.

"Because you're standing on your front porch." She perked up and started looking up and down the street. "And if you're naked on your front porch, we're going to have a problem." With the lack of street lights, she would never make out the Rover in the dark from that distance. "Get rid of your company, Cassidy!" I saw her look back and forth from the phone to the street before she rushed inside.

After a few minutes I saw the door open and Calvin and a girl walked out. Wait, was that Jane? "What the hell is *she* doing there?" I grabbed my cell and texted Jane.

> Keep your trap shut about me, cuz.
> Love, J.

She was in the truck now and it wasn't long before I received her reply.

> Got it bad, do you?! You're not alone.
> She couldn't be more obvious if she
> pushed us out the door!
> Love, J

Calvin and Jane drove down the street and around the corner. I made my way closer to her house, climbed out of the Rover and strode to her door. I dialed her again.

I checked the door and was pleased to find it unlocked. I caught a glimpse of her in the kitchen. *Time to have some fun.*

"Don't lie to me, Cassidy!" She jumped almost a foot off the floor once I slammed the door and turned the lock before I rushed her.

I was on her so quick and hard that I knocked the wind out of her. Pinning her against the kitchen wall, I was already erect as my mouth claimed hers as my own. The kiss was so fanatical that my head was spinning and I could almost taste the champagne on her lips. She moaned into my mouth and rubbed against my erection as she pulled away for air. I could smell her arousal and repositioned her against the kitchen wall. Grinding my hips into her, feeling like I couldn't get my mouth or body close enough, I knew I had to possess her.

"James, is everything ok?"

I was practically smothering her; I needed to tone it down, "I just needed to see you, feel you, and remind myself you're real."

Cassidy grabbed my face and pulled my eyes to hers. She looked at me like I was crazy. "I'm here. I'm not going anywhere. I'd be crazy to. Remember, you're the only one to make me orgasm during intercourse."

I gazed at her, my mood immediately lifting as I flashed half a grin. She seemed to know exactly how to lighten the mood. "How about I do it again?" I started kissing down her neck, "and again, and again."

Like she couldn't say no to me, "You had me at again."

She wanted it; it was written all over her. I found my way under her camisole as she took my jacket off impatiently. I had to have her. I reached down and wrapped my hands under her thighs and pulled her up so she straddled my waist. I carried her to the counter. I needed more of her and ripped her sweater and camisole off and over her head. Her breasts were taunting me in that lacey bra of hers. I had to taste them. I was rougher than I planned, but she didn't object. My control was at its limit.

"James…"

Acting like a crazed animal I tugged and sucked on her breasts through the bra so rigorously that I was sure it was almost painful, but she didn't ask me to stop. I pressed into her and she was quiet, breathing rapidly. "I need you now, Cassidy. Fast and hard." She looked hungrier than I had seen before, exquisitely lost in lust as she began removing my belt. Once my belt was removed she pushed down my trousers, needing me as much as I needed her. Her fingers searched for the elastic of my boxers and found none. The only thing waiting for her was my erection and she grabbed on and squeezed until I growled. "Fuck. You're killing me."

"Sir, I'm shocked. Commando?" She was smirking at me, feigning innocence as she began stroking me.

I shrugged my shoulders, "I *forgot?*" Her assault on my cock continued and I was ready to burst. Closing my eyes, I let my head roll back and savored her touch.

"I think you had this planned all day, Sir."

Looking back to her I saw that she had tilted her head sideways, narrowing her eyes at me. She was such a tease. "I had some things planned today too," she leaned in and began licking my neck.

She swiped her tongue all up my neck and all the way to my earlobe, and then sucked it in her mouth. She was going to kill me. Suddenly I was thrown back; that would be the only time she would catch me off guard. She jumped off the counter in a heartbeat and dropped to her knees. I would surely burst if her mouth touched me. I yanked her back up and she was visibly disappointed.

She reached for me again and was pulled to her feet before she had a chance to taste me. "Hey!"

"I said now! I don't have the patience for your teasing tongue right now." I tried to smile, but any control I had mustered had faded; I was entirely serious.

"You're no fun. How do you know my tongue is teasing?" She asked with pouty eyes and lips.

Pursing her beautiful lips and batting her eyes I responded, "Stop trying to distract me with that beautiful mouth." Pushing her back toward the kitchen counter, I reached for her as she readied her lips for a kiss and instead I reached behind her to unclasp her bra with a flick of my wrist. Turning her around, I pushed her face down on the counter. She jumped as the cold granite pierced her skin, but recovered quicker than I expected her to. I ran my hands down from her shoulders to her waist and then removed her shorts. I was greeted by her lovely round ass. "Looks like I'm not the only one going commando."

"I told you I had things planned too," she was panting against the counter, her body heaving its own rhythm.

Her glorious ass, so round and perfect, was begging for a spanking. SMACK. "Ouch. Oh, God."

She was startled and just as quickly as she had tensed up she relaxed again when my kisses began to cover her ass and the beautiful mark that now adorned her. I ran my hand up the inside of her damp thigh and covered her mound. "You're so wet. Do you want me, Cassidy?" She was so responsive.

"God, yes."

"Yes what?" I continued to rub her clit.

"Yes, sir. I want you, only you."

A shudder ran through me at her words. I pulled the condom out of my shirt pocket, kicked my shoes off, and slid the condom on. I positioned myself at her opening and started rubbing my wrapped head all over her clit. She groaned and I was certain it was one of the best things she had ever felt.

I was gliding my cock all over her clit and she immediately pushed back against me, enjoying what I was doing. "Are you ready?" I slammed into her before she finished nodding her approval. I stilled just long enough for her to take a deep breath, pulled back and crashed into her again. She moved her arms up; gripping the other side of the kitchen counter to compensate for the power I exhibited.

It was like she was made for me. I could feel her pulsing around me as I pulled back and rammed into her again. I needed her closer. Yanking her closer as her arms fully extended across the kitchen island, my strength was the only thing keeping her from falling off the counter. Holding her hips, all that could be heard was the smacking of flesh on flesh and our breathing that was in tune with one another.

nine

Unloaded

~ JAMES ~

SHE LOOKED STUNNING SPRAWLED on her front as she begged me to give her more. I had pulled her hips off the counter toward me to keep her still and continued pushing into her. She met and greeted each thrust with equal precision. I could feel her body tensing as I removed my hand from her hip to caress her lower belly and then down thru her curls. She bucked against me as I began massaging her tight nub.

"Oh James, that feels so good."

Her pussy reared up as I pushed her toward her climax. She clenched around me and pressed back into me. The frenzy was building up in her and then she was crying out, possibly before she was ready.

"James, if you don't stop, I can't."

"Now Cassidy. Never hold back." Almost immediately she began convulsing around me. I couldn't take anymore as my own release had me nearly trembling behind her. She let go as the spasms took over her body. Every nerve was flinching and she grew silent. With the blood pounding in my cock, I came too, shaking behind her. I fell onto her back painting kisses on her shoulders as the last of my release filled the condom.

"Cassidy, are you okay?" I had hoped that I wasn't too rough. She did better than I could've hoped with the power I had exhibited on her, but would she be able to handle more than just my strength? I reached up to release her hands that still clung to the counter. Pulling her up, I turned her around to face me and she looked completely sated.

"I'm wonderful."

It was quick, hard, glorious and over too soon. I kissed her lips tenderly. She had seen a couple sides to me now and seemed to enjoy them all. Wrapping her arms around me she realized I was still wearing a shirt and still semi-erect. She yanked the condom off and threw it in the garbage before I could stop her and my cock jumped at her touch.

"Let's go." I dragged her through the living room and to the stairs as she started to panic. She let go of my hand, jumping to the step in front of me, forgetting she was naked.

"James, my room, well, maybe we could go back to your place."

She DID NOT want me to see her room? I wondered if it was a wreck and lacking as my eyes narrowed at her and I tilted my head in question.

She looked worried. "What's the problem Cassidy? Now I'm even more curious." What the hell was wrong with her? Maybe she was a slob and didn't want me to see her panties on the floor, but maybe I wanted to see them. I threw her over my shoulder and continued making my way up the stairs.

She seemed to surrender and didn't fight me as I carried her up the stairs. Walking into her room I was floored by what I saw. "What the fuck is this?" This was not what I expected to see. I set her back on her feet. "Is that a twin bed? Are you twelve?" I couldn't contain my amusement and began laughing.

She smacked me on the chest. "If I'm twelve you're in big trouble."

"Why in God's name are you sleeping on a twin bed?" The things I had in mind for her would never work on a twin bed.

Shrugging her shoulders she replied, "I don't know. It's not been on the top of my list and it's always been just me, for the most part."

"Well, it'll have to do. Just means I'll be on you, in you and touching you all night." I looked deep in her eyes so she'd understand my meaning as I ran my index finger down the center of her chest. I pulled my shirt off before dragging her toward the bathroom. "First, I want to shower with you."

"That would be lovely. The shower too!" She understood my meaning and placed a chaste kiss on me before we sauntered into the bathroom.

I was savoring the heat of her body against mine as the water pelted our bodies. Her arms were entwined loosely around my waist and her head was resting on my chest. I had never felt more at ease with a woman. Her skin felt like satin under my hands as I ran my hands up and down her back. Her complete silence began to eat at me. "Cassidy, are you ok?"

She didn't hear me and asked, "I'm sorry. What did you ask?"

I had pulled her from her trance, "Where were you just now?"

"Honestly?" She looked up at me and I hoped the look on my face made her believe she could tell me anything. "I was thinking about the first night I saw you at the Blue Horse." I couldn't help but tense a little. "Why did you wait so long to introduce yourself, to make a move?"

With concern all over her face, I couldn't help but wonder where she was going with this. I put her head back on my chest and smiled. "I don't know. You scared the shit out of me." How could I tell her that from the first moment I saw her, my instinct told me to run and my heart and body told me to grab her and *then* run? I felt her stiffen. *Shit.*

"Scared you how?" She leaned her head back, searching my face. I was glad to know I wasn't the only one scared.

"I knew my life would never be the same and it scared me. I'm only sorry I didn't claim you first." I stroked her cheek and she leaned into my palm, cradling herself back into my arms.

Though it was barely audible she said, "Me too."

I needed her to look at me so I tilted her chin up. "Cassidy, if I had known what was going to happen that night I'd have done anything to stop it." *Dan didn't deserve to breathe the same air as her.*

"James. You don't blame yourself, do you?" I couldn't stop the guilt that crossed my eyes and I knew that she saw it, too. "Wait, did you have anything to do with it? The charges were dropped."

She began swatting at my arms around her shoulders and I noticed her eyes were glassy; though the water would disguise any tears that poured down her face.

How could I not blame myself? I bent down to the level of her eyes. "Cassidy I blame myself because it happened in my establishment. I promise you that's all." She let out a gut wrenching sob as I pulled her closer. She had been through enough and I didn't want to hurt her with all the unnecessary details. "I'm so sorry."

Her shaking began to subside with the security of my arms around her. "Please don't blame yourself. It'll break me apart all over again. I'm sorry I doubted you," she said into my chest.

I wished that I could erase all her hurt. I tilted her face toward mine and kissed her softly. She opened for me and her tongue was already seeking mine. I wondered if she would always have this effect on me.

My cock was already aching for her as she ran her hands through my hair. I pressed my erection into her belly and realized she had turned the water off as she opened the shower door. She pulled me to the bedroom without bothering to dry off, only one thing on her mind.

Holding my hand, she opened the top drawer of her nightstand and pulled out a condom, lying it down on top. She lowered herself, laying down on the bed like a willing sacrifice. I took in her body, the curve of her belly, breasts, and thighs. Her hair was wet and clung to her damp body. She was the perfect mixture of innocence and experience. I grabbed the condom and sheathed myself before I joined her on the bed.

"Slow and easy this time, Cassidy." She *needed* me to go slow—it was written all over her face—and for once I *wanted* to take her slowly. My hands moved to her temples and gently massaged them before I ran my long fingers through her wet hair. I kissed almost every inch of her face while she stroked my arms. She started running her fingers through my hair and it nearly drove me wild. My hair was one of my weaknesses, like Samson. She brought my mouth down to hers and devoured my it. She led the kiss, licking and sucking my tongue and lips before pulling my bottom lip between her teeth gently biting down. I groaned as I pressed my cock against her. She made me want to thrust into her at full force. Maneuvering to her opening, I moaned in pleasure at the heat that radiated from her pussy.

"Take me, James."

She was my little piece of heaven. I slid into her with guarded control, slow and deliberate, as she arched her back to press closer to me. We repeated the movement over and over again and I could sense that she was losing control.

"James, oh God, it's so good."

The orgasm built in her as I watched her eyes glaze over. She looked lost in ecstasy. I reared up higher to penetrate her deeper.

"Oh Jesus." .

I loved making her feel out of control. I grabbed her leg and threw it up to my shoulder as she cried out, hitting her deeper.

"Ahhhh! Please don't stop," She was pleading with me and frantic as she waited for her orgasm to take her.

"Have faith baby." I pulled up as high as I could and drove into her further. The only part of her body left touching the bed was her upper back and head. I continued to drive in slow and deliberate. I put a little more force behind my thrusts as she squeezed me into oblivion. She was ready to burst. "Come for me." After a few more strokes I caught her holding her breath as she went stiff. I sensed the change in her and quickened my pace, knowing it was the final piece to the puzzle that she needed.

I unleashed on her as she began screaming and panting her release and she continued convulsing while her hands gripped the sheets. Her pussy was clenched so tight around me that I couldn't contain myself anymore. I worked my hips frantically before she begged me to stop. She was drawing every drop from me. I let her leg fall to the bed as I eased my mouth down to her lips. "You're amazing, Blackbird."

She scoffed, "You do all the work."

"If this is work then I'd like to do this job forever. It's like you were meant to be mine Cassidy." My throat constricted as I realized my slip up. I had said the words before my brain could even process them. I shouldn't have said it, though it was true. She was mine. Letting her go would surely end me. She didn't seem to notice and I rolled us to our sides, still inside her. I ran my hands up and down her back as her body stilled and her breathing slowed.

"You've always been mine, from that first night. You belong here, with me." I wasn't sure if she heard any of my words. I waited a moment and realized she was fast asleep.

I was startled awake in the early morning hours. Waking up with someone was still foreign to me. I had been known to share my bed, but not my slumber. Cassidy was still fast asleep. I eased away from her and covered her up before I wrote her a note. I then gathered my things and headed out the door.

~ CASSIDY ~

I AWOKE AND knew immediately that he was gone. My heart sank. I reminded myself that we had just gotten together and maybe we weren't really *together*. I stretched and lay in bed for a while, recalling the night before. I liked slow and steady James almost as much as I liked no holds barred James. He was amazing in bed; it was clear to me what I had been missing all those years. Passion. He simply had it, while the other 'lovers' I'd been with never did. I decided I would tackle the last few boxes floating around the house after I took a quick shower. I went to get out of bed and saw a note sitting on the nightstand.

> Sorry, I didn't want to wake you.
> Amazing night. I'll talk to you soon.
> XO ~J

His note gave nothing away and I couldn't help but wonder what 'soon' meant. I got out of bed, pulled my hair up, and got in the shower. After I had spent plenty of time under the hot water, easing my pleasantly aching muscles, I exited the shower, pulled on some comfy clothes and headed downstairs. I then spent the next thirty minutes setting up and programming my new coffee maker and was soon enjoying a great cup of coffee. After collapsing all of the empty boxes and throwing them in the garbage, my place was starting to feel like a home. I headed to the living room and sat in front of some unopened boxes.

A couple hours passed and all of the boxes were emptied except for one. I still hadn't found my damn iPod. I dug through the last box, not recognizing the belongings. I looked on the outside of the box to find there was no writing on it designating who it belonged to. After a few moments it dawned on me whose box it was.

Holly.

I felt like an intruder looking through her belongings. Most of her stuff was donated a few weeks after her death. She had no family, just Sam and I. As I continued to pull items out I came across a picture frame and removed it from the box. I flipped it over to see that it was the photo of the two of us that she kept in her room.

It was taken my last night at the diner. Neither of us were looking at the camera. She had her head thrown back in laughter, probably at something I said.

I wasn't even aware that I was crying until the tears hit my leg. I was also on the cusp of laughing; the night that picture was taken was a great night. I pulled out a little keepsake box and opened it up to find tickets and movie stubs. Some of the events Holly and I had attended together and others we hadn't. I had no idea Holly was so sentimental.

I continued my investigation of the contents of the box. GOLD! My iPod had been found, buried in the bottom. I jumped up and ran over to the stereo, docked the iPod, pushed play and cranked it up. I grabbed my laptop, pulled up iTunes and started downloading some of the summer's biggest hits. Holly always said I was a pop music whore and I couldn't deny it. I loved my top 40! I also setup a new playlist titled 'James'.

ten

Ride

~ CASSIDY ~

I WASN'T SURE HOW MUCH TIME had passed, probably a couple hours. I was busy cleaning, organizing and re-organizing with the stereo blasting. I thought I finally had the kitchen organized the way I wanted. I was sweeping the floors when *I Love It* by Icona Pop came on. I couldn't help but start singing and bouncing around to the beat. I turned toward the front door and was briefly startled.

Knowing how loud I had the music on, I wondered how many times he might have knocked and if he used the spare key or if I left it unlocked.

"She sings!"

James was there, just watching me, leaning against the entryway with his arms folded across his chest. He had a huge grin on his face, totally amused. Normally I would've stopped in my tracks being totally humiliated, but instead, he inspired me to continue on my tirade. He pushed off the wall and closed the distance between us.

I tried to play it cool and pranced my way over to him before I gyrated my ass against his thigh as I continued to sing. When the song ended I went to turn the music down, but he caught my arm just before I was out of his reach.

Grazing his lips across mine he whispered, "I missed you."

"Hmm." I eagerly kissed him back. "You were up early." It was a statement, not a question. I took in his appearance. I hadn't seen this James before. His hair was down and I admired him from head to toe as he pushed some strands out of his face. He was wearing a black V-neck shirt, a black leather jacket, dark jeans that hugged him perfectly, and black boots. He had my entire being humming with his hotness. If I hadn't known better I would've guessed he had shown up on a Harley.

He threaded his hand through his hair as I checked him out. "Get dressed, Cassidy. I'm taking you for a ride." I looked at him with a question in my eyes. "It's a gorgeous fall day and I want to spend it with you. Come on." Leading me to the stairs, he patted my ass as I headed up. I stopped, turned and before I could say anything he said, "Totally casual. You'll want to wear jeans and boots if you have them." I nodded and headed back up the stairs and into my room.

I liked casual James. I rummaged through my closet and pulled out my favorite jeans, a grey t-shirt, and after throwing half a dozen pairs of shoes out of the way I found my favorite pair of army boots. I threw them on and went to the bathroom to put on a little makeup and brushed my teeth. I noticed that the music wasn't quite so loud anymore.

~ JAMES ~

I TOOK IN my surroundings and could tell she had done a lot of work. The only boxes I saw were empty and evidence of her just moving in was now gone. Walking over to the stereo, I turned the music down and answered my ringing cell phone. The call confirmed that her car was ready and I gave instructions for it to be dropped off at her house in the next couple hours.

It was then that I spotted the pictures on the mantel and glanced through them. There was a picture of a younger version of Cassidy and two guys, one older and the other her brother. The older gentleman had to be her dad. On the other end of the mantel was a picture of her and Holly. I picked it up and admired the candid moment and then immediately flashed through every moment of that horrible night at the bar again. I scolded myself for not warning her off Dan sooner. Dan swore he was clean but the toxicology reports from that night revealed otherwise. The fucker even went as far as to hide some of his stash in my office at the Blue Horse.

~ CASSIDY ~

I LOOKED IN the mirror and took the pony out before running my brush through it. I decided to leave my hair down but threw an elastic band around my wrist. After putting on some eye shadow, mascara and gloss, I took a deep breath and headed downstairs. Grabbing my purse and a jacket off the coat rack, I turned and found James standing by the fireplace. He was holding the photo of Holly and me. "Ready when you are."

He must not have heard me come down the stairs as he looked to me slightly startled. He put the photo back before he walked over to me. "That was quick." I simply smiled and glanced nervously down to my feet before motioning him to the front door. James went through the door as I dug through my purse. When I found my keys, I locked the door and placed the keys back in my purse. Finally lifting my head to find James, my jaw dropped.

I froze instantly. "Holy hell!" He was straddling a big black bike. He looked like a fucking god on it, just smiling at me. He turned it on and revved the engine. Goosebumps flew across the back of my neck as I took a deep breath and walked down the stairs.

James revved the engine again for optimum effect as I walked down the stairs. "Have you ridden before?" I shook my head 'no'. "Really? Well, come here." I walked hesitantly toward him as he handed me a helmet. He was helping me put it on while giving me some instructions. "You're going to want to keep your feet here and not here."

He pointed out a few things and I nodded in agreement. Cal had a bike and had offered to take me for a ride, but I had always refused. I climbed on, rather ungracefully, slipping once, and put my hands in my lap.

I sensed him laugh as he had to reach behind himself for my arms. "You're going to want to hold on, Cassidy."

After pulling my arms around he asked if I was ready. I responded, "I think so!" He revved the engine and I jumped a little as the tingly vibration ran under my seat and through me. *Dear Lord!* Before I could say anything more, he let the tires squeal as he took off down the road, causing me to grip him tighter.

James quickly headed to the north freeway to get out of the city. It really was an awesome fall day. We'd been graced with an unusually warm fall. Soon winter would be upon us and the bike would likely go into storage until spring.

Soon we were in the country and the colors were breathtaking. I ran my hands up to his chest and rested my head on his shoulder. Suddenly my nostrils were assaulted by the smell of cinnamon and apples. "OH, yum!" My stomach growled in response.

"You hungry?" I replied 'yes' in his ear. The cider mill was right around the next curve.

After we parked, James grabbed my hand and intertwined our fingers as we headed toward the barn. I glanced over at him to find he was smiling which in turn made me smile. The cider mill was packed as was to be expected on the Sunday before Halloween.

After waiting in line we made our way to the register to grab some donuts. The girl working behind the counter asked us if we wanted half a dozen, a whole dozen, or more.

James looked to me and I said, "I'll take a half dozen. I'm not sure how many *he* wants, though." James looked taken aback.

I could hardly contain my laughter when I looked to him. He looked baffled. "I'm kidding. Half a dozen will do. I'll share." I nudged him with an elbow in his side and he laughed. We also purchased half a gallon of apple cider, snagged two cups, some napkins, and made our way outside.

He led me back to his bike and away from the bustle of all the families enjoying that lovely day. "Did you really think I wanted all six donuts for myself?"

James looked as though he wasn't quite sure how to respond to me. "Umm, I don't make it my business to question one's eating habits."

James looked at me mystified. I had just put him in dangerous territory and I knew it. I couldn't help but bust up laughing. "Don't look so serious. I'm just harassing you. I could certainly eat them all, but you make me want to share."

I started cracking up and he relaxed. I knew exactly what I was doing. I reached in the bag for a donut and he snatched the bag away from me, "Hey…" I puckered my bottom lip as James put our purchases in the saddlebag.

I watched him as he opened a compartment on the side of the bike and placed our purchase inside. He came out holding one donut and guided it to my lips before snapping it away. He dared take a bite out of it as my eyes got big.

Like the gentleman he was, James handed me the remainder of the donut which put a big smile on my face. "I know a little place right up the road. Bear with me."

He placed the helmet on my head before putting on his own. He then turned to me and asked if I was ready. "You got a little something…"

I wiped his lips with my thumb and then proceeded to lick my thumb clean. James let out a groan. It was sexy as hell and I knew exactly what I was doing.

His eye color seemed to immediately grow more vibrant. "Wait, I missed a spot." I stood up on my foot rest to get a better angle on his face and trailed my tongue across his bottom lip and finished with a soft kiss. I was gazing down at him quite pleased with myself.

I probably would've let him devour me right then and there, damn the audience of families. I was looking into his eyes with a big grin on my face. He put his arms around me and grabbed my ass. "Be careful, Cassidy. I wouldn't want us getting arrested for indecent acts." He then smacked my ass.

After he pushed me back down in my seat, he raced down the road once I had placed my hands around him. I ran my hands down to his hips and was starting to trace them over his thighs before he grabbed my hand while shaking his head.

James grabbed my hand before I reached his groin and placed it to his abdomen, "Stop distracting me!" We were only driving for a couple of short minutes when he pulled onto a back road. The road led to an empty field and I noticed a sign declaring we were on private property. He ignored the sign and drove onto the land. He steered us toward a big tree that sat on top of a small hill and parked nearby. I got off the bike and admired my surroundings. The fall colors were breathtaking.

I took in my surroundings while he pulled the donuts and a blanket out of the saddlebag. I took the donuts and cider from him as he laid the blanket out under the tree.

"The sign said private property."

"I'm not concerned; I know the owner," he responded casually and I nodded in approval before I took my seat on the blanket. He sat down next to me and proceeded to pour cider into the cups and then handed me one of the cups. We opened up the donuts and each took one.

"Mmm, it's so good." I was truly enjoying the donut and so was James. "It's so beautiful out here."

We were both grinning like little kids. I leaned back on my hands with outstretched legs and enjoyed the warmth on my face. He looked like he wanted to pounce on me and was doing everything he could to resist. I wondered if he was trying to prove that he could be a gentleman anytime, anywhere.

"It is. I love it out here." He continued assaulting me with his eyes and I couldn't help but feel nervous.

"You're not the only one admiring the view." I rolled my eyes and shook my head in disagreement. "You really can't take a compliment, can you Cassidy?"

"I don't know. Guess I'm not used to it."

"Not used to it?"

"I could try to get used to it." I smiled at him as he closed the distance between us.

James leaned in and brushed his thumb across my cheek. Ever so slowly, he leaned in and paused with only a breath between our lips. I was aware that I had stopped breathing.

My breath caught as James was about to press his lips to mine; I wanted it so much. "I'm not going to kiss you again until I know more about you." I let out a moan as he leaned back against the tree.

He was really enjoying himself. "What do you want to know?" I grabbed another donut and pulled a piece off, slowly putting it in my mouth while locking my gaze on his. I tried enticing him, but it was evident he wasn't going to give in. I decided to start talking before he started asking questions I didn't want to answer.

"I have an older brother who's a cop. Dad's a Ford retiree. I grew up in the suburbs. I'm a party planner, but you know that. If you want to know something specific you'll have to ask."

Then he asked the dreaded question. "What about your mom?"

I was pretty sure I visibly flinched at the mention of my mom. Ugh. He didn't miss a beat. "Mom's gone, has been a long time. Next question please."

He must've figured I didn't want to discuss it further because he changed the subject. "Any past relationships?"

"Nothing serious, at least not mutually. You?"

"Nothing serious, at least not mutually." He flashed me a smile. "What do you want for your birthday? It's Saturday, correct?"

That smirk flashed again and I couldn't help but blush every time I saw it. His question caught my attention. "How do you know when my birthday is?"

"Purse. Elevator."

"Oh. Um...I don't know. I haven't really thought about it. It's not like I expect any gifts. I've been so busy with work and the auction." It dawned on me then that he would probably be at the auction on Friday. It was being held in *his* hotel after all. It was as if he could read my mind.

"I'll be there," he said. Going back to our conversation about my birthday, he asked, "What about a new, *bigger* bed?"

I scoffed, "Ha! Mr. Benedict, don't tease. I'll take the bed from 1204 if you don't mind. Best night's sleep I've had in a long time. Though, that *may* have had something to do with you." I shivered just at the thought of our time in that bed and flashed him my sexiest stare. He brought something out in me that I couldn't quite explain. I had never felt so confident around a man before. I smiled at him, hoping that I was tempting him.

"I'll have to see what I can do."

I laughed because he couldn't possibly be serious. *Could he?* I got on my knees and crawled over to him. He didn't move a hair as I straddled his knees.

"I like a lady on her knees."

"I *bet* you do. What about you? When's your birthday? Anything catch your eye that you want?" He grabbed the back of my thighs and pulled me closer.

Grasping his shoulders to steady myself, he buried his head in my neck and inhaled. I moaned and in turn buried my head in his hair, running my hands up the back of his neck. He exhaled into my ear, "I have what I want right here and now." I moaned and brought my head down to his while running my hands through his hair.

"You're a temptress, Miss Charles." He grasped my waist and pushed me off and up to my feet as he followed.

"You bring it out in me." I felt like I was going to combust and let out a disappointed groan.

He popped another donut in his mouth, gathered some of our belongings and headed back to his bike. I was horny as hell and was starting to fancy the idea of James naked in the autumn sun. He was bringing out a whole new side of me that I hadn't known existed. I gathered the blanket and followed him over to his bike.

"It's getting late and we both have to work tomorrow."

James handed me my helmet while taking the blanket from me and putting it away. I looked to the horizon and noticed the early signs of the sunset approaching. "Shit, my car."

"It will be back at your place by the time we get back." James motioned me to get on the bike. He fired it up and headed back to town. I couldn't help but wonder why he was suddenly being so distant. He was acting all gentlemanly, like you would expect on a first date. Of course, that was our first date, technically. I was thankful to be headed home because it was starting to cool down quickly.

eleven

Anchors

~ CASSIDY ~

"**A**RE YOU HUNGRY?" WE'D JUST WALKED in the door at my place after I looked over my car. He even had my stereo replaced. He was too good to be true.

"What did you have in mind?"

"We can order takeout or I have some Chinese left over from last night. I can cook, but I don't have much."

"Whatever's easy."

I headed to the kitchen and pulled out some plates, forks and got the leftovers out of the fridge. "All I have is champagne, water, and soda." He took water and I did the same. After the food was heated up, I took my plate and headed to the living room with him following behind me. I sat on one end of the couch facing the opposite end where he took his seat. We each had a few bites before he broke the silence.

"Why a phoenix and the blackbird? You have a thing for birds?" he asked with half a grin.

His question took me off guard a little. I shrugged my shoulders. "It's silly, really." I looked to him and his curiosity wasn't budging. I could tell by the look on his face he wanted to know. I sighed, "When Holly and I met I was in the middle of reading all the Harry Potter books. She was peering over my shoulder one day and saw me reading about the phoenix. She had questions and I explained them. She said that we were both like the phoenix, each in our own regard. Overcoming hardships in our past, having to let it go so we could move on with our future. We were planning to get matching phoenix tattoos before she died. She actually drew my tattoo. I had it done on her birthday in September." I looked at him and he was listening intently to me with a sincere smile on his face. Slowly, James turned his smile into that sexy smirk that turned me on and made me uneasy all at once. "I told you it was silly."

"It's not silly. It's lovely. When are you getting the colors added?" He took another bite of his food and I did the same.

"I've been meaning to schedule the color appointment, but I've been so busy with work. And I still haven't decided what colors I want to use." I winked at him. "Why the dragon?" I looked at him nervously.

"Similar to you, it has to do with someone close to me that I lost." Before I had a chance to inquire more, he set his plate on the coffee table, closed the distance between us and took my plate from me, placing it next to his. He unfolded my legs before he sat back down on his end of the couch grabbing my ankles and setting my feet in his lap before unlacing my boots. "And the blackbird?"

Everything about him was smoldering. "A few things. I love the song by Alter Bridge. My grandmother's maiden name stands for raven, a blackbird, or so she told me. Some people say they're a bad omen, but my grandmother used to tell me that blackbirds were our ancestors watching over us, like guardian angels."

He nodded his understanding. "I like the song, too. Seeing the tattoo on your wrist all those months ago reminded me. I listened to that song over and over these past few months. Do you have any other tattoos?"

"Maybe." He growled and I snickered. "Holly and I got matching tattoos several years ago, my first, then the blackbird two summers ago after my grandmother died."

"Where is it?" Both of my boots were now off as he tossed them to the floor. He locked his hands onto both ankles and yanked me closer to him. "Tell me, Cassidy."

I was already panting and feeling flush. "You're getting warm." He grinned and removed my socks in unison. "Warmer." James began running his hands all over my right foot and I immediately tensed, trying not to bust out in laughter.

"Maybe I'll tickle it out of you." He traced a finger from my heel up to my arch and my hips bucked as I grasped the cushion beneath me.

"Please don't!" He examined my entire foot before running his hand up the back of my calf, massaging as he went. I rolled my head back and savored his touch. He dropped my leg and started examining my left and I knew when he had found it. I felt his weight shift and then the hot sensation of his tongue as it licked the outside of my ankle. "Mmm." Goose bumps covered my body.

"How did I miss this? Why an anchor?" He sat back down all the way and pulled me even closer to him. My feet were resting on his hips as he resumed massaging my calves. I had to force myself to look at him.

"We were all the other had for a long time. Cal was in Afghanistan and Holly didn't have any family. It was just the two of us." I sighed and let my head drop to the side resting on the couch as he continued kneading my calves.

"So was her anchor in the same spot?"

"Actually, she got wings on her back." He didn't have to ask the question. "We were inspired by a sign we saw once in a store window. *'You are the anchor that keeps my feet on the ground and I am the wings that keep your heart in the clouds'* or something like that. I was her anchor, she was my wings."

"That's beautiful." His hands left my legs as he guided me to lie on my back and hovered over me. I didn't resist.

"Thank you." He was above me and I was longing for him to kiss me. I moved my hands to touch him and he moved out of reach before I was successful.

His hands were on the waist of my jeans as he worked his way under my shirt. My breath hitched as he ran his hands over my belly before undoing my pants. "Lift your hips." I did as I was bid as he tugged my jeans from my hips. He sat back down as my jeans joined my socks and boots on the floor. His hands made their way to my thighs and began massaging. He was dangerously close to my panties and I was worried he would set me off without much more effort. I realized I was tense when he whispered, "Breathe, Blackbird. Relax." He sounded almost as breathless as I felt.

His hands ran along my hips then up under my back and I was suddenly face to face with him. James had pulled me to his lap and I immediately flanked his sides with my legs and circled my arms around his shoulders. He buried his face in my neck and inhaled deeply. I believed he found my scent as intoxicating as I found his. His scorching tongue worked its way to my ear where he bit, tugged, and sucked on my lobe.

"Ohhh, God."

I was panting in his hair as I sought relief by trying to grind into him. His hands were all over my back and it felt like he left a trail of burnt ash along my skin.

"James..."

He tugged my shirt over my head and began kneading my breasts through my bra. His chest was heaving along with mine. I needed him on top of me, in me, on me. I tried to lie back and he stopped me, instead wrapping his arms tightly around my back, placing his hands on my shoulders as he pressed me into his erection. Bursts of electricity shot through my body at the momentary relief of his cock pressed against my pussy. I circled my hips against him and grasped his back like my life depended on it.

"Shit." He thrust up in response to my movements.

"James, please kiss..."

I didn't get to finish my sentence. His lips attacked mine and I was in heaven. I was truly putty in his hands. I continued to rub myself against him and worked on pulling his shirt up. I found the expanse of his back and it was hot and dewy.

Bang, bang, bang.

I brought my hands to his chest and leaned back momentarily. He obliged and I tugged his shirt off and added it to the growing pile of clothes on the floor. He was simply stunning to look at.

BANG, BANG, BANG.

"Cassidy, don't make me bust down the door. I know you're in there." I bolted upright and nearly leapt off James's lap. *Dammit, Cal!*

"Shit. It's my brother. He *will* break down the door." We were both catching our breath. I climbed off James's lap and threw a shirt on. "Don't move." I was surprised with my own tone and James just smirked at me.

Bang, bang, bang...

"HOLD ON, CAL!" I went to grab my jeans and realized the shirt I put on wasn't my own. It was more than long enough and it would have to do. I looked to James and he looked good enough to eat, that damn smile on his face, just lying there, nearly naked. If this didn't send the message to Cal that I was 'busy', nothing would. I rushed to the door, unbolted it and threw it open. "WHAT!?"

"What are you doing with *HIM*?" He was shouting at me. He tried to walk past me and I braced both hands on his chest in response.

"What do you mean *him*?"

"You know what I mean. He's the owner of the Blue Horse." He looked me up and down, noticing the shirt and my near nakedness. If he was angry before, he was fuming mad now; I could almost see the steam puffing out his ears.

"Dammit, Cal, get OUT!" I shoved him back, which took all my strength. "I'm twenty-seven years old and I'll date whomever I want. This isn't up for discussion. I'll call you tomorrow." I pushed him again, just far enough that I could slam the door. I immediately locked the deadbolt and looked out the peep hole.

He was throwing his hands in the air as he walked back to his patrol car. He tended to stop by when he was on duty and things were slow. Knowing him, he ran the plates on the motorcycle when he pulled up. *Dammit.* I took a deep breath, smoothed down the shirt I wore and headed back to the living room.

He hadn't moved. It should be illegal to look that divine. I plopped down on the couch next to him. "Sorry, he's a little over protective. Big brother syndrome and all; it doesn't help he has a badge to go with it."

James didn't say a word. He simply moved so fast, that before I knew it, I was on top of him again. We were sitting up, face to face, as I straddled his lap once more. I was taking in his appearance when he put his nose to mine. "Dating, huh? Why didn't you tell me you were dating someone? This might be a deal breaker, Cassidy."

Shit. I immediately tried to retract my statement. We hadn't discussed dating or anything relationship oriented. "Sorry, I, it's just that I didn't know what to tell him. I didn't mean to imply..." He started cracking up. "What are you laughing at?" Now I was annoyed.

"Whoever this bloke is that you're dating, tell him to get lost, you'll only be dating me from now on." He was rubbing his nose up and down mine when I realized the joke was on me. "That is, if you *want* to date me. I'm perfectly fine with just the fucking."

I sucked in my breath and attempted to get off his lap. I was appalled. He made it sound so dirty.

He seized my arms, "Cassidy, I'm joking. I'm sorry; I didn't mean to offend you. You're the only girl for me, have been since that first night I saw you at the Blue Horse."

I relaxed and looked into his eyes. He wasn't lying. "Really?"

"Cassidy, don't ever doubt it. We'll deal with Cal and anyone else who might have a problem with it. Okay? Now, where were we?" He gently pressed his lips to mine. I eased my body back into his and accepted his kiss.

I panted, "Okay," between kisses.

James wasted no time in removing his shirt from me. I settled in closer to him and ran my fingers through his hair. I tipped his head back so I could have better access to his mouth as his hands began kneading my shoulders and neck. I dropped my head to his shoulder as he released the tension from my shoulders. Running my hands across his ribs and down his abdomen, I reveled in the dusting of hair that covered him. I paid special attention to the happy trail that disappeared into his jeans.

I started to undo his belt as he lifted my head and brought my mouth down to his. My body was screaming in expectation of him. I'd never had a craving like that before. I was convinced I could live off him and him alone. I pressed against him and he met me with a thrust of his own as a burst a pleasure ran through me. I bit his lip harder than anticipated and he groaned. "Sorry."

"Don't be sorry." He pushed me back a bit while one hand encircled my neck and then ran down the center of my chest. "A front clasp, I was wondering how you got this on." He fiddled with the clasp, and before I knew it, my breasts sprung free and were greeted by his hungry mouth.

I finished undoing his belt and began working on the button to his jeans when he lifted me up and stood. I grabbed his wrists and stopped him, "Please, let me."

He took a deep breath before relaxing. I sensed that he needed me as much as I needed him. I freed the button before palming his erection through the denim. James threw his head back and gripped my shoulders. I found the zipper and pulled it down slowly before I worked my hands into the waist of his jeans. I tugged them down to his knees and realized he still had his boots on.

"Sit down."

He sat back on the couch and I noticed how tight his boxer briefs were, his erection straining against the material. I knelt down in front of him and pulled his boots and socks off before freeing him of his jeans. On my knees, I placed myself between his legs and started massaging his calves. I could feel the tension slowly roll off him. After a few minutes, I worked my hands up to his thighs and dug my knuckles into his muscles. His head was leaned back against the couch when I snuck my hands into his boxer briefs, up to his hips, and then yanked them down. He lifted slightly to ease my way, his eyes cloudy with desire.

I swear his cock bounced as my eyes took in his superb nakedness. With his underwear discarded, I returned to my previous position, but closer. My breasts were resting on his lower abdomen as I began kissing his chest and rib cage while my hands lightly caressed his back.

"Cassidy, you're making me crazy." His hands began rubbing my scalp.

"I thought it only fair to return the favor." I smiled up at him and he looked like a man possessed. He wouldn't let me continue this much longer. I moved down and his cock was standing at attention against his stomach. I grabbed him and gave him a squeeze. His hips jumped up as he groaned and I squeezed him again. Dipping my head I ran my tongue from the base of his glorious cock to the tip where I began circling the head.

"Dammit, woman." He was out of breath and I loved it.

I greedily took him into my mouth while fisting around his base. I glided down his length several times. I didn't normally enjoy this task, but with him I never wanted to stop. I squealed when he quickly pulled me off him and dragged me to his lap. I was on my knees as he bit my left breast.

"Owww!" He kissed, licked, and sucked the pain away almost as quickly as he had delivered it. "God, James, please."

"What is it, Cassidy? Tell me what you want."

His hands were running down my back and into my panties, digging into my ass cheeks as he lifted his hips to press against me. I jumped as a surge of pleasure made me dizzy. I grabbed hold of his face and attacked his mouth. I took my fill of him until I had to pull away to catch my breath.

"I want you inside me, desperately. Please. Here. *Now*."

He placed his hand on my lower belly as his fingers made their way under my panties and into my short curls. I was frozen in time. The only thing I could feel was the heat of him and my heart as it pounded in my chest. His fingers went further down and grazed my swollen nub. "Oh." I placed my forehead on his and closed my eyes as he gently rubbed my clit. "James…" he dipped a finger deeper and slid inside me.

"You're so wet. Show me what you want." He gripped my ass with his free hand, raising me up and down so that I was riding his hand.

"More, I need more." Our eyes were locked as he added a second finger. I eagerly gripped them with my walls as he slipped his fingers in and out. It felt amazing. Suddenly, there was more of him that I wasn't prepared for. "Oh that's, ohhh, too much." He had added a third finger and it was almost unbearable. Almost. I could feel the frenzy building inside me.

"Slow and easy, Cassidy."

I steadied my pace to give my tight pussy a moment to adjust to his fingers before I rode him again and again. I had my rhythm down and my head was thrown back, "Now stop moving." I was startled to stillness at his words and started to plead with him before I was silenced.

I was up on my knees bracing myself on his shoulders. He was running his slick fingers up, down, in and all over my sex. The pressure was building and felt wonderful. I recognized the sensation of a bead of sweat as it slid down between my shoulder blades. He pulled me closer and I could no longer see his face. His head was buried in my breasts and the hand that was gripping my waist had now joined his other hand in its exploration of my sex, but from behind. I jumped a little as he gently circled my *other* opening.

"Relax, I won't hurt you." The act was entirely foreign to me. The hand in front swept into me again, gathering my juices before sliding out to my rear. He continued circling my tighter hole with one hand while pumping me with the other.

The feeling was so alien, but I was enjoying it. "James, it feels so good, but I don't want to come without you." I pulled myself away slightly before I grabbed his cock. "Please, I want this."

~ JAMES ~

HER PANTIES WERE barely on, with both my hands inside them. She would be my undoing. I never knew it could be so intense. "Please, I want this." She was milking my cock with her hand. "I need you, all of you inside me, now." She was panting in my ear and I lost all sense. I pulled my hands from her soaking center and ripped the panties from her body. She gasped and then cooed in my ear as I shrugged my shoulders. "I liked those."

"I'll buy you new ones." I had her sit on my thighs as I cupped her face. "I need you, too." I kissed her slowly and deeply as she pulled her legs up while scooting closer. Her ankles were now gripping my ass with her hands in my hair. Her mound was pressed against my erection. She lifted slightly and guided her opening over my tip. Our kiss halted for a split second as she gazed into my eyes. She looked absolutely lost, like she was on another planet. Before I could push her away to get a condom, she sheathed me with her tight pussy. She began shuddering from her own force, "Cassidy."

"I'm sorry, I had to have you, and I couldn't wait. I don't know what came over me." She was wheezing and pulling away looking regretful. "I've never done this without protection, you're the first." She was pulsing around my cock and I thrust my hips up and deeper into her. "Oh, God, that's not helping." She circled her hips seeking pressure on her clit.

"I'm clean, Cassidy." She smiled against my lips and kissed me. "You're the first I've done this with, too. You're on the pill, right?" She nodded and deepened the kiss. We started rocking in unison, both lost in the sensations. The only sounds were her sensual moans. I could already feel her beginning to tremble. She was close.

"Breathe, Cassidy, slow it down. Let me catch up." She groaned and slowed all her movement. She placed her hands on my knees and arched back. I drank her up. She was exquisite stretched out on top of me. "You're beautiful." I gripped her waist and slid her up and down my cock as she threw her head back. She was so tight around me.

"James. Feels. So. Good." She lifted her hips to meet mine. I couldn't resist the temptation and began rubbing her clit. She jumped slightly on my throbbing cock, "I can't wait if you do that, you have to stop."

I stopped my thrusting and grabbed her breasts, twirling and tweaking her nipples. She brought herself back down to me and sucked my lower lip between her teeth. Her hands were on my chest pinching my own nipples.

I grunted as I slammed up hard into her and she met me full force. "Cassidy, fuck."

She could sense my own desperation and slammed down on me harder. "Harder, James, faster." She was whimpering with her arms clinging to my back as she mewled in my ear. She was so close.

"I don't want to hurt you."

"You won't. Please. Oh, God."

Her words had me teetering on the edge, too. I clutched her waist as we slammed into each other over and over again. Before I knew it, she was crying out into my mouth, every part of her shuddering around me. "Fuck, Cassidy…"

"I want to feel you come inside me." Her words sent me over the edge and I unleashed myself inside her as I buried my face in her neck.

She was limp against me as I thrust a few more times. Her pussy was trembling around me. I ran my hands over her body, eliciting more quivering from her. I lay lax on the couch, draped in a sated Cassidy. Her hands were lazily trailing up and down my sides. "You're amazing, Cassidy."

"I think you're the amazing one. I never knew sex could be this good. God have I missed out."

"You won't be missing out anymore." We lay there for a while, basking in our afterglow. After a few minutes I felt her shiver. "You're cold."

"A little." She was still curled into me.

I tightened my hold on her. "Let's get you in a hot shower." I stood up with shaky legs and carried her up to her room.

twelve

Bubbles

~ CASSIDY ~

H E SET ME DOWN ON THE VANITY and then turned to me, "Bath or shower?"

"Are you joining me?"

"If you insist," he winked at me.

"Bath, please." I watched him as he leaned over and turned the water on. The muscles in his back were rippling and begging to be touched. I got down from the vanity and crept over to him. I pressed myself to his back wrapping my arms around his chest. He tensed momentarily and then covered my hands with his. He spun in my arms and embraced me.

He whispered into my hair, "You're going to change my life, Cassidy Charles, aren't you?" Before I could comment on that he smacked my ass and pushed me toward the toilet before he walked out.

I took advantage of the privacy and relieved my bladder. When

I was finished I dug around in my cabinet for some bath products. I found my orange scented bubble bath and pulled it out as he walked back in. "Do you mind?"

I waved the open bottle under his nose and he smiled. "I don't, it smells like you."

I walked over and poured some into the running water and watched as the bubbles formed. After grabbing some towels and other bath necessities, I placed them by the tub. It was now that I noticed how large the tub was. Thank goodness! "Do you need to use the bathroom?" He nodded so I headed into my bedroom and glanced at the clock. Where did the time go? I heard the toilet flush and then the bath water was turned off.

He appeared in the doorway, looking like he was carved by Michelangelo himself. "Ready?" I nodded as I walked to him. He took my hand and led me to the tub, stepping in first and sitting down. "Come here." I stepped in, still holding his hand, and sat down between his legs. I wasn't used to this kind of intimacy. Reading my thoughts again, he pulled me back to him and gathered my hair over one shoulder while kissing the other. "Relax, Cassidy."

"I'm trying." I leaned back into him and his arms encircled my waist. His knees were cocooning me and I began tracing lazy circles over his thighs. "How old are you?"

"Does it matter?" He was running the loofah across my shoulders.

"Of course not, I'm just wondering when your birthday is since you know when mine is."

"December 31st. I'll be thirty three this year."

"New Year's Eve! How fun. Always a party to go to." I swore I felt him tense up behind me.

"If you say so." I didn't question his lack of enthusiasm. "I'm going out of town tomorrow." My heart sank at his words. *Get a grip, Cassidy.* "I'll be back by Friday, in time for the auction and charity ball."

"Okay. Where you headed?" I was purely curious, making conversation.

"Just some business to deal with, it's no big deal. I'll miss you, though."

I smiled at his words. "I'll miss you, too."

He pushed me forward and continued washing my back. When he was finished he pulled me back against him and started washing down my front. I flinched as he hit a sensitive spot by my hip.

"You really are quite ticklish. I think I'll enjoy that." Before I fully understood his meaning he was digging his fingers into my hips. I squealed as water was splashing everywhere.

"No, please stop. Agh. James, please." He was laughing, too, and I wriggled my way around to face him. He finally stopped his attack as I steadied myself against his chest. Suddenly everything was quiet and we weren't laughing anymore.

He pulled me tight against him. "I mean it, woman. I'm going to miss you...terribly." Before I could respond he kissed me. It was a kiss that I was meant to remember and knew that I would, just like all his kisses. Ever so slowly and softly he teased my lips with his tongue as he glided it across my lips before retreating. I begged for more as I felt him grow hard beneath me and I squirmed against him. We were insatiable. "You won't be able to walk tomorrow, Cassidy." He smiled against my lips.

"I don't care to walk ever again." I tugged on his hair and he deepened the kiss. That was his weakness; I'd figured it out by the way he reacted each time I would pull on it. I reached between us to stroke him as I continued the pursuit of his lips. His head then fell to my shoulder as he groaned while his hands were massaging my backside. I continued my playful tug of war on his penis and he shifted me slightly so I was straddling his thigh. I couldn't help but move against it. I leaned down and began kissing his neck and shoulder. He was rocking me on his thigh while I increased the pressure of my hand on his cock. We groaned in unison as I bit down on his shoulder.

"Cassidy, the things you do to me." He grabbed me tighter and tensed. "Shit." In a split second he had moved me and thrust into my already swollen flesh. It knocked the wind out of me as I clung to his neck crying out. He stilled, waiting for me to relax around him.

When I could breathe again, I sought out his mouth and tugged on his bottom lip while I pulled his hair. I lifted slightly and slid back down, tensing as I went. Like a wild animal he unleashed on me while changing our position. My back was now against the other end of the tub and he was on top of me, pounding away. Only a few moments passed before he succumbed to his release.

"Cassidy, I can't…" He was yelling and tensing over me as he shot into me.

He kept his head buried in my neck for several moments as he panted. I was shushing him while stroking his back. "Are you okay?"

"I'm great. A selfish clod, but I'm great." His breathing was calming and he brought his eyes back to mine. "I'm sorry, I lost control." He kissed my nose before separating us. I flinched a little from his brutal lovemaking. He looked to me with concern in his eyes. "You're hurt."

"Just a little tender. I'll be fine." He shook his head, stood and got out of the tub. "James?"

"Up with you." I went to stand up and realized I was a little more than tender; I felt like I had just run a marathon. I tried to climb out of the tub and slipped, but he was there to steady me before I fell. "You're not fine. I'm an ass."

I smacked his shoulder. "You're not an ass. I'm just not used to so much intense sex. Is it always like this with you?"

His eyes were hooded and I curled myself into him. "You've

brought out the randy teenager in me, Cassidy. I'll try to calm down on the intensity."

"James, I like it this intense, don't think otherwise."

He pulled away from me, grabbed a washcloth and headed to the sink. He turned on the cold water and saturated the cloth before wringing it out and walking over to me. He knelt in front of me, "Spread your legs, this will help." I spread my legs as he held the cold cloth to me. At first I recoiled before the cool sensation seeped into me. "Feel better?"

"Yes, it's wonderful." My hands were on his shoulders as I braced myself. He began wiping softly before heading back to the sink. The cloth was no longer cool so he ran more cold water over it and then repeated his task.

"To bed with you."

I pouted as he smiled at me and pulled me to my tiny bed. He yanked the covers down and sat me down before bending down in front of me. "You're not going to break me."

He looked up at me, digesting my words, and I leaned down to kiss him. He stroked my mouth with his tongue ever so softly. I couldn't help the moan that escaped past my lips. "You're insatiable." I smiled my agreement as he trailed kisses down my chest and abdomen. He pushed me to lie down on the bed as his lips kissed my hip bones. I convulsed as goose bumps danced across my skin. "Gentle this time, Cassidy."

He spread my legs as he continued kissing his way across my hips. "Yes, please." I felt his hand feather down my lips to the back of my leg as he spread me even wider.

He started blowing cool air all over me and I could feel myself open for him. I was rolling my head from side to side, reveling in the sensation. "James, please." I was rewarded by his scorching hot tongue.

One long stroke pierced my opening and glided up to my clit. "Mmm, James."

He began circling my clit with expert precision. Soft, yet so direct, as my juices flowed. He licked back to my opening and his tongue dove in. My back arched off the bed as he held onto my hips. He used slow heavy laps up and down my lips several times and then he started sucking on my clit. One finger gently slid in and began circling.

I felt like I was floating. Every nerve ending was tingling with desire. I didn't know being so gentle could feel so good. "Breathe, Cassidy." He started circling his tongue around my nub again while his finger did the same to my vagina, while slowly moving in and out.

Just a little more pressure. I started rocking into him needing more and I carefully felt him add a second finger. The inevitable spiral began to unfold inside me. "Oh God, I'm close."

He began flicking my clit and humming against it. His fingers pumped a little harder and it set me off. I started to buck against him, but he held me down and found my breast. He was pinching a nipple, sucking my clit and pumping me as my body exploded with pleasure and I screamed out his name. My toes were even tingling. He was a god. How was it possible to be so good? I didn't care. He continued working me until I was twitching all over and pleading with him to stop.

~ JAMES ~

SHE WAS ABSOLUTELY beautiful and a more giving lover than any I'd had, and there had been a lot. She liked it rough, whether she knew that or not was the question. I wasn't looking forward to being away from her for so many days. *What was wrong with me?* Cassidy was what was wrong. I should have run in the other direction that first night I saw her at the bar. She was a witch and I was definitely under her spell.

She was still coming down from her orgasm and twitching against the sheets. Her hands were clenched on my head, trying to pry me off her. Once her breathing slowed I peeled myself out and off her. I swung her legs into her bed and climbed in next to her. I grabbed the covers and lay down with her, rolling her to her side as I curled my chest around her back. She was mumbling incoherently as I held her, soothing her until I was sure she was sound asleep. I kissed her head before I left.

I made my way back to the hotel and packed my suitcase. Dad and I tried to visit with Mom at least once a month and I hadn't seen her in several weeks. Dad mentioned that it wouldn't be long now before we had news. Everything was packed and by the front door. I headed to bed for a few hours of sleep before I stopped in at the office.

SLEEP WAS POINTLESS. I made it into the office by seven a.m. Jennifer came in as I was going through my emails.

"James, you're here early. I wasn't expecting you this week."

"Morning, Jennifer. I just want to check on a few things before I leave. The jet's on standby." She nodded in understanding. "If Miss Charles from B & C calls this week please get her anything she needs."

"Yes, Miss Charles. She's a lovely girl! No problem, James." She headed to her desk just outside my office and got to work.

I set my automatic reply in my email before I shut down my computer and packed up my laptop. As I walked out of my office I set a box down on Jennifer's desk. "Please see this is delivered by courier today. See you next week."

"Sure thing, James. Give your mother my love."

I nodded as I headed to the elevators. The doors opened and Calvin was standing there in his uniform screaming into his phone. He flew right by me and headed to Jennifer's desk. "I'd like to see Mr. Benedict." He put the cell phone in his pocket.

"I'm sorry, sir, is there a problem?" Jennifer was looking at me, expecting me to make my escape or to intervene. Calvin was looking all around, completely oblivious that I was who he was looking for.

"Officer Charles, I believe you're looking for me."

He turned and glared at me, unaware he had just walked by me. "Mr. Benedict. Yes, a moment of your time, if you don't mind."

"Jennifer, call Smith and let him know I'll be down shortly." I walked back into my office as Calvin followed and I motioned him to sit on the couch, then shut the door behind him.

"This won't take long." I set my briefcase down and turned to him. He had closed the distance between us and was pointing his finger in my face. "Stay the hell away from my sister."

I moved away and sat down on the other couch across from where he stood and ripped my hands through my hair. "Calvin, if you'd calm down and give me a moment to explain; I think I deserve at least that."

He was battling with himself as he took a few strides before sitting down across from me. There really wasn't much of a family resemblance except for their eye color. "Talk."

"Officer Charles, or can I call you Calvin?" I was goading him when I knew I shouldn't. If I had a sister I would have been fuming mad about her dating me, too.

"Officer Charles will do. What the hell were you doing at my sister's place?"

I raised my eyebrows at him. I knew he didn't really want the answer to that question.

"Dammit, that's not what I meant. Stay away from her."

"Officer Charles, calm down. I know what you must think." I let out a deep sigh. "I'm not who you think I am. I care deeply for Cassidy. There are some things you should know."

~ CASSIDY ~

"God dammit, Cal. CAL?!" *Shit.* I couldn't believe what he was doing. I was on my way to my office and had to pull over. I tried dialing James but he didn't answer, so I called Lena who answered immediately.

"Lena, can you get me the number to Benedict Holdings? I can't find it in my phone. No, not the hotel, ok thanks." Once the text came through I dialed the number and headed back into traffic.

"Benedict Holdings, Jennifer speaking."

"Jennifer, it's Cassidy Charles. Yes, I know, ok, that's not why I'm calling." *Shut up lady!* "Did a tall blonde cop just walk in, by chance? Yes, shit, ok. Umm, no I'm on my way." I disconnected the call and threw my phone down on the passenger seat. I started hitting my steering wheel while shouting, "Shit, shit, shit! Damn you, Cal, you overbearing ass."

I pulled up to the office building almost twenty minutes later in sheer panic. I had no idea where to park, forgetting about the underground garage. I hoped and prayed they both still had their teeth. I glanced across the street and saw Andy doing valet at the hotel. I squealed my tires as I did a U-turn and pulled into the valet at the hotel.

"Miss Charles, nice to see you." I threw him the keys without a word and dodged a few cars while I ran across the street.

I was greeted by the security desk and a man in uniform I didn't recognize. I asked to see Mr. Benedict and in return got a suspicious look at my request. "Jennifer is expecting me." He got on his phone and pressed a couple of buttons. A short moment later he hung up the phone and pointed to the elevator while he mentioned I needed to go to the 23rd floor, unaware that I already knew that. I could only imagine what threats Cal used to get past the security desk.

It seemed like forever before the doors opened to the floor I sought. I rushed out and saw a desk with a woman in her fifties sitting behind it. "You must be Miss Charles?" I nodded as I recognized her voice. I started looking around in a panic. "Dear, you look like you've seen a ghost, are you ok?"

"Yes, I'm fine. Is James still here?" She waved toward his office doors, doors that were closed. For the first time I noticed his name on the door. Jackson James Benedict III, God that was a mouthful. I looked back to Jennifer who motioned me in. Hesitantly I pushed on the door. The scene that greeted me had my stomach turning. What the hell was going on?

They were both sitting forward, opposite each other, laughing. Cal spotted me first and jumped to his feet. "That's my cue. James, it was a pleasure." James stood and they shook hands. "I'll see you on Friday."

I was dumbfounded. What had just happened? Cal kissed my cheek and whispered, "He's one hell of a guy, sis." I was left staring after him as he left.

"Morning, Cassidy." I turned to James who was smiling like he knew the best kept secret in town and was waiting to see what I would offer to find out what it was.

He gathered up some papers from the coffee table and put them in his briefcase before he turned back to me. My hands were on my hips and I was utterly baffled.

"What the hell is going on?" I was genuinely concerned and he just shrugged his shoulders and strode over to me.

"Your brother likes me. He's a smart guy." He pulled my hands off my waist and brought them to his lips. He kissed each in turn. "Cassidy, you're going to be late for work."

"I'm already late. I thought for sure I'd walk in to a brawl. What did you say to him?"

He pulled me close and kissed my nose. "I told him the truth."

"Which is?"

"The truth."

"For the love. You seem quite pleased with yourself." He kissed me chastely. "I thought you were going out of town?"

"Smith is waiting for me downstairs." Our hands were entwined as he held them behind my back, leaning into me seductively. "Did you sleep well?"

I blushed immediately and smiled. "You know I did. When did you leave?"

"Late. Let me walk you out." We headed out of his office and past Jennifer after he grabbed his briefcase. Her head was buried in her work as we entered the elevator. He pulled me tight against him. "You in an elevator with me, tsk, tsk, tsk." He bit my ear and I giggled as I grabbed onto his suit jacket. "I can't get enough of you, lady."

"Good, that means you'll keep coming back for more."

He jerked back and looked at me, "Always!" The doors opened and he was all business again as we walked out the front doors. "Where's your car?" I pointed across the street. He laughed as I explained my parking dilemma. He waved to Andy who responded by hopping in my car and driving it over. "I don't want to jeopardize your job. I'll be in touch." He embraced me and kissed me deeply.

I was vaguely aware of Andy's reaction after he pulled my car up.

When James was done kissing me, Andy acted like he hadn't seen a thing. I then saw James's Rover pulled up behind my car and a man in black shades was standing by the driver's side door. He simply nodded to me.

"That's Smith." I mouthed 'oh' as James shuffled me into my car. He leaned down, "Think of me." He kissed me again as he ran his hand up my leg before buckling me in. He cupped me gently and I clenched my thighs around his hand before he quickly pulled away.

"You're the devil," I glared at him. He smiled, closed my door, and I drove off once I'd regained my composure. It was going to be a long lonely week. Thank God work would keep me busy.

~ JAMES ~

I watched her drive off and then climbed in next to Smith before he headed to the airport. Calvin was more than receptive to what I had told him, more than I thought he would've been. He was a little shocked and told me that Cassidy should know, but he would let me handle that. It couldn't have gone any better, really. It was going to be a long week. Friday couldn't get here soon enough.

thirteen

Revealed

~ CASSIDY ~

I WALKED INTO WORK THIRTY MINUTES late. Lena rushed into my office asking, "Everything ok?" She handed me my coffee.

"All good. It's still warm."

"I ran it through the microwave."

"Thank you, Lena. Is she here?"

"Not yet, you're in the clear." I plopped into my chair, relieved by her words. Though Cecily was late to work on numerous occasions, she didn't appreciate tardiness from her employees, and she always seemed to be on time on the days we were late. The joys of being the boss.

"Have we collected all the auction items for Friday?" Lena sat down at the other side of my desk as we dug into work.

A couple hours later, we were both on calls; Lena was on her cell and I was on my desk phone when Linda came in. She dropped a package on my desk, and behind her, a pair of legs carrying a massive bouquet of peonies walked in. I ended the phone call and couldn't help the smile that spread across my face.

"Flowers for Miss Charles." The delivery man poked his head from behind the floral arrangement.

"That's her!" Lena chirped as the flowers were placed on my side console. I came out from around my desk and signed for them. "They're beautiful. Who are they from, Cassidy?"

"Thank you." The delivery man made his way out, followed by Linda who was scowling at me. *The old bag needed to get laid*, I thought as I opened the card.

> Blackbird,
> I'll never forget our firsts.
> Miss me.
> XO ~J

"Well?"

Blushing, I examined the peonies closer. The bouquet was a mixture of purple, pink, red and blood red peonies with some greenery. They were stunning. I closed my office door before taking my seat. "Lena, this has to stay between you and me." I'm not sure why I even bothered to preface the conversation with that statement. One great thing about Lena was her ability to keep a secret.

She was squealing with delight. "I couldn't believe it when I saw you in his office with him. O.M.G. Cassidy. He's a big fucking deal! A big fucking *hot* deal!" Her enthusiasm was contagious and I started laughing with her. "Does Cecily know?"

"She saw us dancing at the masquerade on Friday and said we needed to talk. So I'm not really sure."

At that same moment, Anthony barreled through my door and threw a newspaper down on my desk. Anthony was Cecily's PA, gay, black, and wonderful. He and Lena were the closest people to me since I lost Holly.

I didn't normally pay attention to the papers, especially the society pages. Anthony *lived* off them. I picked up the paper and examined the picture.

"What the fuck?" It was a picture of James and me at the ball. We both had our masks on, but the caption read: JB3 MYSTERY WOMAN! "JB3?"

Lena and Anthony both said in unison, "Jackson James Benedict the third; JB3!"

Realization hit me like a tidal wave. *James was JB3?* That was bad. "Oh, holy hell." I may not have paid attention to *all* the society pages, but I knew who JB3 was. Millionaire playboy, new girl every week, bachelor extraordinaire. I heard Lena and Anthony talking about him all the time. I really knew how to pick them.

"Holy hell is right, girlfriend. If the picture was in black and white no one would know it was you, but in color, giiirrrl. You can't hide that mane of red hair. And since when are you and JB3 a thing?" He spotted the bouquet and read the card. "XO, J? Giiirrrl! Caught you a big fish with that one."

My head was in my hands and I could feel the headache coming on. "Fucking hell."

"Mmmhmm, hell fucking him, I bet it's more like heaven." Lena immediately started cracking up as I turned fifty shades of red. "NOOO? I was kidding. You're sleeping with him? Honey, do tell! It's time for lunch anyway. Let's go!"

Anthony was right, it was time for lunch. I grabbed my bag as Lena, Anthony, and I headed to the Coney Island down the street. I filled them both in on the way.

By the time our lunch arrived I had spilled the beans including our run-ins at the Blue Horse from the summer. I spared no detail except for some of the intimate ones.

"What am I going to do? He's JB3. I don't know if I can handle this."

Anthony was fanning himself. "Honey, if you don't want to handle that, I will!" We all started laughing. "Please tell me he's got a little dick. I don't think I can bear it knowing he's that good looking and hung."

My face gave me away without any hesitation. I hated that I so easily blushed.

"Damn. Giiirrrl, you hold onto that with both hands, literally." Then he winked.

We went back to eating as I pondered all the thoughts running through my head. He could have any girl he wanted, he was so far out of my league. Anthony asked me what was wrong. "Um, I'm me and he's, well, JB3! I'm from a blue collar family and he's not. He's high society." They looked at me like I was crazy. "Once I knew who he was I knew he was loaded and I tried not thinking about it." More to myself than to them, I mumbled, "This is a disaster waiting to happen."

Anthony grabbed my hand. "Girl, you a catch. You're real, not some fake society bimbo. Has he given you any reason to doubt him?"

"It's been three and a half days. He's gone out of town or at least that's what he's told me."

"What does your gut tell you?" Lena was asking now.

"I believe him."

"Then leave it. He comes with some high toting baggage, but you can't let that define your relationship. Girl, you deserve this." Lena agreed and I was feeling better.

After paying our bill we headed back to the office. Anthony's phone started buzzing. "She's baaack!" We all quickened our pace knowing Cecily was waiting for us.

We walked in to see Linda scowling again, "Cecily wants to see you and you." She pointed at Anthony and me. We both sighed as we made our way to her office.

Her door was open and she was standing by her desk finishing up a phone call. She waved us in and motioned me to sit. *Shit.* She ended the call and barked a few orders at Anthony before sending him off.

"Close the door, Anthony." He gave me a sympathetic look before closing the door.

She took her seat, then a sip of her water and stared at me. I hated when she did that. Finally she spoke. "Great job on Friday." I visibly relaxed as she smiled. "Stop doubting your talent, Cassidy. You're great at what you do."

"Thank you. I'm grateful for the opportunity." She continued staring at me before shuffling a few things around on her desk. She picked up a paper and put it in front of me so I could see. It was the picture from the ball of James and me. "Oh, God."

She chuckled. "If you're looking to bring attention to yourself, he's the quickest way to do it." All I could do was shake my head. "I don't really care what's going on, but keep it separate. I don't want this affecting your work. You have a promising career ahead of you. Stay smart, Cassidy."

"Absolutely, of course, Cecily. Thank you for understanding."

We went over a few more work related things before I went back to my office. I scrolled through my email hoping for some worthwhile correspondence, but there was none. I spotted the box at the end of my desk that I had forgotten Linda put there because I was distracted by the flowers. There was no return address, just my name and B & C on the label.

It was a good sized box. Opening it, I discovered another box with Frida's labeled on it. What the hell? Suspiciously, I opened it up and pulled back the pink tissue paper. Several pairs of satin underwear, bras, and camisoles greeted me. I didn't see a card and began looking for one when Lena popped her head in. I slammed the box shut, but not before she saw it.

"Is that from Frida's?"

"Don't. Just hush. What's up?" *Why the hell did he send me lingerie at work?* He really was the devil.

She was smiling from ear to ear and I knew then she saw what it was and I knew I was as red as a rose. "From James?"

"Lena, what do you need?" I was totally embarrassed and she knew it.

"I'm heading out to pick up the last of the donations. I'll see you in the morning." I looked at the clock and wondered where the time had gone; it was already after four in the afternoon.

"Great. Thank you, Lena. Have a good one." She winked as she closed my door. I sagged into my chair and peeked back into the box of lingerie once more. It was a gorgeous mix of satin and lace, but mostly satin. As I rifled through, I finally found a note.

> I owe you some new panties.
> I couldn't resist the rest.
> ~James

I felt myself blush at the realization that JB3 just bought me a new wardrobe of undergarments. *JB3.* I never realized they were one in the same. I had heard most of the stories, but never paid them much heed. It was the job of the press to exaggerate, right? I couldn't resist...I knew I shouldn't...

I pulled up my internet browser and typed in 'JB3'. A slew of links popped up. This was bad. The first one was a link for the local paper. One after another I started clicking away. Almost every picture was of James and random girls. Only one face repeatedly appeared next to his. She was a pretty brunette named Melissa Westin.

Not being sure how much time had passed, I was rubbing my temples when my cell started ringing. Pulling it from my purse I saw it was Cal. "Hello."

"Hey, sis. You okay? You sound stressed."

Sighing deeply, "I'm a fool, Cal." I felt sick to my stomach.

"What are you talking about?"

"James…he's JB3." I was practically in tears.

"He's who? Cassidy, it's after six. Are you home yet? I was planning to pick up a pizza and thought we could have dinner before my shift."

I loved my brother, overbearing ass and all. "I'll be there soon. Just use the spare." I disconnected the call and put my cell back in my purse. Gathering up my box of lingerie, laptop bag and purse, I decided to leave the flowers because my hands were so full.

When I got home, Cal was getting out of his truck with a pizza box in one hand and a six pack in the other. I walked up the steps, unlocked the door before I hung up my purse, put my laptop bag down and ran upstairs with my box of intimates. Before heading back down, I changed into some more comfortable clothes.

Cal was sitting on the couch and handed me a plate of pizza as I sat down. He was in uniform from the waist down, sporting a white t-shirt on top. Cal started eating, waiting for me to break the silence. Spotting that he brought my favorite, Mike's Hard Lemonade, I grabbed one and downed half the bottle while he eyed me suspiciously.

He sighed, "Cassidy, what's going on?"

"I told you, I'm a fool. He's a notorious playboy. I'm just a notch in his belt."

He just scowled at me. "Cassidy, while at first I would've agreed with you, after talking to him this morning, I don't think that's true.

He really cares for you, he told me so. What happened between then and now?"

"He's plastered in all the papers and now I'm there, too." I got up and grabbed the article from my laptop bag and tossed it in his lap.

"JB3? Are you the mystery woman?" He was smirking. "What's the big deal?"

"Are you kidding me? Really? After what we've been through; I deal with enough crap from those entitled asses I throw parties for, but to be dating one of them?" Now I was just talking shit because I was totally freaking out.

"Cassidy, I know what's going on here." I looked at him doubtfully. "You really like him. You've never cared about what others thought before, not since high school. You're just making excuses because you're scared you're going to get hurt."

I started crying. "I am not!" *Damn, I hated when he was right.*

"Ok, if you say so." He went back to eating his pizza and I did the same. After a few minutes he got himself more pizza, water, and me another drink. "I can't tell you what to do. We all have a past; you know that better than anyone. His just happens to be well documented. Don't let his past dictate your future. I know *you* have things you'd like to sweep under the rug."

Cal had a point. "You're right. Sorry I freaked out. Thank you."

"Any time, sis. You know I'm here if you need to talk...or kick some ass, even if it's yours." He grinned and ruffled my hair.

Smiling, I smacked his hand away. "Knock it off!"

"I need to go. You're good here?" Nodding my agreement, I stood up and he gave me a giant bear hug until I was giggling.

"Put me down!" He obliged and headed out the door and I followed after him. I didn't even ask him about his conversation with James. "Hey, what did you two talk about this morning, anyways?"

He just shrugged his shoulders at me. "Bros before hoes, Cassidy." He was laughing as I rolled my eyes at him. He got in his truck and took off.

Unbelievable. Bros before hoes. What about sisters? Cal had never liked any of the guys I dated. Of course he had never met any of them either. This could be interesting.

Turning on my iPod, I selected *Stars* by Grace Potter and the Nocturnals. The song reminded me of Holly. I cranked it up before I sat back on the couch with another slice of pizza. I let the music flow in me as I just vegged out. I was replaying the events of the weekend over and over while lying on the couch. Several songs later, one I hadn't heard in a long time started playing. How ironic that it came on at that moment. I sat and listened to it, loving it all over again. When the song ended I got up and hit repeat, replaying the song. Alter Bridge's *Blackbird* boomed through the speakers. I listened to the song one more time before turning it off and heading up to bed.

~ JAMES ~

My PLANE LANDED and it was already late. I decided Mom could wait until morning and headed straight to the hotel. I managed to get some shut-eye on the plane and decided to get a workout in. After changing my clothes, I headed down to the hotel fitness center. I was alone in the gym, which wasn't surprising given the late hour, and pretty much had the run of the place. I jumped on a treadmill after lifting some weights and put my ear buds in and selected my 'workout' playlist.

Cassidy was all I could help to think about as my legs pounded away. She didn't seem to care about my reputation, or she was clueless. Guessing by the lack of magazines and papers around her place, I was convinced she was clueless. I knew it could get ugly. And Melissa…I couldn't even think about her. Worst. Mistake. Ever.

A while later, I slowed the treadmill to a stop and noticed I ran over ten miles; my goal was five miles every other day. I'd definitely be hurting in the morning. Seeing it was close to two a.m., I grabbed a towel, a bottle of water, and headed back up to my room. After taking a shower, I checked my email, and after firing off a few, I was thankful to be feeling drowsy. I climbed into bed and let sleep take me over.

Light filled my room when I awoke. Grabbing the bedside clock, I was surprised to see it was almost eight in the morning because I rarely slept more than three to four hours in a row. I stretched, showered, and dressed in the span of twenty minutes. Wearing jeans and an oxford, I left my hair down and headed out the door. The valet brought the rental around and I jumped in to head to the clinic.

I checked in at the front desk and then made the trek to my mother's room.

"Jimmy!" She held my face between her hands and kissed me before hugging me. "Oh, it's good to see you, my boy. Let me look at you." I felt like I was twelve years old again. "Something's different. Tell me how you are. I was just headed to the cafeteria for some breakfast. Come on." She wrapped her arm around mine and we walked in silence for a few moments. She was too thin, but looked better than she did at my last visit several weeks ago; she had some color back in her cheeks.

I got an omelet, bacon, and some orange juice while mom grabbed two croissants to go with her eggs, fruit, and coffee. When we sat down she placed one of her croissants on my plate. "Jimmy, they're delicious, you *must* have one." I nodded as I dug in to my breakfast. "So, tell me about this Cassidy."

I started coughing, practically choking on my bite of omelet. She was grinning from ear to ear. After I composed myself I glared at her.

"Talking to Dad, are you?" She put a cheesy grin on her face and waved her hand at me in her usual 'carry on' manner. "There's not much to tell."

"I know better than that, Jimmy. Your Aunt Bev emailed me a copy of that picture in the papers of you two. I'm sorry I missed the masquerade, it looks like you had a marvelous time."

"Knowing Aunt Bev, *she's* the one who took the picture." I sighed. "She's wonderful. She's laid back, funny, beautiful, passionate…"

She was beaming at me across the table. "You're really taken with her. Oh Jimmy, that makes me so happy. I never thought I'd see the day when someone turned your head. And she's not after you for your money?" It was a question everyone would ask.

"She's the most genuine person I know, Mom. I don't think she quite comprehends all the baggage I come with."

"Dad said she's a doll. I can't wait to meet her and find out for myself." I looked at her with my brow all creased. "Honey, I'm coming home. The holidays are coming and I miss my family."

"What do the doctors say?"

"Jimmy, please let it go." She wouldn't look at me and started devouring her breakfast.

She was evading the question. I slammed my silverware down a little too hard and she jumped. "Sorry." She tilted her head at me and feigned a smile. "Mom, what do the doctors say?" I tried softening my tone.

"Jimmy, we knew it was a long shot. I have some tests today and should have results in the next day or two. If this is going to be my last Christmas, I want to spend it at home."

I pushed my half eaten plate away from me. "Mom, don't say that." Resting my head in my hands I felt her squeeze her frail frame around my shoulders.

"My sweet boy. We've been fighting for years; I was told I only had *months*. It's been a good fight. No matter the results, I want to go home. There'll be no more discussion." My throat was constricting and I squeezed her hand. Defeated, I acknowledged my understanding and she sat back down to finish her breakfast.

fourteen

Rainbow

~ JAMES ~

WE PROCEEDED WITH A DAY FULL of tests for Mom. I gave her every appropriate detail about my time with Cassidy and she was the happiest I'd seen her in a long time. After dinner we went back to her room, and I could tell she was exhausted, so I insisted she go and get some rest and she did.

I left her room to head out to the gardens to call Dad. "Dad, it's me. Yes, she's resting. Did you know she's planning to fly home with me? Yes, I understand…"

Dad told me, "Son, I know how hard this is. Your mother and I made this decision together. She wanted to be the one to tell you."

I could hear his voice cracking and it nearly sent me over the edge. "Ok. We'll see you in a couple days. Love you too, Dad." I sat down on the nearest bench with my head in my hands as the tears fell from my eyes to the grass below.

After an hour of feeling sorry for myself I decided to go back to Mom's room and found she was still sleeping. I left her a note telling her I would be back in the morning, went back to the hotel and headed straight to the bar.

"Whiskey, make it a double." The bartender nodded and fetched my drink. I downed it in one gulp and the fire burned me all the way to my toes. The bartender looked at me. "Water, please." I knew better than to have any more. Glancing at the menu, I decided to order a steak and salad.

After struggling about whether or not to order another drink, I spoke to the bartender who made the arrangements to have my dinner sent to my room. I was scanning through emails and on the phone when room service knocked. I opened the door and the waiter brought the meal in on a cart. After handing him a few bills, he bowed and left the room.

"Smith, just do what you need to get it done. Sabrina and Delaney should have all the necessary information. I want it done by Friday night, sooner if possible. You, too. Thanks."

Sitting down, I made hasty work of my meal before getting back to work; it was the only way to keep my focus off Mom. I worked into the wee hours of the night and decided to go for another workout. After another long visit to the gym, I showered and hit the hay.

"WHAT DO YOU mean there's no change? She's been here for four months." I was on the verge of hurling myself on the doctors. Of course I wanted her home, but home *and* in remission.

"Mr. Benedict, I understand your frustration. While the cancer cells haven't spread, neither have they receded."

"James, please sit down." I was burning a path in the small office as I paced back and forth. I did as my mother asked and she put my hand in hers before looking back to the three doctors standing in front of us. "I've told my son that I'm going home. We'll be leaving tonight. I appreciate everything you and your staff have done for me. We knew this was terminal five years ago."

The female doctor nodded her head. "We've discussed this in great length at our sessions, Mrs. Benedict. We all respect and honor your decision." The doctors took their turn hugging my mother before leaving the room. Mother just looked like everything was fine. It couldn't be farther from the truth.

"Jimmy, go back to the hotel. I just need a few hours to pack and say my goodbyes. I know you need to make some phone calls." Good ol' mom, ordering me around like it was business as usual.

"I'll be back in a couple hours."

We left the small office and I kissed her on the cheek before she headed toward her room. As I made my way for the car, I pulled out my cell and called the pilot to put him on standby.

IT WAS THE MIDDLE of the night when we landed at home. Dad was waiting for us and Mom was thrilled to see him. They'd always had a very loving and tender relationship. It made me ache for Cassidy. I told her I would be in touch and I hadn't been; she would probably be furious with me. It was near dawn on Thursday morning, Halloween. I couldn't go to her now. I was an emotional mess and I could only imagine how busy she was with work. Smith was waiting with the Rover so I climbed in and he took me back to the hotel.

~ CASSIDY ~

THE WEEK HAD flown by with the exception of missing James. The auction was the next day and I hadn't heard from him all week. Maybe my gut was wrong; I thought for *sure* that I would've heard from him. Besides the lingerie, flowers, and the pictures in the paper, it was like he, *we*, didn't exist. There was another picture in Tuesday's paper of us chatting outside his office building on Monday morning.

After another long day at work, I was walking into the parking garage behind my building. I had worked late to avoid the kids surely knocking on my door for Halloween. It was then that I looked up and he was there, his bike parked behind my car, and he was just sitting on the seat staring at me.

I froze in my tracks. I couldn't help it; the smile that spread across my face revealed how super excited I was to see him. He stood up and put his hands in his pockets with that look on his face that made him irresistible. I took a deep breath and continued walking toward him.

"Cassidy." He looked down to his boots, rocking nervously back and forth when I tried to scowl at him.

I halted a couple arm lengths in front of him and crossed my arms over my chest. "James." I wasn't sure what to do. Never having been in a situation like that before, I was pissed at him for not calling, but so thankful he was there in front of me. He looked up at me and reached for me, but I stepped back to avoid contact. "When did you get back?"

"Early this morning." The anger started rising in my gut.

"I see." He was just standing there; both of us speechless. I unlocked my car with my fob and started toward the driver's door, attempting to walk around him.

"Cassidy, please, help me out here."

Angrily I swung on him, "Help *you* out? I'm sorry, but what do you need help with?" He looked at me like he was surprised by my rebuttal. "You said you would call. It's Thursday and I'm still waiting."

"I'm sorry. I was really busy; there's a lot going on you don't know about." He *did* look sorry, but I was so mad.

"A lot I don't know. You can say *that* again, James. Or should I call you JB3?"

"Goddammit." He started running his hands through his hair and began pacing. "I fucking *hate* that nickname."

"I wasn't expecting to see my face plastered all over the papers. A little warning might've been nice." The frustration was emanating from him. "I feel like any minute reporters will figure out who I am and come knocking down my door." Ok, I was exaggerating a little and just felt bad for both of us.

"Cassidy. I'm sorry. I couldn't figure out if you didn't care who I was or if you truly didn't know."

"Yes and yes." He stopped walking and looked at me like he forgot his original question to me. "I don't give two shits who you are or what the papers have to say about you. They're paid to tell stories. I just wish I knew about it all before you left."

Looking slightly relieved at my statement, he closed the distance between us. He bent down to my level and put his forehead on mine; his hands were on my hips. "I'm so sorry, baby. Forgive me?"

Trying to ignore him, I could see he was pouting out of the corner of my eye. I couldn't resist him; I was a junkie and he was my drug. His scent traveled through me and I was a goner and suddenly flooded with emotion. I rolled my head to the side and buried myself in his chest, wrapped my arms around his waist and squeezed him tight. "I missed you so much. Don't do that again."

I felt him exhale a deep breath before he tilted my chin up and kissed me quickly. "I missed you, too, Blackbird. More than you know." His arms circled around my waist as he stood to his full height. My arms moved to his shoulders and around his neck as I was lifted off the ground, concealing my face in his neck.

I wasn't sure how long we stood there just holding on to one another. This man owned me and it scared me to death. After a few minutes of figuring out our plans he decided to follow me back to my place.

When I pulled up in my driveway I saw a petite blonde walking out my front door. *What the hell?* I threw my car in park, blocking the foreign car in the driveway, and jumped out of my car. "Can I help you?"

"You must be Cassidy. Oh, James, there you are." She walked over to James who was just getting off his bike, both of them completely ignoring me. Kissing him on the cheek, she said, "Everything is all set. I thought I had another day." She gave him a scolding look. "You're lucky I like you." Playfully, she swatted his shoulder before I interrupted, ready to stake my claim.

"I'm sorry, but who the hell are you and what were you doing in my house?" She looked at me like I was the rudest person she'd met and before she could speak James interjected.

"Cassidy, this is Delaney. She's an interior designer and a friend." Delaney was scrolling through her phone like we didn't exist.

"That's nice, but that doesn't explain why she was in my house." *That* got her attention. James looked pleased with himself and Delaney looked offended.

Before I could say any more, he thanked Delaney again and walked her to her car, holding her door for her before making his way back to me. "Are you going to let her leave or do I have to move your car for you?" He was all smiles.

I grunted loudly, got in my car and moved up far enough for her to pull out of my driveway. Once she had left me enough room I pulled into the drive, parked, and got out. "What's going on, James?" I was beyond annoyed and he could tell.

"It's all good. Don't worry. I didn't redecorate the *whole* place, just made a few modifications." He was looking haughty as he ushered me through the door.

"It doesn't *need* any modifications." He frowned down at me and I gave up the banter as we entered my house, too busy trying to see what the modifications were.

"Are you hungry?"

"Dammit, James. If you don't tell me…" He started laughing before pulling me up the stairs behind him.

We reached my room and I walked in, immediately stopping in my tracks. My room had been *completely* transformed and smack in the middle was a brand new bed, a *big* four poster bed. The bedding was an exact replica of the bedding from his hotel, specifically the suite I stayed in. I was utterly speechless.

Walking to the bed, I took in the headboard. It appeared to be wrought iron, but was painted ivory with a gorgeous trellis design. I ran my hands over the luxurious comforter while still taking in all the metalwork. This was a bed you could tie someone to. The faint smell of paint lingered in the air and I realized there was a new color donning the walls. There were also some other new pieces of furniture. The bed had to be king sized. I didn't think a bed that size would fit in there, but it did.

"How?"

"Do you like it?" He was grinning from ear to ear, just watching me take it all in.

"Seriously. It's too much, James." I was lost for words. *How did he do this?* "How? She did this in like 10 hours?"

"Your spare key. I've had Delaney, Smith, and Sabrina pulling strings since Monday to get it done. I'll be lucky if Delaney works for me again, though I compensated her well for her time." Looking at me like he was waiting for my approval I just shook my head. "Please tell me you were serious about wanting a bed for your birthday."

I started laughing. "James, if I thought you were really going to give me anything I wanted I may have asked for a million dollars or maybe a Ford Mustang GT500." The look on his face said he could do that, too. He started to speak when I motioned my fingers across my lips telling him to zip it. "It's amazing, you're amazing, and I'm suddenly ready for bed." I winked at him and he grabbed my wrist before tackling me and throwing me on the bed.

Straddling my hips, he had my arms pinned above my head and he quickly looked very serious. "Do you trust me, Cassidy?" I let a chuckle slip before realizing that given the look on his face, he wasn't joking anymore. I simply nodded.

He started unbuttoning my shirt before removing it from me. He was silent and meticulous in his task. Once it was off he placed a hand just above my breast bone and slowly trailed it down to my navel as my breathing quickened. He discarded my heels and skirt next. Groaning, he traced the lace lining on the hips of the new panties I was wearing; ones he had purchased for me. My hips lifted, seeking more of his touch.

"In due time, baby." He inched his way back up my body before whispering to me, "Roll over."

Once I was on my stomach, he began trailing feather light kisses down and across my back. I couldn't help but move my shoulders at the sensation.

"Don't move."

I felt the weight of his body leave the bed and heard the shuffling of clothes hitting the floor followed by more movement. His weight returned to the bed and I sighed as I felt the heat of his naked chest against my back.

Rolling to my side he whispered in my ear, "Get on your knees."

I obeyed without a second thought. Once I was on my knees, I turned my head to look at him and my sight was taken from me. The feel of a cool satin blindfold covered my eyes. "Oh."

"Shh, you're safe." My nipples immediately hardened as I felt the cool air dance across my breasts after he removed my bra. Running a finger over my ribcage and tattoo, he caused my breath to catch. He then gently took my wrists and placed my hands high up on the headboard.

He stood behind me when I felt him reach around me, and I felt something soft and smooth encircle my wrists. I should've felt panicked, but I was surprisingly calm and wet. James tied me to the headboard; I knew this when I felt him tug on my binds. Slowly, he ran his hands down my arms, grazing my breasts as he continued down to my waist, past my hips, and down to my knees. I couldn't contain the shivers that passed over me.

His hands made their way up to the waistband of my panties and began to slip inside as I stiffened. "Shit." I said it louder than I anticipated and I felt him still.

"What's wrong, Cassidy?" His hands were on my waist as his breath hit my cheek.

"I, um, well." This was not the conversation I wanted to be having.

"What is it, baby? I'm not going to hurt you." His voice was calming and reassuring.

"It's that time of the month." I was mortified.

"Your what?"

"For God sakes, James, I'm on my period." He grew silent. "I should be done later today or tomorrow."

"It's fine. I can work around that. These can stay on, for now." He circled my ass with his palms through my underwear. "Now, relax." He started caressing my back again and the warmth seeped back into me. "Do you know what a safe word is?"

Goose bumps washed like a wave over my body. I had fantasized about this for so long, if only to experience it once, owning a collection of books on my e-reader, some fiction and some not. I was completely enraptured with kink, BDSM and the Dom/sub relationship, believing that I myself might have had a bit of 'sub' in me. But how did one go about finding those things out? I hadn't ever considered it would have ever happened for me. I nodded my head.

He grabbed my hair and pulled my head back. "How do you know?" His breath hit my cheek and I couldn't quite ascertain if he was angry or enthralled.

Stuttering before I could properly put the words together, I explained to him that I had a collection of books on the topic. I told him about my curiosity and I swear I felt his lips curl into a smile against my neck.

"Have you ever been whipped, Cassidy?" I shook my head no. "Spanked?" I gave the same answer. "Have you ever been tied up?" Again, same answer. "Do you fantasize about it, Cassidy? You can tell me." This time I hesitantly whispered my reply and nodded my head. "I'm honored to be your first and your teacher. Are you prepared to be my student?" His hot breath was blowing in my ear again and it sent pools of warmth between my thighs.

I trembled again as his hands sent ripples of pleasure all over my naked flesh. "Yes, only you."

"Good girl. Only with me. Do you have a safe word? If not, I can give you one." He tugged on my hair again.

"Rainbow." My breath was coming fast as he took my ear in his mouth.

"Only with me."

My body felt his sudden absence and I heard him moving around the room again. Soon the enchanting tones of Enigma were filling the air. I wanted to laugh at his choice, but their music was quite hypnotizing. His hands were gathering my hair as he pulled it back, braided it and tied it off once he joined me back on the bed.

"I've waited for this day. I knew it since that first night I saw you. My imagination didn't do you justice." He kissed my shoulder and then he was gone again. I wasn't quite sure what he was referring to when he said he 'knew it.'

My senses were in hyper drive as I worked on getting my breathing under control. The faint click of a lighter told me he was lighting candles and his footsteps picked up again. I heard him place some things on the nightstand; I could only begin to imagine what those items were. My ears became sensitive and I could hear the occasional car drive down the road and kids giggling in the distance. I pulled my focus back to the music and was startled back to attention when I heard a piercing 'smack' echo through the air. I inhaled sharply, wondering what that smack was—a paddle, crop, or whip—I had no idea, and in turn grasped the headboard as I felt something cool and hard run up the insole of my foot.

"Relax. Don't move. You must obey me in all things, Cassidy."

It was an order, not a request, and when my breathing slowed the sensation continued up my calf and to my thigh. He ran it to my inner thigh and across the center of my panties as I moaned trying to get closer. *Smack.*

"Be still, Cassidy." I felt his hot hand soothing the spot on my thigh he had just whipped. It took every fiber of my being to hold still. My entire thigh was tingling with pain and pleasure and the sensation was spreading out from the point of contact. "Your coloring is exceptional."

His voice was husky and low and had me panting. "I want you to focus on your breathing, understood?" I confirmed with a nod.

The caress from his tool of choice began again. He started at the insole of my other foot and worked his way up my leg till he was rubbing my lips through my panties. I was convinced he must be able to see me pulsing through them. Moaning impatiently, he moved and began circling my buttocks before moving up my spine. It was sweet torture and I knew it had only just begun. His weight shifted, his hand cupping my chin, pulling up and back. My cheek was placed against the warmth of his abdomen and I was aware of his erection just below before feeling the cool tip of his device slide over the top of my breasts. I shivered in response and heard his growl above me as my nipples puckered.

The *smack* that came to the back of my thigh was welcome misery. I groaned, reveling in the wonderful sensations it sent vibrating through me. "Does it feel good, Cassidy?"

"Yes." My voice was barely audible.

"I know it does. Spread your legs wider."

I did his bidding and felt the burn begin in my thighs from kneeling in that position. The light caress of a feather started its torturous journey across my abdomen. I wanted nothing more than to clamp my legs together. The feather began gliding along my inner thighs and the drumming in my core was more intense. His hot breath weaved its way from below my ear, down and across my shoulder and then he repeated the action on my other shoulder. Then it was with cool breath he played his game and then again with his flaming tongue. He was driving me mad, the feather still between my thighs and grazing my panties.

His torture was sweet and masterful as I began to shake. My body was tensing and relaxing over and over as my impending orgasm rose on the horizon. Just from touch, I had never experienced anything so intense like that. His fingers were tip-toeing their way up my spine to the base of my neck before he wrapped my braid around his hand and pulled me back again. My scalp was tingling, and the warmth emanating from him along with his scent was intoxicating.

It was then he removed my blindfold and I was greeted by almost complete darkness, the room lit by a single candle. I had trouble focusing and felt tipsy, like I had one too many drinks. I closed my eyes in hopes it would help me to regain my bearings. James was on his knees behind me and I felt him bend lower. The distinct feel of his erection between my legs nearly sent me over the edge. He was thrusting against my satin and lace covered mound with ease. "Oh, God." My head went slack against his shoulder.

He groaned before purring in my ear, "You're doing very well for your first time. You're close, aren't you?" Before I could respond he removed himself from behind me, and if not for my bound arms, I would have fallen to the bed below me.

"Stand up." By some miracle, I managed to stand and turned my head to look at him. He was in all his glory; naked and fisting his erect penis and I wanted to kneel at his feet. His eyes were boring a hole into me, "Do you like what you see?"

My eyes traveled the expanse of his body again as I replied, "Yes."

The candlelight danced over his skin. His hair was tied back and that was the only thing that disappointed me. He released his shaft and climbed the bed to stand behind me. He untied my wrists and then began rubbing them. Turning me to face him our bodies were barely touching. His face neared mine and I was hungry to taste him.

"James?" I was desperate, but he put his index finger on my lips and shook his head.

"Back on your knees."

He held my hands to steady me as I knelt before him, his erection taunting me. I looked up to him and his eyes gave nothing away. We stood this way for what felt like hours.

Finally he rewarded me with speech, "Good girl," as he cupped my cheek. "Your control and obedience are exceptional." I half smiled, wondering what he would do next. Grabbing his penis once again, "Keep your hands on your knees." He ran the silky tip of his erection across my lips once and did it again as I let my tongue slip out. He inhaled sharply. "Cassidy!"

I pulled my tongue back in my mouth as our gazes met again. "Sorry." But I wasn't sorry, not one bit, and he knew it.

"Open up." As I opened my mouth, he placed the head of his cock between my lips. "Suck me." I was more than eager to oblige, taking him in as far as I could without gagging, and started circling my tongue round and round while sucking. "Jesus, woman." He was fisting the base when I felt the bed jump. I averted my eyes to see his other hand was bracing the headboard behind me. His eyes were closed and he looked to be in agony, sweet agony. Pulling my lips back to his tip I dove onto his length over and over again as his hips gently rocked in unison with my motions. Feeling brave, I took a chance and gently grazed him with my teeth. I could feel him pulse against my tongue and I moaned. "You'll be my undoing, woman." I wasn't sure if he was talking *to* me or *at* me.

The pulsing of his cock increased against my tongue, telling me he was close. Just when I thought he would reward me with his release, he pulled out of my mouth and dropped to his knees. Instead, he grabbed my face and rewarded me with a brutal, all-consuming kiss as my nails dug into my thighs. Moaning, our tongues were dueling, our lips sucking, and our teeth were nipping.

"More."

I wasn't sure what I was asking for more *of* but I felt him smile against my lips. He abruptly pulled away from me again and left the bed. I looked to my new nightstand and noticed it had three large drawers. On top was a large white feather with a silver handle, a black and red riding crop and the blindfold. My nipples hardened as I gazed knowingly on the tools he had used on me.

"Come here." Standing at the end of the bed, he motioned me toward him. I scooted down to join him. When I placed my feet on the floor to stand, my legs were like rubber and gave way under my weight. He braced me before I fell and got on his knees in front of me and began rubbing my legs vigorously while I held onto his shoulders. "Take some deep breaths. We just need to get the blood flowing through them again."

"Mmm, that feels good." My head fell to the side and rested against one of the bed posts as I closed my eyes to savor his touch.

"Better?" Opening my eyes and smiling, I nodded at him. "You're exquisite."

Once he stood, he kissed my forehead while I inhaled his intoxicating male scent deeply. His hands circled my waist before he spun me around, looping his arms around my chest. He was sending my nerve endings into overdrive as he caressed my rib cage, which we had both learned was an extremely sensitive pleasure point for me. I twitched and moaned against him as waves of pleasure teased me.

"I love what my touch does to you." He started biting the tender flesh between my neck and shoulder.

"Only your touch." I was out of breath and my brain was hazy.

"Yes, only my touch." He grabbed my hand and pulled it to the post closest to us. "Hold on and don't let go." Positioning me with my back to him, he spread my legs and pulled my hips back before rubbing my ass. *SMACK!* I inhaled sharply as the burn spread out over my flesh. I watched as he walked to the nightstand and grabbed the crop and feather. He smiled wickedly before he disappeared behind me. "Don't move."

Taking a calming breath I felt the feather moving down my spine, and in the same instant the sting of the crop met my skin. Soon the feather was smoothing over where the crop had stamped its mark on my delicate flesh. The cycle repeated over and over until I lost count, never imagining I could get pleasure from this activity, but I did.

He trailed the crop over my panties again. "James...oh, God."

I was on the cusp and didn't know how much more I could take. I was startled by his speed; he'd plastered his chest to my back and surrounded me. One hand massaged my breasts while the other was circling over my lips, through my panties. He growled in my ear, "Come for me." His pelvis was grinding against me and I could feel his erection against my inner thigh as I pushed back against it, as he pressed my clit though my panties.

A moment later I welcomed the tidal wave that breached my shores. I was crying out and convulsing uncontrollably as he showed me no mercy, pinching my nipples and grinding against me. When the shudders finally started to subside, I was swept into his arms, my entire body was numb except for the faint throb of my sex; sound and sight had left me. All I could feel was his warmth against me as he laid us in the bed and cradled me against his chest. Sleep easily took me.

fifteen

Closer

~ JAMES ~

Her legs were tangled with mine and her breathing was slow and steady. She was everything and more and she did better than any other sub I had ever attempted to teach. She was a natural, whether she knew it or not, and I couldn't get rid of the nagging feeling that she belonged with me. I didn't think I would ever be able to let her go. I fell into a deep sleep wrapped around her.

~ CASSIDY ~

Memory flooded me as I began to wake, stretching out looking for him. James was gone. I suspected that I should get used to it. Why did he leave? I rolled to my back and let out a disappointed sigh.

"You ok?" I almost jumped off the bed at the sound of his voice as I heard his chuckle coming from the doorway.

My eyes adjusted to find him leaning against the doorway with a big plate of food. "I thought you left." He was wearing pajama pants that hung loosely on his hips and nothing else.

"Do you want me to leave?"

"NO!" I took a deep breath, not meaning to sound so desperate. He smiled as he strolled toward me. Turning on the bedside lamp, he turned and sat down on the bed holding a plate full of cheese and fruit. My stomach growled at the sight of food as he placed the plate under my nose so I could grab a couple chunks of cheese and some grapes. "What time is it?"

"Just after midnight." My face crinkled up. "Did you expect it to be later?"

"I don't know what I expected." Picking up a strawberry he placed it in my mouth and I grabbed his thumb with my lips while devouring the strawberry.

"Insatiable." His eyes became hooded as he took in my naked form.

"Only with you." I smiled coyly before feeding him a grape and he returned the favor, grasping my wrist to suck on my index finger. I groaned before he released my hand as we both stared at the other intently.

"You did well. Better than I anticipated." Leaning in, James caressed my cheek before kissing me. "Shower with me."

It wasn't a request. As he set the plate on the nightstand, I grabbed another handful of food, sharing some with him. I watched as he discarded his pajama pants on the way to the bathroom, baring his ass for me. And what an incredible ass it was.

"Shit! I was supposed to pick up my dress tonight for the auction. Oh God, I won't have time tomorrow." I started freaking out.

He yanked me to his chest, "It's already taken care of, don't worry." I started to question him, "Cassidy, I've already handled it."

"Thank you. You're a lifesaver." I kissed his chest as he hugged me to him briefly and I felt his cock jump against my belly. "I want to please you." I palmed his erection as he walked backward to the edge of the tub. Sitting down, with me standing between his legs, I took his action as approval.

I dropped to my knees on the bath rug while I raked my hands down his chest. Grasping him delicately, I ran my tongue from base to tip before sucking him between my lips. His thighs flexed as his erection pulsed and it didn't take long before his hands were freeing my braid and fisting in my hair. I had never enjoyed giving a blow job so much until now.

"Cassidy." It was a plea.

Increasing my pressure and speed as my free hand ran up and down the muscles of his leg, I could feel the telltale signs and relaxed my throat before the explosion overcame him. He cursed my name as every muscle of his began to tense. He poured down my throat and I took all of him with pride. When his seed had ceased flowing, I removed my mouth and continued stroking him with my hand from root to tip. His breathing had slowed and he appeared to be sated as he pried my hand from him and pulled me to his lips.

"Thank you."

"It's my pleasure." I smiled lightly. "Get in the shower, I have to pee." He turned the water on, and after a moment, stepped into the steaming water just in time for me to release my bladder. I flushed the toilet without thinking.

"Dammit."

I rushed to the shower and threw the door open. He was scowling and standing to one side while the scalding water hit the floor.

"I'm so sorry. I don't know what I was thinking. Are you okay?" He started laughing before grabbing me and jerking me in with him.

"You trying to mark me, woman?" I joined in with the laughter.

We finished our shower and he insisted we sleep, promising to stay with me. I fell asleep in his arms, blissfully happy.

~ JAMES ~

As morning peeked through the curtains I was immediately aware of her. I was on my stomach and could feel the feather running up and down my body. She was straddling the back of my calves, and her firm breasts pressed against my back as she leaned over me, trickling kisses against my shoulders. I allowed her exploration to continue until her breathing slowed and then her hand began fingering through my hair. I couldn't stop the shiver that passed over me.

"How long are you going to pretend to sleep?" She whispered in my ear before biting my lobe.

I caught her off guard and regained the power as I turned on her. She was on her back, smiling up at me as I pinned her to the bed. "How long are you going to pretend you have the power?" I smiled at her and dropped my lips to her neck.

"Forever if it means you'll top me." Still kissing her neck, I heard her voice get light and labored as I groaned at her words.

"You're trying to top from the bottom. Be careful, Cassidy. We don't have time for another lesson this morning."

"Even if I beg?" She was tugging on my hair as her legs circled my calves. As I ground against her she hummed softly.

"I'll be taking you this evening, period or not." She purred, begging for me to take her and I jumped off the bed before I lost my control. She whimpered at the loss of me as I made my way to the bathroom, attempting to relieve my bladder. It took longer than usual given my erect condition.

When I walked back into the bedroom I saw that she had thrown the covers over her head. I smiled before grabbing them and ripped them off her. "Up with you, lady."

"Hey!" She flung herself to her back and glared at me, "I'm pouting."

"I see that. Keep pouting and I *won't* take you tonight." She flinched at my harsh tone. "I see you have an exercise bike and I added a treadmill. Let's go." I grabbed her ankle pulling her to the end of the bed as she tried to hide the smile forming on her lips.

She stood and stomped past me. "You're cruel."

I smacked her ass before she made it into the bathroom. "You have no idea."

She turned back to glare at me and I winked at her as she stuck her tongue out and closed the bathroom door. I threw on some shorts from the bag Smith dropped off and headed to the guest bedroom.

A few minutes later, she walked in wearing shorts and a sports bra, pointing at the treadmill I was running on. "Where did this come from?"

"I told you, I added it yesterday with the bed. It's mine and was in storage. We can go out running together if you prefer." She looked disgusted at that thought and hopped on the bike.

We both abused our chosen pieces of equipment for the next forty five minutes. I was pleasantly surprised by her endurance.

"I should shower. I have to be at the hotel by nine a.m." I nodded and she wiped her forehead with her arm and left the room, her mood suddenly gloomy. I turned off the treadmill, waited a few minutes, and when I heard the shower running, made my way to the bedroom.

I stripped off my shorts and opened the shower door without her knowledge. She was just standing there, eyes closed with her face turned up to the water as it hammered down on her. I slinked in behind her and lowered myself enough to place my head on her shoulder as I circled my arms around her waist.

"Don't be angry." Startled, she inhaled sharply at my surprise appearance and quickly relaxed when my hands began caressing her belly.

"I'm not angry. I'm a wanton hussy." I heard the humor in her voice but scolded her for using such words in reference to herself. "You've done amazing things to my libido."

Her temple was resting against my jaw as I said, "Is that a bad thing?" She moaned as I caressed the sweet spot by her hip.

"I hope not." She sighed and pressed back against me. "James, please."

"Please what, Cassidy? Tell me what you need." She started circling her bum against my erection.

"I need you."

Groaning at her words, I ran my hand up her inner thigh as the other gripped her hip. She caught me off guard and turned in my arms and our lips were like magnets, finding each other immediately. She was hungry for me as her hands tangled in my hair pulling me closer to her. I slipped my fingers through her folds and she tensed momentarily before burying her forehead into my chest.

"Oh, please don't stop."

"I said tonight, not this morning."

She jerked back and looked at me like she might cry.

"But, you've changed my mind."

She smiled and practically jumped up my body as I pulled her up against me and then leaned against the shower wall. My cock was wedged against her mound desperate to penetrate her. She reached between us, shifted her hips and positioned my head at her opening as my hands cupped her ass. Her baby blues pierced my own green eyes as I slipped into her ever so slowly.

She moaned in ecstasy. "I love your pussy." She clenched around me even tighter at my words.

I slid us down to the floor, not losing contact with her. "Closer, I need more of you." She was almost delirious in her desire.

"Here." I grabbed her calf, guiding her off her knees, and pulled her leg up until her foot was flat on the shower floor, her other leg followed suit. I stretched out my own legs giving her all of me. She trembled as she pushed down on me to my full length, causing me to shudder as I hit her womb. I bent my head and sought her breasts as she began rocking against me and quickly picked up her pace.

"Slow down, Cassidy." She looked to me and hesitated, but she conceded.

"I'll never have enough of you, ever."

She was frenzied and passionate, so passionate. I put my hand over her heart and pushed her back as she placed her hands behind her, just above my knees. Her breasts were on display and I suckled them in turn as she rode me slowly and deeply. Soon she began to shake from the exertion and she pulsed around me more frequently. I slid my thumb to her clit and she cried out as her nails dug into my knees.

"Harder, please."

Her head was thrown back and I reached around her back with my other arm. "Faster, Cassidy."

Seeking confirmation, she looked to me before gripping my shoulders and picked up her pace. My own orgasm was close and I growled her name. She found my hair and tugged as I thrust up into her harder. I could feel her clit harden and her whole body went still before she began screaming out. I lost control of my own hunger and pummeled up into her relentlessly as my cum rocketed out of me. I bit down on her shoulder as she was cooing in my ear.

Several minutes later, I pushed her sensitive core off me. "Thank you." I was surprised by her words as I pulled us to our feet.

I kissed her forehead before running my hand across her cheek,

"You don't have to thank me. You make me lose control. *I* should thank *you.*"

We finished our shower in almost complete silence. When we were done toweling off and dressing, she looked to the clock and cursed. "I have to go." She looked to me and I already knew her question.

"Give me five minutes. I'll drive you there." She nodded without question and then I heard her running down the stairs. When I got down there she was pacing by the front door sipping on her coffee. "You should eat something."

"I can't exactly eat and carry all this on the back of a bike." She pointed to a small duffel bag, laptop bag and her purse and I started laughing. "What's so funny?"

"Look outside, Cassidy." She opened the door and saw that the Rover was there. She turned to me, asking how, and I told her, "Smith made the trade last night. You should eat something. Go grab a banana." She returned from the kitchen with two bananas and smiled as I gathered up her bags and we headed to the hotel.

~ CASSIDY ~

THE FINAL PREPARATION for the auction went off without a problem. I used the hotel key James gave me and headed up to his suite to get ready. "Hello, James." I didn't get a response and knew he must not be there.

As I took in my surroundings, I noticed several picture frames on a side table. As I examined them, I saw Mrs. Whitford, her husband, Jane, and some other women in one frame. *Why does he have a picture of Mrs. Whitford's family?* There was a picture, front and center, of a lovely older woman. Her coloring was similar to James and I wondered if it was his mother.

Grabbing a bottle of water out of the fridge, I then headed upstairs to get ready. I found my dress lying on his bed with my shoes and another small box. I picked up the box I didn't recognize and taped on the outside was a small card.

> *You'll do wonderful tonight.*
> *I'll see you at dinner.*
> *~XO J*

I opened the box and inside I found a beautiful pair of drop earrings. A black gem graced the top of each with another larger black gem hanging on the end. The gems were connected by a strand of diamonds. They were stunning and I was speechless.

I got undressed and grabbed some fresh undergarments before heading into the bathroom with my duffel bag. I laid out my makeup and plugged in my curling iron before I pulled up my hair and hopped in the shower to rinse off. After I was dry I meticulously tended to my hair and makeup, like Lena had showed me last week, and after close to an hour I was dressed and ready, earrings and all.

I made my way to the ballroom and everything was perfect. It wasn't long before I was escorting guests to their tables and fielding any questions they may have had about the auction. Spotting Mrs. Whitford and Jane, I made my way over to them.

Jane and I were exchanging pleasantries when a big smile took over her features. Before I had a chance to see who she was smiling at I was suddenly assaulted from behind.

"Kudos, Cass, this looks great!"

"Calvin! Put me down." He released his arms from around my waist and set me back down. "Are you trying to give me a heart attack?" I hit his shoulder while we both laughed. "You look great. I'm so glad you could make it!" He deserved a night out and I was dying to see what, if anything, was happening with him and Jane.

"Well, don't keep us waiting in suspense, Cassidy, introduce us!" Mrs. Whitford was eyeing my brother like he was prime rib.

I chuckled and introduced Mrs. Whitford and Cal to each other.

"Are you single, Calvin? Janey here could use a hunk like you in her life."

Calvin laughed nervously and responded 'yes' as Jane scolded her mother and apologized to Calvin for her mother's rude behavior. I noticed Cal wink at Jane as I spotted Lena rushing to me.

She had panic written all over her face as she pulled me aside, "Cassidy, we're down a bachelor. Cecily is going on and on about how there must be ten, there are always ten!"

I stood there for a moment, racking my brain for a solution. Cal came over and asked me if everything was alright. "Yes, Cal. Everything is perfect. I need you to come with me." I winked at Lena as I pulled Cal away from Jane and we headed toward Cecily.

~ JAMES ~

"Aunt Bev, you're sure you got this?"

"Don't patronize me, child. My handiwork is well evident. Ask half the couples in this room and they'll agree that I played a part," she chastised me, hitting me across the chest with her auction program.

"Don't exaggerate. It doesn't suit you." She looked like she might strike again and I quickly made my exit after kissing her cheek just as Cassidy spotted me. The MC came overhead and requested that the bachelors make their way backstage; the bachelor auction would begin in five minutes. I threw Cassidy a smile and made my exit.

~ CASSIDY ~

I WAS SCANNING the room looking for him. He had been eye fucking me all night in his usual fashion, but had yet to approach me. His hair was down and I was itching to run my fingers through it. We were not seated at the same table for dinner and honestly, I was frustrated because I didn't get to enjoy dinner at all; I was too busy putting out fires.

There he was, chatting with Mrs. Whitford again, and the minute he saw that I was heading his was he ran off. *Chicken-shit!* What the hell was he playing at? The rest of the men in the room took their leave as well. It was a long standing tradition that the married couples, or at least the married men, left at this point in the evening. I presumed he left, not wanting to have anything to do with what was about to happen. I would have to wait until after to catch up with him.

As I made my way to Mrs. Whitford she smiled brightly and said, "Cassidy, just who I was looking for. Please join me and Jane so we can enjoy the bachelors."

Before I could even respond, she was dragging me toward the stage and Jane was just smiling sweetly. We were in the second row of tables, center stage. I tried to get Jane's attention, but she was busy talking to another woman.

"Mrs. Whitford, how do you know James?"

"James? Such a lovely man. You fancy him? The feeling is mutual, take my word." The woman wouldn't let me get a word in edgewise and she was avoiding the real question. She knew more than she was letting on and it was making me crazy.

"Cassidy, I'm so excited. I can't believe you're throwing Cal to the wolves! Do you know who the other bachelors are? Cecily wouldn't tell me! This is going to be great!" Lena was overjoyed and took the seat next to me.

You could feel the estrogen clogging the air. Lena knew as much about the bachelors up for auction as I did. The MC—a local news reporter—had made her announcement that the bachelor auction was ready to begin.

The lights got turned down, spotlights hit the stage, and it suddenly sounded like a pack of hyenas had been released into the wild. I snagged a roll from a bread basket before the wait staff cleared it away and I started to feel sorry for Cal, just a little. *It's Raining Men* by The Weather Girls started playing overhead and I had to admit, I was bummed that I didn't have money to bid—James wouldn't like that very much—unless of course he was up for bid.

sixteen

Bachelor

~ JAMES ~

"**I**'M NEVER GOING TO FORGIVE MY sister for this." Cal was checking his tie and running his hand through his short hair.

Six bachelors had already been purchased, with number seven on the stage. Cal was number nine and I was lucky number ten. I think that was the loudest I remembered the crowd ever being. I felt my cell buzz, alerting me of a text.

All set ~Aunt B

"Calvin, how are you?" We shook hands.

"Good, man, and you? Cassidy know you're one of the bachelors?"

"Not yet. Does Jane know you're up for grabs?" He shook his head 'no' and we had a few laughs. I assured him that the ladies would be all over him, especially Jane.

"Cassidy told you about Jane?"

"She did. You should know one more thing." He looked at me intently. "Jane and I are cousins. She's been through a lot in the last year. Don't hurt her."

He scoffed and said he could say the same to me. "Cassidy's really done a great job with tonight's events." He changed the subject as bachelor eight was welcomed to the stage.

"Yes. She's excellent at what she does." He looked at me as if he knew I wasn't just referring to her job.

"Have you told her yet, James? I really think she'll take it better than you think she will."

"Soon." He nodded and the backstage attendant ran over and escorted Cal to the side of the stage; he was almost up. I waved to him, "We'll catch up later. They'll love you."

~ CASSIDY ~

THIS DRAMA WAS crazy. Grown women were spending thousands of dollars fighting over one date. *Save a Horse, Ride a Cowboy* by Big & Rich was now playing and I knew I shouldn't complain. The more they spent, the more money I raised for the hospital. Cal was then called to the stage and looked nervous as hell. Lena and I couldn't help but giggle and Jane immediately perked up, and she wasn't the only one. She looked at me questioningly and I just shrugged my shoulders and winked. This was going to be interesting. Mrs. Whitford, on the other hand, hadn't stopped smiling since the guys started coming on stage. *Horny old bag!*

"Please welcome Calvin Charles to the stage. Calvin is 6'3" likes long rides on his Harley, camping, and enjoying the more natural things in life. Laid back and easy going, he prefers a night in rather than a night out. You can tell by how well he wears that suit that he's a fitness buff. He's also an elite member of our police squad and an Army Vet. Ladies let's hear it for Cal! Let's start the bidding at $1000...yes, do I hear $1500, $1750....."

Lena was squeezing my forearm and I was shocked; Calvin was a natural. He removed his jacket, threw it over his shoulder and started strutting across the stage. *Oh dear Lord.* He removed his tie and then threw it at me. I was humiliated, a little disgusted and laughing my ass off at the same time.

I mouthed at him to 'stop'. He shook his head and started unbuttoning his shirt and his bid jumped even higher.

"$3000!"

I looked over to see who had jumped the bid and it was Jane! She was in a battle with some cougar in the back. I looked back and forth between her, Cal, and Jane and Cal was eating it up. The bid was currently Jane's and she had him for $3750.

"Once, twice, sold! Congrats to the lovely lady in red! I believe the lucky lady is Miss Jane Whitford. Congrats to Jane and welcome home."

Mrs. Whitford was ecstatic as Jane rolled her eyes at her mom. She won him just in time to save my eyes; his shirt was unbuttoned and he was in the process of removing it. Jane walked to the side of the stage and Cal descended as he took her hand and they walked to the back of the ballroom. *Go Cal!*

"Now for the top prize of the night. Get out your credit cards, ladies. Back by popular demand, ladies, he's finally returned to us. The one, the only, Jackson James Benedict III, better known as JB3!"

What the FUCK? No wonder he was avoiding me all evening. My heart immediately sank and I was pissed off as the cheers and whistles became ear piercing, a reminder of his popularity with the ladies. I looked back to the stage and saw James walking out.

"Fucking hell!" Lena and I said it at the same time. I was glaring at him and he had the nerve to smile at me.

"Cassidy..."

"Lena, I love you, but shut up!"

Jackson James Benedict III, lady-killer, playboy extraordinaire, JB3, and my lover. What had I gotten myself into?

"6'4.5" former West Point Academy star football player. He enjoys concerts, rides through the country, and traveling to exotic lands. Are there any exotic ladies in the house?" The MC was clearly a fan and continued taking liberties. The list went on and on, though she forgot one; he was an incredible fuck. I chastised myself for my thoughts, discovering he was built like a football player because he *was* one, though I missed where he went to school. This couldn't be happening. He was eye-fucking me in front of everyone causing me to blush in response as the bidding began at $5000. There was no way...

"$5000!"

It came screeching from behind and reached $10,000 in seconds. *These bitches were out of their minds. $10,000 for one date?* Before I was even aware of what was happening, Mrs. Whitford joined in on the bidding. He was still eye-fucking me. What the hell was going on? Did he expect me to do something? I'm broke. I was so muddled I felt my head begin to ache and noticed Lena's mouth was hanging open in disbelief.

"$25,000!"

"$30,000!"

"$35,000!"

Soon the bid was at $50,000 and it was down to some waif of a brunette side stage, some lady in back, and Mrs. Whitford. The brunette was glaring at me and I pointed to Mrs. Whitford.

"$50,000!" The MC had ceased speaking as numbers were being thrown out without hesitation.

The brunette yelled, "$60,000."

The room dropped to a quiet hum and the MC chimed in about making history, and JB3 beating his previous bids. James looked away from me for a split second, nodded at Mrs. Whitford who was sitting right next to me.

"$100,000!" Dead silence.

I swear I saw James's eyes bulge for a millisecond. Everyone was staring between Mrs. Whitford and the brunette and I looked back at James.

The MC asked Mrs. Whitford if she was sure and she yelled back, "I made the bid didn't I?" A light chuckle broke through the room.

"Going once..." Everyone was staring at the brunette now.

"Going twice..." The brunette threw her hands up in disgust.

"Sold for $100,000 to Mrs. Whitford. I hope you're not spending $100,000 just to spend time with your own nephew!"

Nephew?! Mrs. Whitford yanked me to my feet and hollered, "He's not for me, and she's the lucky lady!"

OH. MY. GOD.

It dawned on me then that they were cohorts. I looked to the brunette who was glaring at me like I just pissed all over her cookies. The MC concluded the auction and asked the bachelors and their winning bidders to head to the dance floor. My head was still spinning as James made his way over to the three of us. Giving Mrs. Whitford— *HIS AUNT*—a kiss on the cheek, he thanked her before looking at me.

She returned the kiss, "Anytime, James."

Lena's poor jaw was going to be aching if she didn't pick it up off the floor. James took my hand and escorted me to the dance floor as words finally made their long anticipated appearance on my lips.

"When were you going to tell me that you're Mrs. Whitford's nephew?" He merely chuckled and took us to the center of the dance floor.

He grabbed my hand and pulled me tight against him with his other hand on the naked flesh of my back. I did my best to hide the shiver than ran straight to the apex of my thighs. I started to speak when I met his eyes, and instantly his lips were on mine and my entire body melted into his.

The kiss was over far too soon and he whispered, "You look amazing in that dress, but I can't wait to get you out of it."

The music finally began, *Wild Horses* by The Sundays, and he took the lead and started moving us slowly to the beat. I was dazed and moved along to the command of his body, noticing the lights were still so low that I could barely make out the faces of those around me. It was the perfect setting for seduction and the song was fitting. Wild horses couldn't drag me away from him.

I gently placed my cheek against his shoulder and indulged my senses. James smelled how I thought a man should; all sex and power and fresh laundry with a little musk. I was still trying to put all the pieces together. That meant Jane was his cousin. *How had I missed that?* I wondered if Cal knew, but I was captivated by the song and sighed in resignation. Closing my eyes, I let James and the song carry me away, losing track of time and space while floating in his arms.

Suddenly aware of all the people staring at us, I looked around and realized the song had long ended and we were still in our embrace. "James, please." My voice was barely above a whisper as my eyes pleaded with him to let me go. He released me as I looked for the nearest exit, uncomfortable with all the prying eyes.

Spotting the exit to the gardens, I started to head that way, knowing some fresh air would help, but I never made it outside. I was bombarded by inquiries—some genuine and some about James and I—before Cecily found me and hugged me. She had never hugged me before.

"Amazing work, my girl. Well done! Take Monday off and enjoy your birthday weekend. You deserve it."

I thanked her, shocked by her generosity. She walked away with a gentleman I didn't recognize as I looked for James again, but didn't see him.

It was just past midnight. I had sent Lena home almost an hour ago when Cal congratulated me and inquired about James.

"It's a long story for another night. Jane?"

He just waggled his eyebrows at me and I smacked his shoulder. He gave me a quick hug, kissed the top of my head, and took his leave. I noticed Jane waiting for him in the hall and smiled to myself as they walked away hand in hand.

Besides a few hotel staff, I was the only one left in the ballroom. It no longer resembled the glorious space from several hours ago. The months of hard work had paid off. We raised more money than ever before—thanks to James and Mrs. Whitford—though I was still upset that he hadn't told me. I decided to make my way to the terrace to get that breath of fresh air I so desperately needed.

As I turned, I ran into the brunette who was bidding on James. *Oh crap.* "Sorry about that. Excuse me." I tried to walk around her and she blocked my path. "Can I help you?"

She was glaring at me and I noticed she was a little shorter than me, thinner—maybe too thin—long dark hair, blue eyes, and fabulous tits.

"Cassidy is it?" I nodded. "Stay away from him. He's spoken for." She was standing there all erect and prissy.

"Excuse me; I don't think we've met."

"Melissa, Melissa Westin."

"Stay away from whom?"

"You know who. James. We have a long history. You're just a phase like all the others. In the end he always comes back to me." She was quite proud of herself.

Recognition hit me that she was the brunette I'd seen him photographed with during my internet stalking of him; the only girl I remembered seeing more than once.

I didn't have time for the petty bullshit. "If I'm just a phase, like all the others, why do *you* keep taking him back? Kind of pathetic isn't it?" That should've shut her up but she looked ready to strike.

"Ladies, everything ok here?" James came up to stand next to me and I noticed him glaring at Melissa.

"Everything is fine." I wasn't going to get him involved in her ridiculous power play.

The bitch started crying.

"Cassidy, please excuse us." He put his hand on Melissa's back and they walked off.

Were you fucking kidding me? I was speechless. Clearly he knew her, and not just casually. Now I felt like a fool. How did I not see that coming? She was bidding on him and he hadn't even told me he'd be a part of the auction. I decided I had to get out of there and headed to the elevator. All my belongings were in his room. I would just grab my stuff and leave before he returned.

~ JAMES ~

"Melissa, this has to stop." I was trying to be stern yet gentle as she went on and on about us and what we had and how I was throwing it away. She was an easy comfortable fuck at one time, but I couldn't tell her that was all it ever was. I was an asshole and I used her. I knew that.

"What has to stop? Who is she?" She was sniffing and wiping her tears away.

"This was never going to work between you and me. It was a mistake." She flinched at my words. "I'm sorry I hurt you."

"A mistake that you made over and over again? That doesn't sound like a mistake to me." Now she was pissing me off. "I'll let you tie me up, I'll try again."

"ENOUGH!" I was escorting her to the front of the hotel, "We haven't been together in over a year Melissa." We made our way outside and I flagged down a cab.

"You'll be back. You always come back." I handed the driver a wad of twenties and pushed her into the cab before I walked back inside and the cab pulled away. Melissa hadn't shared my bed in over a year, granted it was on and off for several years, but I couldn't care less about her feelings. I had to make things right with Cassidy; I saw the look in her eyes. I walked to the elevator and took in a deep breath and let out a bigger exhale as the doors opened.

I was practically trampled as soon as the doors opened. "Shit." Her voice and scent registered with me immediately.

"Cassidy, where are you going?" She looked utterly defeated the minute she saw me.

"I'm going home." She pushed out her jaw while repositioning her bags on her shoulders.

Looking ridiculous and irresistible all at once, she was still wearing the blue dress and hauling half a dozen bags. I grabbed her arm and pulled her back into the elevator. "You'll do no such thing."

"Let go of me." Though she knew it was pointless, she tried fighting me off. After the doors closed and the elevator began moving, she stopped resisting. I gathered up her bags, which she handed over willingly, though she wouldn't look at me.

We made it back to my suite and I placed her bags by the stairs as she made her way out to the balcony. I figured she could use a few minutes alone and turned on the sound system before I headed to the kitchen to grab some water. She left the door to the balcony open and I leaned against the frame as I just watched her for what must have been several minutes; a couple more songs played as I looked at her. She was just staring up into the sky.

I laughed inwardly as *Wicked Game* by Chris Isaak came over the speakers. I walked to her side and remained quiet. She knew I was there, but didn't acknowledge it.

"You're going to break my heart, James Benedict the third." It was a statement, not a question.

Turning to look at her, she was still staring into space. "I think I'm the one who should be worried about a broken heart." She turned and glared at me.

"Who is she?" Her tone was foreboding.

"Melissa?"

"I know her name. Who is she?"

"You have nothing to worry about."

"So I *should* be worried. Perfect." She was being obtuse now.

"Dammit, woman..." I reached for her.

She pulled away, "I'm not your woman." Her voice was cracking.

"Cassidy, I promise, she's in my past. She's having a hard time letting go. I reinforced it to her tonight."

"What did you mean when you said that you've tried staying away from me?" She was staring back to the stars, "You said it in the elevator the night of the masquerade."

"I know when I said it." I ran my hand through my hair and turned my back to lean against the balcony wall. "Cassidy. Given the circumstances and everything that happened that night, I didn't think it appropriate to pursue you. I struggled staying away from you once I knew who you were. With the investigation and, well, everything else."

"You mean Dan?" She was looking to me again and scoffed in disgust. "Dan was a mistake. I was lonely, he was there. End of story." Her words were cold and distant. "Wait. Once you knew? What do you mean?"

"It's not important."

"IT *IS* IMPORTANT." As she stared at me I could see her mentally putting the pieces together. "Oh God, I'm going to be sick." She started pacing. "Did you have something to do with me getting the promotion and the auction? Cecily said…"

"God no, you did that on your own. I swear I haven't interfered with your job in any way." I took a step toward her. "Cassidy."

She was mumbling to herself, recounting the events over the summer. "I don't understand, unless…It was you, wasn't it? *You* paid for the funerals."

She had found me out. "Yes." There wasn't much else to say. After I found out Sam and Holly were both orphans with no family I did what anyone would do given the circumstances.

"Why did you keep that from me? What's the big deal?"

I was wringing my hands, knowing there was more to it all. "Cassidy, it's late. It's nothing to note."

"Nothing to note? You were innocent of any wrongdoing. Why did you stay away? You paid for the funerals of two strangers. Cal and

I did everything we could to find out who did that so we could thank them." She closed the distance between us and placed her hand on my cheek. "Thank you. How can I ever repay you?"

"That's not necessary. You should get some rest. You've had a long day."

"No more secrets, James. They destroy everything they touch." She placed her hand in mine as she pulled me back inside and up the stairs.

seventeen

Dreams

~ CASSIDY ~

I HAD BEEN THERE BEFORE. HOLLY AND I WERE *dancing and laughing. The lights were low and the room was spinning around us. Before I knew it I was dancing alone. I found myself wandering down a dark hallway to a door.*

"Holly. Where are you?"

I hadn't seen her in so long; we had so much to catch up on. I walked out the back door and was blinded by the bright lights. As my eyes started to focus I found her. She was with Sam as she waved me over. I headed toward her as a hand wrapped around my wrist and pulled me back.

I looked back to see who was holding my wrist, but I couldn't make out his face. While I was trying to identify him, I heard the familiar POP, POP, POP. I viciously pulled away from the one holding my hand just in time for Holly to fall into my arms.

"Holly!" She was coughing up blood and choking as I wiped her hair

out of her eyes. "Holly no, please stay with me. Help will be here soon. Don't go. I need you."

~ JAMES ~

CASSIDY WAS SOUND asleep, and I was downstairs in the office, when I thought I heard her voice. I stopped to listen for a moment and heard nothing. It must've been my imagination as I scanned through the messages on my phone while downing the contents of my glass.

"Holly!"

Shit. What the hell was going on? I dropped my phone on the desk, along with my glass, and bolted up the stairs. I could still hear her talking and sobbing and when I reached the bedroom she was thrashing on the bed.

"Don't go. I need you."

As I approached her, I could see the tears streaming down her cheeks. I climbed on the bed and gathered her in my arms. "Cassidy. Cassidy, you're safe. I'm here." I wasn't sure if she was awake or still dreaming, but the sobs were racking through her. "Shh." I continued rocking her in my arms for several minutes when she bolted upright.

She started punching and pushing at me. "Cassidy, it's me. You're ok. It's ok."

As her eyes finally focused on mine, I knew she was awake. She dropped her head into her hands and started shaking. I pulled her back to me and set her in my lap before grabbing the sheet to wrap around her naked back. After a few minutes the shaking had ceased and she was quiet.

"I'm sorry I woke you." Her voice was raspy and broken.

"Don't be sorry. I was awake. What were you dreaming about?" I continued rubbing circles up and down her back.

"I, uh, it was Holly. I was with Holly. I haven't dreamed about that night in over a month, if not two."

"I'm sorry." Had I somehow brought it upon her by talking about the funerals? Maybe I should've stayed away.

"Don't be." Pulling her head up far enough to look up at me, I could see her eyes were swollen and red and there were still tears gathered under her eyes. I wiped them away with my thumb then licked her salty sadness away. A faint smile gathered on her lips. "I miss her so much."

"I know you do." I held her for several more minutes with her head resting in the crook of my neck. "Cassidy?" She barely responded and I recognized the rhythm of her steady breathing. She was asleep, or close to it, as I scooted us down to lie on the bed.

I started to pull away from her, "Please don't go," she whispered.

"I'm not going anywhere, Blackbird, ever." I grabbed the rest of the blankets and pulled them over us before I tucked her backside into my chest. She sought out my hand and entwined our fingers before tucking our joined hands to her chest. Dan had fucked up too many lives. I should've intervened sooner.

~ CASSIDY ~

I WAS BEGINNING TO WAKE and became aware of his absence as I sprawled on my back and felt the coolness of the room skittering across my naked chest. As I went to stretch, I realized that I couldn't move my arms and frantically yanked my arms.

"You're safe." His deep whisper immediately calmed me and filled me with want.

Something cool clasped around one ankle and then the other. The bed dipped beneath his weight and soon he was straddling my hips, careful to keep his weight off me. My eyes focused on his and I saw his hair was tied back and he was naked. His semi hard shaft was resting on my belly and I groaned as I attempted to lift my hips.

"Enjoying the view, Miss Charles?"

I smiled at him, "You know I am." I felt my nipples harden as his eyes swallowed me whole and his fingertips grazed over my skin, sending shivers through my core. Just a look, touch, or a kiss and I melted for that man.

"You trust me."

"Implicitly." I wasn't sure why, but I did, and I knew he would never intentionally hurt me. "And it scares me to death. I think I'd rob a bank if you asked."

He chuckled. "I won't ask you to do that." He circled each nipple with a finger. "But I *will* test your limits and build your trust even more."

I inhaled sharply, more out of anticipation rather than fear.

"I think you like that idea."

How did he read me like that? I didn't have long to contemplate it before his lips smothered mine. All worries of morning breath brushed aside as he nestled between my thighs. Dying to be closer to him, I hated that I couldn't touch him and swiftly he jumped off me.

"You're a sneaky minx." We were both panting. "I've had a change of plans. I'm going to unhook you and I want you to roll to your front."

When I nodded my consent he quickly released me and I rolled to my stomach. He attached one arm and slid his warm palms down, across my shoulders and up my other arm to hook it to the bed. I buried my face in the sheets and found his scent lingering on the pillow. His hands were gliding down my back then he removed my panties and I waited for him to restrain my legs, but it didn't happen. He left the bed and before I had a chance to look for him, he was back and I felt a hand on the back of each leg.

"Get on your knees, lady, but leave your chest on the bed."

I took my position with his assistance, my ass in the air and fully exposed to him. I blushed knowing that his eyes were devouring me and couldn't help but try to press my legs together.

"Not so fast. Spread them wider." I was thankful I couldn't see his face and that he couldn't see mine. I was mortified. "You're beautiful." His hands smoothed over my bare ass and down my thighs as his thumbs ever so gently brushed my labia on each side.

"Oh," I groaned into the bed and swiveled my hips, seeking more of his touch. *Smack!* "Shit!"

"Hold still."

"Yes, sir." My tone was mocking.

"Don't push it, Cassidy."

I immediately smiled, wondering what was wrong with me. I wiggled my hips a little more and was rewarded with another *smack!*

"That's your last warning. You move again and spankings will cease and I'll leave you here." Immediately I stilled. "Good girl. Someone enjoys being spanked."

He began caressing my cheeks simultaneously before playing the game where he would smack one and then the other before rubbing them. This game continued for a long time, until my ass was numb and on fire at the same time. Every smack spread more tingles further through my body. I swore I might come from him spanking me alone and the drunken dizzy feeling was taking me over again.

"James." I was panting and didn't even know what to ask for.

"You're close, aren't you?"

I nodded into the pillow as he inched closer to me and I felt him rubbing the head of his erection across my moist inner thighs. It took all my strength not to move as his chest was now hovering over my back. Reaching around, he tugged on my nipples before pulling on my hair resting at the nape of my neck.

"Oh Jesus. Please."

"Tell me what you want." His voice was smoldering.

"You inside me, please. Fuck me, James."

He didn't speak, only took action as he slid his head all over my clit as my thighs began to shake. Then he slammed into me; it was utter relief.

"Fuck! You're so wet and tight." I clenched around him even more. "Minx!" He smacked my ass again.

His assault proceeded and I could already feel my orgasm swimming back to the surface. My stomach muscles were tense—every muscle in my body was tense—and I couldn't breathe.

"Breathe, Cassidy." I struggled, but did as I was told and after I released the breath I was holding, I breathed in deep as he reached around and began rubbing my clit while pounding away with stealth determination.

It was my undoing, *he* was my undoing. I screamed his name, and some other obscenities, while he pounded away, my toes curling and I became as limp as a dishrag. I couldn't hold myself up much longer and began slipping, my head still thrumming and swimming through the aftershocks of my release. He pushed us down flat to the bed and continued pumping in and out of my swollen flesh. His pace started to slow some, but he was nowhere ready to let go.

Smack! "Oh. No. I can't take any more, James."

I could almost hear him smile behind me as he continued my punishment. The vibrations immediately sparked my core anew. *Sweet Jesus, he was going kill me with sex.* Before I could comprehend what was happening, I was aware that I was building up again. He was breathing on my neck and reaching up my arm to release my bonds, but never missed a thrust, and soon both my arms were free.

I cried out when I felt the loss of his body, but he flipped me over before I could figure out what he was doing. He straddled me across his lap and was lifting me up while my back was pressed against the cool fabric of his headboard.

On his knees, and wrapping my legs around his waist, he told me, "Hold on, Cassidy."

Somehow I found the energy to wrap my arms and legs around him as my head fell to his shoulder and he plunged back into me. My breath hitched and my nails dug into his back.

"Yes. Oh, James." I sought out his hair and set it free, tugging and twisting my fingers through his dark locks, pulling his head back. I found his lips and bit down on his upper lip after sucking it into my mouth, my energy renewed. *Would I ever get enough of him?*

"Fuck, Cassidy." His own hand found my hair and pulled me off him so he could molest my breasts. "Open your eyes." I opened my eyes to find him staring into them and I felt my orgasm climbing over the horizon. "Happy Birthday, Blackbird!"

"Thank you." He remembered and I was smiling like a fool before his lips captured mine. "James, I'm close, again," whispering between kisses and desperate for him to come, too. Hammering into me harder, I sensed he was close. My whole body squeezed him.

"Cassidy."

Feeling him tense, I ground into him, discovering it was just what I needed and I broke apart all over again. I grabbed his hair and tugged while sucking his ear and he exploded inside me on a growl. Covered in sweat and me, he shuddered inside me for what felt like forever. I was unforgiving, continuing to squeeze him periodically to remind him we were still joined.

"Dammit, lady, you'll pull it off if you don't stop that."

I giggled into his shoulder, "We can't have that. Though, the thought of carrying that piece of you around in my purse is slightly tempting. Eeek!" He was tickling my hips and flipped me to my back as he lay on top of me. "It was a joke, please, stop." I was smacking his hands away, but it was useless.

He stopped his assault and fell down next to me before he gathered me in his arms. "You're going to be sore."

"Then I guess you're doing it right." I winked at him and the look of surprise on his face was priceless.

"Damn straight I'm doing it right." We lay there in our serenity for several minutes. "Let me take you to dinner tonight."

"I can't." His head jerked up as he looked down at me. "Calm down. I made plans with Anthony and Lena from work. I can cancel them."

"No."

"You can come with. Calvin will be there, too." Looking to him, I could tell he was brooding. I began kissing his chest and moved so that I was straddling him. Finding his nipple, I began to lap at it. "Please come."

"You're insatiable." I lifted my head and looked at him, totally relaxed, his arms were up and under his head.

"I can't help it. Look at you. You're irresistible. I mean, WOW." He laughed a genuine belly warming laugh which had me laughing, too. "Please say you'll come."

"I'll come."

I threw myself down to him and wrapped my arms around his neck before kissing him. "Thank you!"

A COUPLE HOURS later, James dropped me off at my place. He said he had some errands to run and that he would be back to pick me up around six. I warned him that everyone was meeting here before we headed out for the night.

Walking through the door, I scanned through my mail and sorted out the bills from the junk, putting the junk in the recycling and the bills on the counter. Chessa jumped up to greet me.

"Hey Chessa, I've missed you." I picked her up and was rewarded with a purr. Carrying her to the door, I grabbed a few of my bags before setting her back down. We were heading up the stairs when there was a knock on the door. "Who could that be?" Chessa ran to the door and I swooshed her away and she headed to the living room.

I opened the door and felt the color leave my face. "Dan?" *Fucking hell.* "What are you doing here?"

"Happy Birthday, Cassidy."

~ JAMES ~

I HAD TO RUN to the office to take care of some business before picking up Cassidy's birthday gift and then I was headed home to check on Mom. Cassidy wouldn't get much more use out of her birthday gift this year, but she would come spring.

Spring.

For the first time I realized that I wanted her here in spring. I tried to shake off the tug that she had on my emotions as I pulled into the drive at Mom and Dad's place.

I walked in and Dad told me that Mom was resting. "She's fine, Son, just tired. She's still adjusting to the time change."

"Ok. Please tell her I stopped by."

"I hear you and Aunt Bev pulled off quite the coup last night at the auction."

We shared a chuckle. "Speaking of Aunt Bev. She went a little overboard, jumping the bid so quickly."

"You know she has no patience. I'm sorry I missed it." He poured me a scotch as we sat opposite each other in his study. "How's Cassidy? Have you told her?"

Swirling the contents of my cup and looking down, I said, "She knows about the funerals."

"You need to tell her about Dan before she finds out on her own."

"I know, Dad. Her brother is aware of most of it and has been keeping it from her until I can tell her."

He sighed, "You're playing with fire, James. When she finds out, and she will, that you and her brother both know; well, so help you God."

Agreeing with him I mentioned, "Today's her birthday. It can wait. Last I heard, he was supposedly in rehab, again."

"Rehab can help the addict, but once a snake always a snake."

I needed to change the subject before I got angry. Downing my scotch, I placed the glass on the table between us. "I'd like you and Mom to meet her, officially." Dad was just beaming at me. "Enough, Dad."

"Anytime, just let us know when. Your mother will be thrilled."

"Yeah, yeah. I should go. I'll be in touch. Give Mom my love." We shook hands before exchanging a hug.

"I think your Mother is right."

"Dare I ask?"

"You care a great deal for this girl." I just stared at him.

"Don't be ridiculous." I headed out the door unable to listen to any more of Dad's nonsense. Wasn't it too soon to be feeling so many emotions for Cassidy? We had only known each other a few months and had only been dating for a little over a week. What the hell? This was ridiculous; I did care for her and I didn't know why I was denying it.

eighteen
Secrets

~ CASSIDY ~

Stepping out onto my front porch cautiously, I closed the door behind me. "Dan, what are you doing here?"

"Hi to you, too. These are for you." He handed me a lame bouquet of flowers.

"Thank you. Sorry, I just wasn't expecting to see you." And I didn't want to see him ever again. I pushed the thoughts aside of his treatment of me after the shooting and narrowed my eyes at him. "How'd you know where I live?"

"I have my sources. I know it's been a long time. I'm sorry I disappeared on you. Can we go inside?"

"I don't think that's a good idea." Normally I would have let him in, but his presence suddenly made my skin crawl. *What did I ever see in him?*

"Do you have company?"

I sighed, "Dan, what do you want? You made it pretty evident that you didn't need or want me around for your recovery. I'm glad to see you're better, but why are you here?" He'd been so cold and callous to me after the shooting and I welcomed it. I didn't need or want him around and it seemed to be mutual.

He let out an exasperated breath, "Cassidy, James is nothing but trouble." I flinched at his words. *How did he know about James?* "He's just going to use you and throw you away."

"Excuse me? You're the one throwing people away."

"We both experienced a trauma. My family circled the wagons. I'm sorry I pushed you away. It was a mistake." He tried to put my hands in his and I pulled them away before he was successful.

"Don't touch me. Dan, what we had, well, it was a mistake. I don't know what you *think* you know about James, but you don't. Please leave."

"I know that he and Melissa Westin have a long and torrid relationship. They have since high school." My stomach started convulsing. "I'm guessing by that look on your face you know who she is." I must have nodded because he continued on. "Cassidy, they're meant to be. You're just going to get hurt. Everyone who gets in between them ends up hurt or dead. Just like Jason."

Gasping at his harsh words I narrowed my eyes at him and he answered the question in my eyes.

He started responding before I even asked the questions, "You don't know about Jason?" He ran his fingers through his short spiky hair before continuing, "Jason was my best friend and James's cousin. Jason and Melissa were a couple before James broke them up. Melissa cheated on Jason with James and Jason was so torn up about the whole thing he committed suicide." He reached for me again and I evaded him.

I couldn't listen to any more of it, "Dan I need you to leave. Please. Thank you for the flowers."

"Cassidy, wait…"

Rushing back inside before Dan could stop me, I made sure to turn the deadbolt. *What the hell just happened?* Dan's words ran over and over again in my head. James and Melissa had been on and off since high school? Jesus Christ, I was an idiot. No wonder she was so upset at the auction. And Jason, who was Jason? Dan said Jason and James were cousins.

It was preposterous. I decided to find my laptop, powered it up and sat on the couch pulling up my favorite search engine. I typed in Jason and James Benedict. After scrolling through a few pages I found a link for Jason Benedict Whitford. Oh, God, this just gets worse and worse. Finding an obituary from fifteen years ago for Jason, I noticed his death was listed as December 31st, James's birthday. My whole body started trembling as I scanned further through the article and stopped at 'brother to Jane'. Fucking hell. I was going to be sick. I ran to the kitchen and emptied the minimal contents of my stomach into the sink.

When my stomach had calmed and the shaking subsided, I returned to my laptop. There was no mention of a drug overdose or suicide, but there wouldn't be. I found a link to a memorial page and clicked on it and there I came across several pictures of Mrs. Whitford, her husband, a much younger Jane and Jason. I scanned through and found one of Jason and James. In fact, most of the pictures were of James and Jason as I scrolled further down. There were none of Dan that I could find, which I thought was odd if Jason and Dan were such good friends like Dan claimed.

Before I knew it, it was after 5p.m. I had to stop obsessing and start getting ready. I put the laptop down and pulled myself off the couch. Of course I was in no mood to go out now, and after spotting the flowers on the floor by the front door, I gathered them up, took them to the kitchen and tossed them in the garbage. I headed up the stairs and proceeded to take the longest shower in history.

~ JAMES ~

I USED THE SPARE and let myself in after failed attempts at knocking. When I entered, I could hear the shower running and I spotted a small envelope on the floor. It wasn't sealed so I opened it up and was immediately fuming mad. The card was from Dan and was a feeble attempt at an apology and a plea to get back together. I put the card in my wallet and pulled out my cell.

"Smith, he's back. God dammit, I don't want to hear excuses. Find out where he's staying. He's made contact with Cassidy. I don't care. Just get it done."

I put the phone back in my pocket and headed to the kitchen for some water, noticing a flower smashed in the lid of the garbage. Opening the lid I found a fresh bouquet of flowers in it. Well, *that* was a good sign. Shit. Who knows what he said to her. It was probably going to go one of two ways. Bad and worse.

Deciding to try my luck I headed up the stairs and the shower was still running. I sat on the end of the bed and waited for a while. *What was she doing in there?* Just as I was about to interrupt her, I heard the water shut off before hearing her move around the bathroom for a few moments.

She walked out the bathroom door and was startled when she spotted me. "James, you scared me. How did you get in?"

She pulled her towel tighter around her body exhibiting that she was nervous and self-conscious. I got up to walk toward her as she started fidgeting.

"Cassidy, what's wrong?" I knew exactly what was wrong, but needed to hear it from her.

She was chewing her nails and I could tell she was trying to figure out what to say. "I thought I said no more secrets."

"Jesus Christ, Cassidy. What does that mean, what secrets?" My adrenaline was pumping as I started pacing the floor.

"I know about Jason and Melissa." She just watched me, gauging my reaction.

I took a deep defeated breath before sagging back down to the bed and put my head in my hands. "Cassidy...I...FUCK. I'm sorry. I should've told you."

"So it's true? You and Melissa, since high school? How could you do that to Jason, your cousin?"

"Whoa, hang on. How could I do *what*? You're talking about things you know nothing about." I was trying to keep my temper in check, "I was waiting for the right time."

"The right time? You had the perfect opportunity last night. You didn't tell me that this thing with Melissa started fifteen years ago. I can't compete with that!" She was fucking mad out of her mind screaming at me. "And your cousin Jason, Jane's brother. I mean, I don't even know how to process this." Her voice began cracking and I went to get up and headed toward her. "DON'T TOUCH ME!"

I flinched at her harsh tone. "Cassidy, please let me explain. I don't know what Dan told you."

"This doesn't have anything to do with Dan."

"The hell it doesn't. He's a snake Cassidy. I know he was here." My temper got the better of me as I turned from her and punched a hole in the drywall.

"What! So now you're spying on me? You don't own me, this is MY house!"

She was screeching in my face, and if I hadn't been so pissed off, I'd congratulate her on her balls for challenging me. "You can't believe anything he says."

"I could say the same about YOU!" She covered her mouth like she regretted saying it or like she was going to be sick. She ran back into the bathroom and started splashing water on her face and I realized she was white as a sheet.

"Cassidy, please let me explain." Softening my tone, I began rubbing the ache that was forming in my hand.

"James, I think you should leave. I don't know what or who to believe. I'm on complete information overload."

"With the WRONG information. Dan can't be trusted!"

She whipped her head up to me, "What are you talking about?"

"Dammit, Cassidy, he's a drug addict and a thief. You can't trust him."

"GET OUT!" She picked up the closest thing to her, a brush, and chucked it at my head. I ducked just in time as it snapped in half after hitting the wall behind me.

"Have you lost your mind?"

"Apparently! But I'm not the one punching holes in the wall. Get out!"

"Hey, what's going on?" Whipping my head around, I saw Cal standing in the doorway to the bedroom.

"Your sister is off her rocker." I was shoved back and realized Cassidy had slammed the bathroom door in my face before locking it.

"I'm not the only one. Cal, I want him out of here NOW!"

Cal had a hint of concern on his face while smiling, too. "Dude, she's a redhead *and* a Scorpio. What the hell did you do to piss her off?" He spotted the hole in the wall by the bathroom, "Come outside, she needs time to cool down, alone, and you could use some fresh air, too."

Knowing he was right, I followed him down the stairs. Cassidy and I both needed to cool off. I reached the bottom of the stairs and Jane was just glaring at me.

"What's going on?"

"Why are you looking at me that way?"

"Please, James. I know you. What did you do? Or should I say what *didn't* you do?"

I sighed, "Let's go outside. I'll fill you both in." We all stepped out the door and to the small front yard, the street lights and front porch our only light.

I filled Jane and Cal in on the surprise visit Cassidy had from Dan that I was confident had taken place that afternoon. Telling them she had asked about Jason, Melissa, and high school, Cal acknowledged the info I had already divulged to him. Jane, being fully aware of Dan and his slithering ways, put it all together in no time.

"So Dan and Cassidy were an item?" Cal and I nodded. "Damn. And she doesn't know about his drug use?"

"Apparently not."

"And you knew this, too?" She was looking at Cal now.

"As of a few days ago."

"Hey!" She smacked us both up the side of the head like a mother scolding her kids.

"You stupid asses. What the hell is wrong with you two? No wonder she's pissed off. I'm pissed off *for* her."

We were all standing there quietly as I looked up to see Cassidy glaring down at us from her bedroom window. Cal and Jane caught sight of her too and Jane let out a big breath.

"How much does she know?" We both shrugged our shoulders. "You're useless. I'll try to fix this." She marched back up the stairs and went inside. Turning, she said, "Does she at least know you own the townhouse, not my mom and dad?"

"Dammit, Jane." Cal looked at me all confused.

"I'll take that as a NO." She disappeared inside before slamming the door shut.

~ CASSIDY ~

I GLANCED OUT the window just in time to see Jane slap them both and couldn't help but laugh. James spotted me and I removed the smile from my face. A moment later Jane disappeared from my view and I went back to the bathroom. Picking up my discarded brush that was now broken, I started pulling the tangles out, which proved difficult with the handle no longer attached.

Then there was a knock at my door. "Cassidy. It's Jane. Can I come in? I'm alone."

"It's open." Coming out of the bathroom, broken brush in hand, I sat on the bed. I had already pulled on some jeans and a light sweater. She made her way in and closed the door behind her. "I assume you're here to plead your cousin's case?"

She laughed, "Cassidy. He has no excuses, but I am here to make sure you have the story straight."

That caught my attention, "I'm listening."

"They told me that you were dating Dan Young and that he was here today." She sighed once I confirmed. "Cassidy, I don't know what Dan told you, but he can't be trusted." I began to speak and she stopped me, "Please hear me out." I accepted defeat and let her speak.

"Jason was my older brother by a year. Jason, James, Melissa, Dan, and I all went to high school together and we ran in the same circle for the most part. Jason and James were inseparable, like brothers. Dan and Melissa were the wild kids; drugs, parties, you understand. Jason started dating Melissa, therefore Jason and Dan started hanging out. Jason didn't listen to any of us that they were bad news. Still with me?"

"Yes."

"James's freshman year of college was Jason's senior year in high school. James was home over Christmas break. Melissa and Dan were seniors, too, and I was a junior. Anyway. Jason was on the verge of flunking out. He was partying almost every night with Dan. Melissa was even getting fed up with Jason since it meant she wasn't the center of Jason's universe anymore. James stayed at my parents' house the night before New Year's Eve, eager to talk to Jason. They had made plans and Jason never showed. I confided to James my fears.

In the early morning hours we all woke to Jason and James yelling at each other. Jason threw a punch and they started fighting. We let them fight it out, but Jason grabbed a bottle and smashed it against James's head. That's how James got the scar."

"Oh no." It was barely a whisper, but she heard me, nodded and continued.

"My parents had to pry them apart. It finally became evident to them that Jason was out of control and needed help, but it was too late. James stormed out, covered in his own blood, and shortly after, so did Jason. That's the last time we saw Jason alive. We searched for him all day and night. James *still* blames himself for it."

"But he tried to help." We were both crying as I couldn't begin to imagine losing Cal like she lost Jason.

"We all know that, but he's a stubborn, overprotective ass and thinks it's his job to keep everyone safe."

"I'm so sorry, Jane."

"Thank you."

"But, what does this have to do with Melissa and Dan today?"

She exhaled, "I don't know what Dan told you, if anything…"

I filled her in on my visit with Dan.

She was turning red, "He's a liar Cassidy. When I went to Melissa's that night looking for Jason, Dan was with her, IN BED. She told me I had just missed Jason, but that he was fine. I suspect that Jason caught Dan, not James, in bed with Melissa."

"Oh. My. God." I put my head in my hands.

"Melissa and Dan were too strung out that night to even realize how far gone Jason was. He was head over heels for that tramp. We were all kids, but if anyone is to blame for what happened, well, it's not James. Anyway. Cassidy, James's biggest problem is that he has a huge heart, and people take advantage of that. The worst mistake he ever made was thinking Melissa had changed. And maybe she has, but Dan? Dan will always be a snake. He made some ridiculous speech at Jason's funeral about them being best friends. Needless to say, he was escorted out. Melissa didn't even show up."

I was utterly mortified, "I didn't know. God, I feel like an ass. I had no idea."

"Cassidy, we all have ghosts in our closets. It's nothing to be ashamed of. There's more you should know."

I didn't know how much more I could handle, but asked her to continue anyway.

"Dan was dealing the night of the shooting." She paused and waited for me to get her meaning. "The drugs found in James's office were Dan's. He swore to James he was clean and that's the only reason James let his band play at the bar. Dan is dangerous. You need to stay away from him."

"Jesus, I'm an idiot." *How could I have been dating a dealer? What the hell was wrong with me?*

"James has been looking out for you ever since that night. He's completely smitten with you, Cassidy. I've never seen him like this." Just then there was a knock at the door.

"Who is it?" Jane went to the door, opened it and I saw James peek his head inside. He looked wretched. They exchanged a few whispers, "Cassidy?"

"He can come in." Jane made her exit. "Thank you, Jane."

"No problem. Oh, and by the way. Cal knew about Dan on Monday and James is your landlord, not my mom and dad."

My head snapped up as I saw her smile at James and he in turn slammed the door in her face. "What?"

"Cassidy?"

"You're my landlord, but I thought." I let out an exaggerated screech, "Is there ANYTHING else?"

He was on his knees in front of me, clasping my legs, "Cassidy, I'm so sorry. I was just trying to protect you."

"I'm sorry, too." Placing my hand on his cheek, I ran my thumb over his scarred eyebrow and he closed his eyes. "This is all so stupid." His head shot up. "We're fighting over ridiculous shit."

He relaxed and laughed, "You forgive me?"

Leaning my head to the side I smiled at him. There really wasn't anything to forgive because we were fighting over things from his past that we had no control over. Dan, well, Dan could go to hell.

"You're my landlord? This could get complicated." I pursed my lips and raised my eyebrows.

"How so?"

"Um, need I go into the various complications that arise in relationships? For instance, the last hour we just went through?"

"No."

I put my arms around his neck as he grabbed me tightly and stood with me clinging to him. "I won't break, James. I'm stronger than you think. I forgive you. You can trust *me*, too."

He pulled back and looked at me, "I'm starting to see that. I'll try harder."

"Thank you."

"You should finish getting ready. Anthony and Lena pulled in just before I came up."

"Ugh. Ok. I'll be down shortly."

"You might want to wear your boots. I'm taking you for a ride, probably the last one for the season." It was then I noticed he was in his worn leather jacket, jeans and boots.

"James?" He turned to look at me, "Kiss me."

He rushed toward me and attacked my mouth as I clung to his jacket while his hands cupped my face. He pulled away too soon as I stood there with my eyes closed catching my breath.

"You ok?"

"Mmm." With a smile on his face he left the room. I let out a deep sigh and made quick work of finishing getting ready.

nineteen

Excessive

~ CASSIDY ~

IT WASN'T VERY LONG BEFORE I WAS heading downstairs and
followed the chatter coming from the kitchen. Lena and Anthony
were drooling over James who was chitchatting with them and Cal and
Jane were nose to nose. Everything was perfect, almost. Glancing at
the picture of Holly on the mantle, she was the only missing piece, and
I wondered how long I would feel her void.

"There she is." Cal rushed over and swept me into a big hug.
"Everything good?" He set me down, looking concerned, and I slugged
him in the chest. "Ow. What was *that* for?" He was rubbing his chest
as I noticed Jane laughing.

"You know what that was for." Jane walked over to him and
whispered in his ear.

"Sorry, Cass."

"I know." Suddenly I was assailed by Lena and Anthony with hugs and gift bags. "You guys, you shouldn't have. Thank you."

Lena insisted I open her gift first so I did and found two travel coffee mugs and a box of coffee for my new coffee maker. "I fully expect *you* to bring me coffee from now on!" We both laughed.

Opening Anthony's gift I grew nervous because of the way he was looking at me and I suspected that his gift would cause me and everyone else to blush. I pulled out a box and was greeted with tissue paper once I opened it. I glimpsed inside and before I could stop him Anthony pulled out a mass of purple satin.

"Whoa, hey now!" Cal was up in arms and Jane covered his eyes as they laughed and I knew I was as red as a tomato.

"Anthony!"

"Giiirl please. He likes it!" He was pointing his thumb at James.

I looked over just in time to see James blush. *He blushed!* We all started laughing. I snatched the lingerie from Anthony and shoved it back in the box.

"Here, Cassidy. This is from your brother and me." Cal started to object and Jane elbowed him in the side.

"Thank you." Unwrapping the package, I discovered a new set of purple king sized sheets with a very high thread count.

"I heard you got a new bed. Hope that's okay?" She winked at me and I gave her a quick hug.

"It's perfect. Thank you."

Anthony passed around champagne flutes to everyone and started to make a toast, but James interrupted him.

"May I?" Anthony nodded approval. "To Cassidy. You've taught me more in the last week than I ever anticipated. I look forward to learning more from you in the years to come. Cheers."

James didn't take his eyes off me and I was already melting when he kissed my cheek. He said 'in the years to come'. I accepted his kiss and pushed his words aside.

"Let's go eat!"

"One more thing." I turned to James who was holding a box of his own.

"James, you already got me a gift." Pushing the box into my hands, he insisted I open it. I pulled out a beautiful purple leather jacket. "Wow. It's gorgeous."

"What's with all the purple?"

It was a lot of purple gifts and we chalked it up to coincidence and that it was my favorite color.

"Here, let me." I turned as James took the jacket from me and slid it up my arms. It was a perfect fit and I turned to give him another kiss. "You look great in it; almost as good as you'll look in Anthony's gift. Ouch!" I pinched his nipple and headed for the front door.

"Let's go. We have some celebrating to do!"

We all stepped outside, Lena and Anthony decided to carpool with Cal and Jane while James and I got on his bike.

DINNER WAS WONDERFUL and full of laughs from everyone. James insisted on paying the bill and I seemed to be the only one objecting. We decided to head to a new bar down the street and once inside we found a corner booth in the back by the dance floor that we could all squeeze into. James and I ended up in the back with Lena and Anthony to my left, Jane and Cal to James's right.

The waitress came and took our drink order. Cal and James ordered water while the rest of us ordered drinks before Lena and Anthony headed to the dance floor.

"Are you having fun?" His arm was around my shoulder as he

whispered in my ear.

"I am. You?" I turned to him and ran my hand dangerously high up his thigh as he nodded.

"Do you want to dance?"

I shook my head and pursed my lips, "I'm good for right now." I slid my hand up higher—he didn't stop me—and soon I pressed my hand against the bulge in his pants as he bit and sucked on my ear and neck.

"Hey, lovebirds."

James and Cal struck up some dialogue as Jane moved around to my side of the table so we could chat. We both rolled our eyes at James and Cal who were now oblivious to us as we heard mention of bikes, cars, and trucks.

"They're meant to be," I smirked as she laughed even louder.

"I guess so."

"So, you and Cal?" I had to ask, I couldn't help it. She smiled while shrugging her shoulders. "He likes you, I can tell."

"Feeling is mutual." We smiled at each other.

Before we were aware of what happened, Lena had pulled Jane to her feet and Anthony pulled me and led us to the dance floor whether we wanted to or not. I looked back to Cal and James who just smiled and waved us on.

A few songs later we were all laughing, jumping and gyrating to Pitbull. I was turning into a sweaty mess and having a blast, having not let loose like this in so long, and it felt great. The four of us were being inappropriate with each other and laughing our asses off.

Blurred Lines by Robin Thicke then came on and you could hear the cheers fill the club. The crowded dance floor became packed as the four of us were pushed aside, now dancing right in front of our booth. James and Cal were doing their best to ignore us so Jane and I upped the ante. We were dirty dancing with one another and now our men were fully entranced with us. James's eyes were hooded as he watched me sashay my body back and forth. I motioned my finger at him, bidding him to join me, but he just shook his head and smirked, clearly enjoying the show I was putting on for him.

As another song ended I looked around, realizing I was alone and my friends were gone. I looked to the table and saw Anthony and Lena gulping down water, but I didn't see James. Before I had a chance to look for him, I was grasped from behind and I started to pull away when I heard 'Blackbird' whispered in my ear.

His hands were on my hips as he pulled my back tight against him. I leaned my head back to his chest, recognizing his scent. *Sex on Fire* by Kings of Leon began playing overhead and I smiled as I let him guide me to the music. I hadn't taken him for a dancer, outside of the slow dancing we did at the masquerade and the auction, but he was good.

I felt the heat of his erection just above my ass and pushed back against him, raising my arms above my head. I found his neck and rested my hands there as he ran a hand across the exposed flesh of my belly and I shuddered.

He dropped his head to my neck as his other hand ran up my side and just under my breast. I was sure we must have been quite the spectacle, but so were other couples on the dance floor. He reached up, grabbing my hand, and spun me out as the tempo picked up and I laughed as he pulled me back to him. Face to face, he positioned his solid thigh between my legs as we continued to sway to the beat. I briefly placed my head on his chest while my hands clutched his biceps as his hands traveled just under the hem of my sweater and spanned across my lower back and down to the curve of my ass. I gazed up to him and his lips took mine; the kiss didn't last nearly long enough, it never did.

He whispered in my ear, "You'll be lucky if I don't drag you to the bathroom, baby." Pressing his thigh into my crotch I gasped, "I have a feeling you wouldn't object."

I squeezed his biceps and before I knew it the song was over. He hauled me back toward the table and everyone was there, but before I could sit, Jane seized my hand and dragged me to the ladies room. I was relieved and took the first available stall. When I emerged to wash my hands, Jane was still standing by the door.

"Everything okay, Jane?"

"Don't panic."

"Ok."

"Dan is here. We have to get Cal and James out of here before they spot him."

"Shit, agreed. What is he doing here?"

"I don't know, but he didn't seem too happy with the show the two of you put on out on the dance floor."

"This doesn't make any sense. He's acting more possessive of me now than he did when we were dating."

"We'll figure that out later. Right now we need to get out of here."

We rushed out of the bathroom and back to our table. It was too late; Lena and Anthony were sitting there paralyzed.

"Where are Cal and James?" They simply pointed behind me, and as Jane and I turned, we cursed in unison.

Cal, God bless him, was trying to hold back James. Dan was laughing and spitting words back at James.

"We have to get them out of here."

Anthony and Lena grabbed our purses and jackets and followed behind us. They had attracted a crowd and a bouncer had made his way over to them. The bouncer and James shook hands and exchanged some words. The bouncer then turned to Dan and escorted him out of the bar and Dan didn't go quietly.

James was visibly angry as Cal patted him on the chest and they turned to see us making our way over.

"We're good here. Show's over." Cal was talking to the spectators.

I noticed a few cell phone cameras flashing. How annoying. I curled up to James and placed my hands on his cheeks. "You okay?"

He pulled my arms down, kissed my forehead before taking my hand in his and nodded as he pulled me back toward our table. When we got there our table had already been claimed by other patrons.

"It's getting late, we can just go." He was teetering on the edge, I could tell. "Hey!" That got his attention, "Take me home, James." I lifted up to my tip toes and whispered in his ear, "You can take your anger out on me." I sucked on his ear briefly before I pulled away.

Chuckling at me, he smiled, "If you insist, lady."

"I insist."

We all made our way through the bar and as we stepped outside the cold autumn air assaulted us. James helped me into my jacket before taking my hand as we walked toward the parking garage. We only made it another ten feet from the bar before Dan popped out from an alley.

"Cassidy! You didn't waste any time, did you? Got yourself the prized stallion."

Jesus Christ. I heard James growl next to me as I stepped in front of him. I wasn't sure who I was trying to protect; James or Dan.

"Dan, get out of here. You're just asking for trouble."

He started sniggering and inched closer. James gripped my shoulders as I noticed Cal stepping up next to us.

I turned to James, "He's not worth it, James."

"He can have you. Tramp. You were a lousy lay anyways."

Cal and James both stepped forward at the same time. Dan must have had a death wish, and before I could stop it from happening,

James's fist landed square in the center of Dan's face. Jane, Lena, Anthony, and I all flinched, though he had it coming.

Dan was knocked to the ground and when he picked his head back up blood was pouring out his nose. "You broke my nose."

"You deserved it." I looked to Jane and smiled at her as she had simply said what we were all thinking. Dammit. I saw some cops running over behind her and turned to Cal.

"Cal!"

He was busy holding James off Dan, but when James spotted the officers he backed off. In the meantime, we had attracted another crowd. Dan was on the ground cursing as I pulled James to the side and checked his hand.

"Are you hurt? You could've broken your hand. You need to start punching a bag instead of walls and faces!"

He smiled while rubbing his knuckles and said he was alright. I looked to see where Cal was and found him holding out his badge and shaking hands with one of the officers. That officer then made his way over to James and me.

"Take the lady home. We'll see to him." The officer pointed at Dan, and I thought I recognized the officer, but couldn't recall his name.

"Thank you." I dragged James away before anything more could be said or done. We all had to make our distance from the scene we had caused. When we reached the parking garage, James turned and apologized to everyone.

"Don't worry about it. If you hadn't punched him, I would have." Cal shook his head, "They're taking Dan to the station. He won't be pressing charges. You okay to drive?"

"Yeah, man. Thanks again. I really am sorry." He and Cal shook hands before we all said our goodbyes.

"I'll see you tomorrow, sis. Noon?"

"Yes. Dad and Lisa will be here around that time." He hugged me again and then we were off.

James took a detour out of the city as we rode for a while and then he pulled into an alcove just outside the city. He put the kickstand down and dismounted before he helped me off the bike, removed our helmets, and pulled me to him.

"I'm sorry I ruined your birthday."

"You didn't ruin my birthday. You sure tried, but it's not ruined."

He pinched my side and hissed at me and I turned in his arms so that my back was against his chest. His arms were draped over my shoulders and I was holding onto his forearms. We found a few satellites in the sky and admired the stars. I started shivering as the night was quickly cooling off.

"Let's get you home, lady. I owe you some birthday spankings."

I didn't object when he dragged me back to the bike and we made our way back to my place.

I woke to the sound of him hammering away on the treadmill and decided to join him. I threw on some clothes and shoes before hopping on the bike, but after thirty minutes or so I'd had enough. My entire body was sore, probably from my sexcapades with James. I was rolling my neck and shoulders when I felt his hands dig into them.

"You're sore. I'd apologize, but then that means I'd regret last night," he leaned in and whispered, "And I'll never regret a moment of you tied up beneath me."

A tremor ran across me and my breath caught, "I don't regret it either."

We were up late as he gave me a proper education on the many uses of satin ties and I smiled as I remembered it. As usual, he was amazing and I was surprised at the things my body happily tolerated and responded to.

"You really are a natural."

"I think you're right."

"Let's get you in the shower. The heat will help relax your muscles."

I cranked on the water and then relieved my bladder while he undressed. I would never get enough of his nakedness; I could stare at him forever. I walked up behind him, kissed his back and he stilled momentarily before turning around. Smiling down at me, he tugged my sports bra up and over my head and then dropped to his knees to remove my shorts and panties. He was running his fingers up and down my legs and stopped at my right ankle.

I looked down, "Everything alright?"

He was frowning. "I was too rough."

I lifted and turned my ankle and saw the faintest trace of a welt and a small bruise taking shape, "James, I'm fine." He wouldn't stop examining me so I resorted to extreme measure and tugged on his hair.

"Hey now," he stood while capturing my ass around his hands and lifted me to him. "You're not playing fair."

We both smiled as I leaned down and kissed him before he carried me to the shower.

twenty

Pressure

~ CASSIDY ~

WE BOTH TOOK TURNS WASHING each other before we exited the shower and proceeded to brush our teeth. Instead of throwing his toothbrush back in his duffel bag, he placed it next to mine. We got dressed throwing each other admiring glances and laughing.

"So, your dad is coming today?"

He caught that last night? He was bent over lacing up his boots. "Yes, a family lunch for my birthday." I didn't say anymore.

"I'd like to meet him." He was smiling at me and knew exactly what he was playing at.

"James, um, I, of course you're welcome to join us." He wanted to meet my dad? I had never introduced Dad to anyone I was dating. Maybe he was testing me. Surely he wouldn't stay.

"Great. I have to get my bike back to the hotel since we're expecting rain and then I'll be back."

Shit, shit, shit. "Ok."

He kissed me and smacked my ass before walking out of my room and down the stairs. I stood there for a moment, dumbfounded. He wanted to meet my dad. I grabbed my phone and texted Cal. He responded by telling me that Jane was coming, too. That should take some of the heat off me.

~ JAMES ~

I WALKED OUT the front door and saw a paper on the front steps and reporters across the street. *Dammit.* I snatched up the paper, threw a smile and slammed the door before proceeding to all the windows making sure all the blinds were closed before looking at the paper.

The front picture was of Cassidy consoling me from the night before after I had punched Dan. The story painted Dan as the helpless victim and I wadded it up and threw it to the floor as I heard Cassidy coming down the stairs. She spotted me on the couch.

"I thought you left." She could see that I was upset, "What's wrong?"

I pointed to the front yard and she leaned over the couch and peeked out the blinds.

"What the… Why are they here?"

She spotted the paper wadded up on the floor, "I'm really sorry. I've always been careful. Someone must have tipped them off to where you live."

She picked up the paper, flattened it out and skimmed through it. "My dad is going to freak out. I have to cancel."

"Hang on. It's not over yet. Do you trust me?"

"Of course."

Pulling out my cell I dialed, "Hey Dad, is Mom up for visitors today?" I continued making arrangements. "Cassidy, is it just your dad?" She told me his fiancée, Lisa, was coming along with Jane and Cal. "Should be eight of us. Great. See you soon."

"What did you do?"

"All taken care of. We're having your birthday celebration at my parents' place." She looked like a deer in headlights. I walked to her and put my hands on her shoulders and looked her in the eyes, "What's wrong?"

"I've never met anyone's parents, James, and my Dad has never met anyone I've dated either."

I laughed, "They'll love you. You better call your Dad and I'll call Jane. Here's the address." Jotting down the address on a piece of paper, I handed it to her.

She hesitantly pulled her cell out of her pocket and started dialing.

"Hey Dad, yes we're still on, but there's been a small change of plans. We're having dinner at my, uh, a friend's house."

A friend! She had to know that she was more than a friend.

"Ok, see you soon." She put the cell down and headed to the kitchen.

"A *friend?*" Looking back to me, she started chewing her nails and shrugged her shoulders. "Cassidy, we're more than friends."

"Well, a lady doesn't presume anything. What should I have told him? Yes, Dad, he's great in the sack. Hung like a horse, too!" She was smiling from ear to ear, "If I'm more than your friend then you need to let me know." She planted her hands on her hips and her eyebrows were raised at me.

I made my move toward her, cornering her in the kitchen, and she didn't flinch. "You're more than a friend, Cassidy Charles."

"Then what am I, James Benedict?"

I had her pinned against the wall and pushed her hair behind her ears, "Girlfriend?"

"Tenant girlfriend is more like it." I tickled her hips. "Hey. You have to admit, girlfriend sounds silly at our age."

Shrugging my shoulders I told her, "You're more than a girlfriend, Cassidy." I leaned in and kissed her when there was a knock at the door.

"Miss Charles, do you have a moment to make a statement about your relationship with JB3?"

"Seriously, they're knocking on my door?" She closed her eyes and dropped her head on the wall behind her, looking defeated.

"Cassidy, go finish getting ready. Grab some sunglasses, too, and we'll leave. I'll call Smith and he'll come and deal with them. Okay?" She agreed and I released her so she could go upstairs.

~ CASSIDY ~

When I got upstairs, I reconsidered my clothing choice and traded my jeans for slacks and my tee for a blouse. I pulled my hair up into a pony and curled a few strands hanging around my face before I applied some light makeup. I was examining myself in the mirror, realizing I was a nervous wreck, when I heard the front door open then close and heard voices. *Who was it?*

I made my way downstairs and spotted Smith and James talking. When I got into the living room I saw Delaney as she pulled a red wig out of her bag.

"What's the plan, James?"

What in the world? I looked to James, wondering what the plan was indeed.

"Cassidy, you remember Delaney, she's here to help." I nodded nervously. "You guys take the bike, they'll think it's Cassidy and me. After they leave we'll take the Rover. Sound good?"

"Easy peasy." Delaney threw the wig on, checked herself in the mirror above the mantel and asked, "How do I look, love?"

Smith walked over to her and kissed her cheek. "I think I like you as a redhead." She giggled.

Smith and James exchanged a high five like a couple of school kids and then Smith and Delaney headed out the door.

James turned to me, "You can close your mouth, Cassidy." He was amused at the look of shock on my face.

"Delaney and Smith?" He nodded. "But, they're, wow, I didn't see that one coming."

Shrugging his shoulders, he mentioned that Smith and Delaney had been together for several months.

"Where'd she get the wig?"

"Let's just say Delaney likes to role play." I immediately chastised myself for asking the question and was disturbed that he knew that. The look I gave him must have told him that. "Calm down. Delaney and I are strictly friends." He sauntered over to me, "I didn't take you for the jealous type."

"Well, I am. Hands off, you're mine! I don't play nice with others." He was grinning profusely as I grabbed his shirt aggressively before pulling his lips down to mine.

"I think I like possessive Cassidy," and he kissed me again.

Surprised by my immediate hunger for him I yanked his shirt out of his jeans and ran my hands up over his abs and chest. I raked my fingers back down his chest before I slid my hands into his front pockets where I dug in to find the side of his erection and rubbed it.

"We'll be late, Cassidy." He tugged on my lip as his hands pulled me closer and he thrust against me.

"So what? More time for us, less time for them to give us the third degree." Pulling his belt open, and then his jeans, I plunged my hands into his boxer briefs and claimed what was mine.

"Baby, we'll be getting the third degree if we're late."

I stroked his cock with mad determination, "Please. I'll be quick. I want you hard and fast." I bit his chest as I yanked down his jeans and boxer briefs.

Moaning, he gave me what I wanted, "I can't say no to you, Cassidy."

"Maybe you don't want to say no." Removing my hands from him, I started discarding my own pants.

He was unbuttoning my blouse, "Why are the buttons so small?" Before I could help him he ripped it open, "Oops." He smirked at me before nuzzling his face in my chest. He pulled my bra cups down and devoured my breasts; one with his mouth and the other with his hand. Biting and sucking, I just knew he was leaving a mark on me.

I managed to free my ankles of my pants and panties, "James." It was a plea and I didn't have to say more. Sucking on my breast as his other hand cupped my wet, naked sex, "OH, yes." He showed no mercy as two fingers pierced my vagina, "Holy shit!" He was digging and circling into me as his thumb found my clit. "Please, wait; I want you inside me when I come."

He growled, "I am inside you."

"Your cock, I want your cock inside me."

Snarling, he removed his hand from me and I sighed at the loss of him. He maneuvered me to the dining table and lifted me so that I was sitting on top and I eagerly spread my legs wide for him. Stroking him again, I polished the bead of moisture all over his tip as he grabbed my hips and jerked me to the very edge of the table. I braced my hands on the edge of the table and looked to his face. I followed his gaze to find he was staring at my sex while stroking his cock.

He inched forward and rubbed his erection all over my clit. I threw my head back at the exquisite feeling. "Cassidy, watch me fuck you."

A shiver ran through me at his words and I looked down just as he pushed into me. The feelings coursing through me were intensified by watching him claim me. It was more than intimate watching as he pulled all the way out and slammed back in.

"I own you, baby."

Breathless and panting I said, "Ditto." It was the only word I could muster. I continued watching him and my release was building with increasing speed. I felt my clit tightening. "James..."

I closed my eyes for a moment, rejoicing in the sounds of our bodies. Clenching around him, I recognized the change in his rhythm, as he was close too. I opened my eyes and saw that he was tense all over and his eyes were glazed over. Watching him as he watched himself fuck me sent me over the edge. My knuckles were burning from gripping the table so fiercely and I lifted to buck into him, my release now inevitable.

My orgasm wouldn't cease. He lifted his eyes to mine, "I love watching you come."

I twitched again, clenching around him knowing he was holding back and torturing me. *How did he do that?* It seemed to go on forever.

"Ahhh, Cassidy."

Finally he threw his head back and let his release claim him. I was still shaking and moaning and I thought I could possibly come again. He pulled out of me and rubbed the head of his cock all over me while his seed poured out of his engorged head. The feeling of his cum bursting against my clit was too much.

"Holy hell," I fell back to the table as he continued circling my tight nub. "Please, no."

"Yes."

His orgasm had subsided, but he continued massaging my clit with his cock. The heat emanating from him was overwhelming and he was gentle yet tenacious. Leaning over me while nuzzling my belly, I grabbed his hair as a second orgasm swallowed me up.

"James, please, stop." Panting and pushing against his head, "I won't be able to walk." My whole body was convulsing and the room was spinning. Encouraging me on, my hearing was momentarily distorted, like I was under water, due to the power of my orgasm.

"I'll carry you." He put in another stroke for good measure and I smacked at him. "Are you well and satisfied, lady? We're good and late." He sounded annoyed.

I jerked my eyes to his and he was smirking at me as my breathing was still quite erratic.

"You ass! It's your fault. You make me this way." He offered up his hand and I took it as he pulled me to my feet, kissing me long and hard. "Thank you, sir. I'm well and satisfied." He smiled at me as my legs were still shaky, but I managed to hold my own.

We cleaned ourselves up and put our discarded clothes back on. I ran upstairs for a new top and opted for a short sleeve sweater. We were out the door and there was no sign of any reporters as we hopped in the Rover and headed to his parents' house.

~ JAMES ~

WE PULLED THROUGH the gates and I glanced over at her. Her eyes were big and she was speechless. "Cassidy, it's just a house."

"That's not a house, it's a mansion." I squeezed her thigh as she grabbed my hand. "You grew up here?"

"I did." I recognized Cal's truck, noticed another Ford truck and assumed it was her father's.

"Wow."

"I take it your dad drives a Ford, too?"

"He's a Ford retiree. He'll *love* your Rover." I noted her sarcasm as she smiled.

"What did he do?"

"He started on the line right out of high school. He eventually finished his engineering degree when I was little. He retired a couple years ago and now works as a consultant."

"And your mom? I know you said she's been gone a long time. Were they divorced?"

She exhaled, "Not exactly." She looked at me knowing I wanted more info. "James, she's dead. It's a long, horrible story for another time."

Why didn't I know this? I mean, I knew her mom was deceased, but a long horrible story? Maybe she was exaggerating. "Cassidy, I'm sorry, I didn't know."

Smiling she said, "It's ok. Lisa, his fiancé, and Dad have been together for several years. They're actually getting married the weekend of Thanksgiving." She looked to the door and we both spotted Cal and Jane waving at us before they disappeared inside. "We should go in, we're being rude."

"Okay. Hey, relax. My parents will love you." I gave her a quick peck before we went inside.

twenty-one
Introductions

~ CASSIDY ~

The house was huge. Good grief. My childhood home could fit inside it times five. He was holding my hand and I was sure I was squeezing the life out of it. We walked through a few different rooms with Cal and Jane trailing behind.

"Cal, where's Dad?"

"I haven't seen him yet. He's here somewhere."

I nodded at his response as James pulled me along. Familiar voices started to travel down the hall. We entered a room that looked like any other normal family room, but bigger. My Dad and Mr. Benedict were standing by the fireplace and Lisa and another woman, who had to be Mrs. Benedict, were on the couch.

"Ah, there's the birthday girl." Always having been a Daddy's girl, even more so since Mom died, he walked over to me and gave me a big hug before kissing my cheek.

"Hey, Dad, how are you?"

He pulled away and eyed James from head to toe. "I'm great. You must be James. I would say I've heard a lot about you, but I'd be lying."

I rolled my eyes as they shook hands and exchanged smiles.

"Mr. Charles, it's a pleasure to meet you. You have a wonderful daughter."

"Please, call me Dave. Indeed she is." He moved over to Cal and Jane. "And who might this lovely creature be?"

"Hey, Dad, this is Jane. She and James are actually cousins." Jane offered her hand and my Dad embraced her instead. "I warned you, we're huggers," Cal was laughing as Jane was pulled into a hug without warning.

"Jane, you've eased my mind. I was beginning to worry the boy would be alone forever." Jane and I cracked up as Cal frowned.

James placed his hand on the small of my back and guided me to the woman on the couch. "Cassidy, I'd like you to meet my mom, Eva." I turned my attention away from my father to James's mother. She was quite lovely and as tall as me, if not taller, and I noticed they had the same dark hair, olive skin tone, and eyes.

"Cassidy, it's an honor to meet you. James has told us so much about you." She stood and kissed my cheek as I looked at James who just shrugged his shoulders. "All good things, I promise."

His dad then came over and we exchanged greetings. "A pleasure to see you again, Cassidy." The last time I saw James's dad was for business; it was a pleasant change of pace.

After everyone was properly introduced, we were escorted to a large dining room. I went to sit at the end of the table furthest from his parents and James interceded. "Cassidy, please sit here."

His father was at the head of the table and his mother to his left. I was placed next to her, with James to my left. My father sat at the other end, with Lisa across from James, Cal across from me and Jane was sitting across from Eva, and next to J.J.

"Aunt Eva, how are you feeling? You look good." Jane looked thoroughly concerned.

"I'm well, honey. No need for concern."

Sensing the tension in the air, I wondered if she was not being entirely truthful. I looked to James, but he was deep in conversation with my father and my attention was pulled back to Eva.

"So, Cassidy, I hear you're quite the event planner."

"Yes, I work for B & C."

"Yes, Cecily. How is she?"

The question threw me off a little, "She's good, as far as I know." Eva nodded as I took a sip of my water.

"So, James and Jane, which one of you will give this old man kids to spoil first? I'm partial to grandkids, but grandnieces and nephews will do, too."

I inhaled my water and started choking while Eva began thumping my back as I looked at the other dinner guests. Lisa was dumbstruck while Cal tugged on the collar of his shirt. Jane wasn't fazed and James, well, I couldn't bear to look at him or my father.

"For God's sake, Dad," James sounded annoyed.

"Jackson, ease up. In all seriousness though, when?" Eva was smiling from ear to ear and my Dad started cracking up.

"You two are incorrigible." James leaned in and asked if I was okay. I nodded, but still couldn't face him and he put his hand on my leg and gave me a reassuring squeeze.

"I think they're worse than Mother." Jane leaned in and kissed Cal on the cheek. "Relax, it's their game." Cal visibly eased, a little.

"I'm an old man and James needs an heir. Better get the show on the road, Son." His dad was relentless.

"You forgot to preface male heir." I was stunned. My dad was playing along now and Cal was laughing. "I don't know what you're laughing at, Calvin. Your clock is ticking, too." Cal paled and now it was my turn to laugh as the jokes and jabs continued through our late lunch.

Once the meal was over, we headed back to the living room. We were all sitting down when Lisa asked the inevitable, "So, how did you all meet? It can't be a coincidence, the two of you dating cousins and all."

All eyes fell to me and almost everyone in the room seemed uncomfortable except for my dad and Lisa. Did his parents know the truth of it all? I wanted to crawl into a hole and felt myself pale as James took my hand, but Cal took the lead.

"Jane and I both paid Cass an unexpected visit and we hit it off."

"How romantic. Cassidy, what about you two?"

Someone shut her up. I didn't want to rehash all the nasty details.

"I met Cassidy a few months ago. She wouldn't give me the time of day. I've been wooing her ever since."

I exhaled at his words—he was amazing—so cool, calm and collected. I didn't even think about what we'd tell them if they'd asked.

"Smart girl." Jackson was smiling as Eva smacked his leg.

Smiling at them, it was obvious they were still in love after all this time. His dad was more relaxed than I remembered him being at our meeting last month when we met to discuss auction details. It was evident he was a man with a heart of gold, like his son.

"Cassidy, dear. We wanted to get you a little something."

Eva stood and caught me off guard as she handed me an envelope. The gift was totally unexpected. "You shouldn't have. Thank you."

"Go ahead, open it."

I nodded and opened it up finding a gift certificate for a massage, mani, pedi, cut and color, and a facial. It was too much.

"James told us how busy you've been. We figured you deserved a day of pampering."

"Really, it's too much. Thank you so much." I got up to give her a hug and spotted James grinning from ear to ear. "I can't wait to use it!"

I went to sit back down and Dad handed me an envelope before I managed it. "While you're up." He winked at me.

"Dad, you shouldn't have. With the wedding and all..." He waved me off.

Inside the envelope was a pair of concert tickets. I blushed and immediately stuffed the tickets back in the envelope. "Thank you, Dad."

"I heard he was coming and I remembered how you used to blare his music in high school. I figured you're old enough to go to one of his concerts." My dad prided himself on knowing all our likes and dislikes when Cal and I were growing up. Cool as he was though, he didn't allow me to go to many concerts unless Cal was willing to escort me.

"Who are they for?" James was curious.

"Yeah, Cassidy, tell him who your high school obsession was!" I threw Cal a threatening look and he tried to subdue his laughter.

"I'll tell you later. Thank you, Dad!" Dad and Cal were having a great laugh at my expense. James seemed to have dropped the subject but was eyeing me suspiciously.

Suddenly, all attention was on Eva. She had dropped herself to the couch and was holding her head in her hands. "Mom!" James, J.J., and Jane were fretting around her immediately.

"Eva, are you okay?" J.J. was crouched down in front of his wife.

"I'm fine. I just got a little dizzy."

"Mom, you need to rest."

Jane was holding Eva's wrist loosely and I could see her eyeing her watch. "Your pulse is fine. I think James is right. You just need to get some rest, Aunt Eva."

Eva nodded as James and J.J. got her to her feet. They escorted her out of the room, leaving my Dad, Lisa, Cal, and I to wonder what was going on.

"I hope she's okay," Lisa stated the obvious.

We weren't left waiting long before Jane returned and assured us everything was ok. "Cal, we should probably head out." Cal agreed. "Cassidy, James asked if we could drop you off at home. He said he'd call you later."

"You said everything was okay. I'd like to wait for him if I can." Jane looked a little perplexed, but she wouldn't elaborate.

"Cassidy, it's no problem, there's room in the truck."

"I'm waiting." I wasn't sure why I was being so stubborn, but something told me to stay.

Cal and Jane didn't offer again and Jane mentioned that she understood. We all said our goodbyes to Dad and Lisa before I sat down on the couch and picked up a magazine off the end table.

~ JAMES ~

WE GOT MOM TO her room, Jane helped her in the bathroom and then we got her in bed. I was making my leave when she called me back to her.

I asked, "Jane, can you and Cal take Cassidy home?"

"Are you sure? I'm sure she'd prefer to wait for you."

"Yes, I'm sure."

"I'm not going to force her, James."

I nodded as she headed back to the living room and made my way over to the bed.

"Jimmy, she's a wonderful girl. I'm thrilled for you." I was sitting on the side of the bed holding her hand.

"She *is* wonderful. I feel like she's breathed life back into me." She squeezed my hand. "You should rest, Mom."

"She's strong but very sensitive. I already sense that in her. She's the one for you, Jimmy, if you let her be. Don't push her away, now or when I'm gone."

"Mom, please don't talk that way. Get some rest. I love you." I kissed her cheek and stepped into the hall, leaving Dad with her. She had always been extremely inquisitive. I shouldn't have asked Jane to take Cassidy home, and as I was walking back to the living room, Dad caught up to me.

"Jimmy, are you okay?" Dad looked genuinely concerned.

"Should I be?" I pulled my hands through my hair violently, not knowing how to even begin processing the loss of Mom. I knew it was coming, but I couldn't bear the thought of it.

"Son, you have to find a way to deal with this." Looking at my father I could see the tears welling in his eyes. "Does Cassidy even know?" I shook my head. "You need to tell her, which will be a start. Let her take this journey with you, it'll help." He put his hands on my shoulders before hugging me.

"I'll try, Dad."

"Son, I promise you'll come out the other end stronger as a person and as a couple if you let her in. Shut her out and you'll regret it. I know from experience. Especially if she's someone you're serious about." He slapped my back and squeezed my shoulder.

We walked back into the living room and I was relieved to find Cassidy sitting on the couch flipping through a magazine. When she spotted me she put the magazine down and jumped to her feet, smiling at me encouragingly.

"Cassidy, it was a pleasure to meet you." My father kissed her cheek before embracing her and she hugged him back.

"Same here. Thank you for having us over."

"Anytime, dear. Happy Birthday. Take care of each other." He excused himself from the room.

She was fidgeting and sensed my unease. "Is your Mom alright?" I just stood there looking at her. "James, please let me in." Her words that echoed my Dad's undid me. I pulled her tightly to me as she wrapped her arms around my waist as I held her. "James, you're scaring me."

"Mom's been battling cancer for almost five years." She inhaled sharply and looked up to me. "I brought her home on Thursday. She's forgoing any more treatment." Her eyes were getting glassy as my own traitorous tear slid down my face and I could tell she was struggling with what to say.

"James, I'm so sorry. Is there anything I can do?"

She tucked her head back into my chest as I whispered, "You're doing it. I'm glad you didn't leave with Cal and Jane. Thank you for staying."

~ CASSIDY ~

WE WERE DRIVING back to my place and the silence was becoming unbearable. James was just staring into traffic, not mentally there. I took my hand and placed it on his thigh and he picked my hand up and kissed my knuckles.

"Watching your Mom fight this battle for years, I can't begin to imagine the pain you're feeling." He looked to me with solemn eyes.

"Death in any form is horrible. Sometimes I wonder if losing her suddenly would've been easier." Feeling myself pale, my throat getting tight, I pulled my hand out of his grasp and started tugging on imaginary specks of lint on my slacks. "Cassidy, I'm an idiot. I didn't mean it."

"I know you didn't. The grass is always greener."

Assuming a smile, I stared out my window and I started remembering the last time I saw her. I was so angry with her. I would give almost anything to take back the hateful words I said to her that night. My door suddenly opened, startling me, and James immediately pulled me to him; I hadn't even realized we were home.

"I'm sorry." His voice was barely above a whisper as he cupped my face when a flash assailed our vision.

"Cassidy, JB3, would you like to make a statement about the attack on Dan Young?" The man holding the camera was short and resembled a weasel with his camera in our faces. James sheltered me under his arm and shuffled me to the front door.

"No comment, Len."

Fiddling with my keys, I noticed 'Len' place his foot on the bottom step behind us when James turned to him, "LEN! I'll call the police. You're trespassing," James growled.

I popped the key in the lock, walked through the door and moved to see Len moving back to the sidewalk. James slammed the door as another flash brightened the evening sky.

Dumbstruck, I watched as James ensured all the blinds and curtains were still closed tightly. I hung up my jacket and purse then placed my birthday cards on the kitchen counter before making my way back to the couch and curling up in my favorite spot. My knees were pulled up and I was resting my forehead on my knees when the couch dipped under his weight as he sat next to me.

"Cassidy, I'm really sorry about all this. I never expected them to take such interest in you, us." His hand was stroking my hair.

Lifting my head to look at him I told him, "It's not your fault. I just wasn't prepared for this. I had no clue what I was getting into."

Looking troubled he said, "I understand if it's too much." He stood and began pacing my living room like he was debating about leaving.

"James, that's not what I meant. How persistent are these people? Should I get used to them being at my door every day?" I needed him to be honest with me so I could prepare myself mentally.

"The buzz should die down in the next couple weeks. You're the new girl on the street. They'll do some digging until a better story comes along." He sat back down next to me and must have seen the shadow of fear cross my face. "What is it, baby?"

"What do you mean by 'digging'?" I started chewing my nails.

Picking up on my nervous habit immediately he asked, "Cassidy, what is it? What are you worried about them finding?" My eyes were focused on my knees. "Your record is clean, Smith said so. What is it?"

"You ran my record?" I shouldn't have been surprised, but I felt slightly violated and he didn't look apologetic in the least.

"Cassidy, I'm your landlord. Of course, I ran your record."

"Oh, right. I keep forgetting that little detail. I'm sure it was strictly business related." He noted my sarcasm and smirked at me.

Pulling my legs out, he stretched them over his lap. "Cassidy, talk to me. You can trust me."

My attempt to evade him was futile. I took a deep breath, blowing it out, "My mom, she's the one who drove off the old Reynolds farm bridge all those years ago."

Watching as the wheels turned in his brain, he looked at me and I knew the instant he remembered the story because his eyes opened just a little bit wider. It was all over the news and in the papers for weeks, if not months.

"Oh, Jesus. Cassidy, I had no idea." I wasn't even aware that I was crying until he wiped a tear away and pulled me to him, cradling me in his lap. "I'll do everything I can to keep this under wraps."

"I'm sorry about your mom. I had no idea that she was sick."

He didn't say anything and we just sat in each other's embrace for a long time. When I felt a change in him—his breathing slow and quiet—I picked up my head and realized he had fallen asleep. Somehow, I managed to crawl off his lap without waking him. I unlaced his boots and then grabbed a blanket and placed it over him.

twenty-two
Twisted

~ CASSIDY ~

Deciding to catch up on some laundry after changing into some sweats and an oversized t-shirt, I threw a load in and returned to the living room to find James still asleep. It was after seven p.m. and I wasn't sure how long I should let him sleep. Electing to heat up some apple cider before waking him, I set the two cups down on the coffee table and knelt in front of him and started removing the boots I had unlaced earlier.

"What time is it?" I looked up at him and his head was still resting on the back of the couch, he was smiling down at me and I smiled back. After I let him know the time, he stretched his arms up above his head, "That smells delicious."

I set his boots to the side before I stood; handing him a cup of cider and watching him take a long sip. "Cecily gave me the day off tomorrow. You want to watch a movie, maybe make some popcorn?"

"That sounds wonderful, as long as you cuddle with me." He winked at me and smiled.

"I didn't take you for the cuddling type."

"Oh, Cassidy, the things we still need to learn from one another." Smiling broadly at him, I took a sip of my own cider. "Did you have a movie in mind?"

"I'm not sure. I figured we can hit the Redbox down the street. I don't have cable or any of the internet movie services."

"You've got a nice TV and Blu-ray player, though."

"Anthony and Lena got those for me when I moved in. Lena's dad works at an electronics store so she got a great deal!"

"You have internet?" I told him I did. "Great, I have all the internet services. Get me your remotes. We can load up mine."

I got him the remotes and sat down next to him while he programmed my multimedia Blu-ray player with several different options. "There. Now you have Netflix and Amazon. Shall we start browsing?"

James changed into some running shorts and a t-shirt before we settled down on the couch. We ended up picking our favorite movies to watch. Goonies and The Princess Bride were both in our top five so we watched them in that order. I felt like a kid again watching them, only I was curled up with James and that made it even better. Frequently we would both repeat our favorite lines; some the same some not. I told him we should do this more often and he agreed; it was nice having a little bit of normalcy. When the movies were over, we were laying down on the couch together just enjoying the quiet and each other.

Curiosity got the better of me.

"So, where did you learn about the BDSM stuff?" My head rested on his chest and I was running my fingers up and down his forearm. "I mean, do you go to secret clubs and stuff?" I chuckled nervously.

"Are you sure you want to know? Think you can handle it?" His voice was deep and soft. I popped my head up to look at him, a little alarmed by his words, and he pressed my head back down. "Relax, Cassidy. If you really want to know I'll tell you."

I hesitated briefly, contemplating if I really *did* want to know. "I want to know."

"It was after Jason's death. I went back to school after winter break and I had so much anger in me that I was getting out of control. I was picking fights in bars and finally got myself arrested. I hired an attorney and she's who introduced me to it all." He must have felt me stiffen, "Don't worry. She just introduced me and showed me the ropes."

Looking up at him, a million bizarre scenarios started running through my mind. "Showed you the ropes? Were you her boy toy?" I scrunched up my face, but my voice was playful as he shook his head with a grin.

"It was strictly a platonic friendship, she was my Mentor. She's married now with kids. I see her occasionally, mostly work related." He continued stroking my back and running his fingers through my hair and it felt heavenly. After a few minutes he broke the silence, "Have I scared you away?"

"No," shaking my head against his chest.

"Then what are you thinking?"

"Mmm, I was thinking about all of it, if I'm doing it for you or whatever. If there's something more I could do for you. I assume you're a Dom and I guess that makes me a sub?"

"Yes, I am, a Dom that is." His tone was gentle. "There's nothing wrong with being submissive, it doesn't make you weak. I sensed it the first time I saw you. It actually requires great strength."

"I just, well, some of the shit I read about is really scary and some of it really turns me on, at least when I read about it, that is. I don't know how I'd react in real life." I hesitated and he stroked my cheek as if to encourage me. "I don't know how to ask this."

"What is it Cassidy? You can ask me anything."

His tone was reassuring so I asked, "Well, how far would you take it with me? I don't want you to hold back, but I don't know how dark and twisted you are, either. You're a little intimidating and I don't know if I could ever tell you no." *Had I just said that out loud?* It was true; I trusted him and I wanted to give him everything he wanted and needed.

"Are you asking me if I want to hurt you? If I'm a sadist?"

"I guess so."

"I *am* dark and twisted, Cassidy, but you already know that. You're the first person, outside the *secret* clubs, who knows this about me and hasn't persecuted me for it. Maybe I should ask you what things turn you on in your books and what things scare you."

Sitting up, I pushed myself off his chest and straddled his thighs. He looked up at me, his eyes transfixed on mine and I let out a deep breath, feeling my cheeks flush.

"I love when you blush. Go on, you can't scare me." Winking and crossing his hands across his chest he waited for me to speak.

"So, there really *are* secret clubs?" I was barely able to control the excitement in my voice.

"Yes, there are. So, what things have you read about that scare you?"

"Well, I don't think I could handle blood play, for many reasons." Staring at my own hands that were playing with a loose string on the hem of his shirt, I looked up and he nodded agreement. "Um, do people really play with electricity?" His look gave me my answer. "That's too scary, no thank you." He smiled. "I'm not really sure, it's not like I've been to any *secret* clubs or parties. Just the things I've read and the things we've done are what I know."

"Would you want to go to a party with me? We could just observe, no pressure or expectations." As if sensing my question before I asked it, he took my hands in his and pressed them to his chest. "It's strictly confidential. I know in your line of work it could make things uncomfortable. Some people wear masks, but everyone signs confidentiality contracts."

Leaning down on his chest so I could be closer to his face I said, "I would go with you; no pressure or expectations." That smile I loved broke the contours of his face and he pulled me down and kissed me.

"Just so you know, full disclosure and all. I'm an odd Dom. I don't have any *one* specific kink. My kink is your kink." My eyes scrunched together in question. "If you want to be hurt, I'll hurt you, purely consensual. I like finding out what turns my sub on while pushing her limits. But I never want her afraid or untrusting. I told you, I'm an odd Dom."

"I think we could all be considered odd in one form or another. I'm happy to be your sub, even if I'm still not really sure what that means."

"I'll see when the next party is. There's usually one around Thanksgiving." He tucked my head into the crook of his neck.

"My dad and Lisa are getting married on Black Friday. I'm the maid of honor, so as long as it doesn't interfere."

"Black Friday?"

Giggling, "The day after Thanksgiving, biggest shopping day of the year; people call it Black Friday."

"Oh, okay. So you're the maid of honor?"

"Yup, and Cal is the best man. Lisa doesn't have any kids and it was really important to them both that Cal and I partake. I'm also putting the reception together."

"Where are they getting married?"

"Oh, it's just a small family thing at the house. We're having it catered, that sort of thing."

"Oh, okay." His tone was a little off and I realized my blunder.

Sitting up to look at him, I asked, "Do you want to come?"

"I'm not inviting myself to your father's wedding, Cassidy. You said it was a small family thing."

"I didn't mean it like that." Pressing my lips together, I tried to contain my laughter. "You're acting like a girl. Of course I want you there with me, if you want." I turned my eyes away from him and he started tickling my hips.

"I'm not acting like a girl. I wouldn't want to miss an opportunity to see you in a dress. Count me in." I was laughing hysterically before he finally stopped. "You could wear that purple corset Anthony got you."

Catching my breath I responded, "I can't wear that to the wedding, I have to wear my dress."

"To the *secret* party, silly."

As I straddled his waist, he reached up to stroke my hair and his hand continued down my neck, caressing the exposed skin above my breasts. His touch sent goose bumps across my body.

"Oh. What else would I wear?"

As he shifted his hips below me I was aware of his rigid cock against my crotch. I casually pressed down against him, still sensitive from our session on the dining table earlier. It sent a ripple of pleasure through my belly and James appeared calm, cool, and collected.

"Oh." I maneuvered against him again, unable to resist the sweet sensations. His eyes closed for a brief second, but he made no move to stop or encourage me.

Contemplating my next move, he shifted up again and I inhaled sharply as his eyes drilled into me expectantly. Losing confidence, I started to climb off his lap and his hands quickly seized my hips and put me back where I was. "Whoa! Not so fast. Why'd you stop?"

"I, well, I thought maybe you weren't in the mood."

He released a boisterous laugh, "You really don't like making the first move, do you?" When I confirmed he said, "I want you, Cassidy. Do with me what you want." I looked into his eyes and leaned down to kiss his face. "I don't always have to be in control. I'm not *that* dark and twisted, but don't tell anyone." He smirked at me and I continued planting kisses on his jaw.

Working my way to his ear, I bit it gently and heard him hiss in response. I licked behind his ear and down his neck to bite the meaty flesh of his muscled neck, nibbling my way down to his shoulder while pulling the neck of his shirt aside. His hands moved under the back of my shirt and seared the skin of my lower back. Pulling my hips down against him, we both groaned. Between my sweatpants and his silky running shorts I could feel almost every ridge of his body.

I pushed his shirt up to expose his abdomen and chest and that amazing V of his. He was covered in a smattering of hair that I just loved and ran my fingers through it leisurely. He made no attempt to stop me so I bent down to taste his flesh, his pecs flexed under my lips as my hands gripped him just above his hips. I licked along his collar bone and back down to his sternum as he remained still, but his breathing was increasing.

When I looked up to him, his eyes were closed. I caressed the stubble on his cheeks with the tops of my hands and traced the faint outline of his scar, realizing the original injury must have been severe. I kissed his closed eyes and when I lifted my head he opened them slightly. They were heavy and a crisp shade of green; I could stare into them forever. The intensity of his glare sent another shudder through me before I cupped his cheek and ran my thumb down the center of his mouth. He quickly sucked my thumb into his mouth and pulled on it until I moaned. Reaching between us, I palmed his erection and his eyes closed once more. Releasing my thumb from his mouth, he pushed his cock harder against my hand.

"I want this off," I said as I pulled on his shirt and he rose up to accommodate me.

I threw his shirt to the floor and began to kiss and bite his well-formed shoulders. I needed to taste and feel as much of him as I could while he allowed me to. I knew that at any moment he would take the control back, and while I was eager for him to do so, I wanted just a little more time to revel in his grandeur.

Scooting down to straddle his knees while nipping at his taut belly, I sat up and ran my hands up and under his shorts while admiring the outline of his erection against the silky navy blue shorts. My hands reached his boxer briefs and I fingered the hem before digging my fingers into his thighs. He moaned, but his expression appeared calm, so I continued my pursuit under his shorts until I reached his waist. He stared at me intently as I tugged his shorts and boxer briefs down in one fell swoop. His cock bobbed against his body and I knew he wanted me. I was hungry for him and fisted his base while licking up to his crown.

"Jesus, lady." His hips thrust against me as I took him in my mouth.

~ JAMES ~

I FELT HER smile around my cock and glide her tongue down my pulsing length like the vixen she was. Her other hand was massaging my thigh when she tucked it under my ass and squeezed. She was devouring my erection as I fisted the couch cushions at my sides. Sheathing her teeth with her succulent lips, she dragged them up and down while sucking away.

Gathering my hand in her red locks, I thrust deeper into her. She tensed momentarily before relaxing around my girth, then pulled back and circled her tongue around my engorged head as I shoved myself back in. Her determined pursuit had me reeling and I wanted nothing more than for her to continue. Fuck, she was good.

"I want to see your eyes," I growled my request as she peered up at me. She removed her mouth and hovered above my cock. A wickedly delicious smile spread across her lips before she licked me again from base to tip while keeping her eyes on mine. "Suck it."

She obeyed, increasing the pressure from before while she bobbed up and down. Her free hand began circling my balls and I was already so close. I thought that mouth of hers was magic as she fisted me vigorously.

"I want to please you." She panted the words before I pushed her mouth back to my cock.

"Harder, Cassidy." She tightened her grip and moaned as I pulled her hair. "Are you ready?"

I felt her nod as the pulsing began. My balls crawled up inside before I started pouring into her. She took me deep as I flowed down her throat; continuing to lick, tug and squeeze as the aftershocks subsided. Eventually she peeled her mouth off me and smiled at me seductively. She made to sit at the other end of the couch, but I snatched her wrist and pulled her down to me.

"Who taught you to do that?" She giggled as I pulled her mouth to mine and I bit and sucked on her lips as she purred. "I can't usually come from blow jobs alone and that's the second time you've done it for me."

"Happy to oblige," she mewled before taking my lip between her teeth. "Maybe the other girls weren't doing it right."

I laughed boisterously at that, "You may be right." I stroked her hair as she rested her head on my chest. "You're quite good."

She spoke, barely a whisper, "Thank you."

"You have me at a disadvantage. You're not naked and I am. That's new for me." Tickling her side gently, I ran my hands over her hips.

"I like you naked." She tongued a nipple before looking up at me.

"Up you go. I owe you an orgasm." She helped me to my feet and I pulled my boxer briefs and shorts back up from their resting place around my calves. She stuck out her bottom lip in a pout at my semi clothed figure before I grabbed her hand and led her to the stairs, pulling her up behind me.

twenty-three
Tranquil

~ CASSIDY ~

I woke on my stomach with his body pressed to mine and I was hugging my pillow under my head. His slow, deep breathing was whispering its warmth over my hair and indicated he was still asleep. His chest was blanketing my back, with his arm around my torso, holding me like I was his possession and our legs were tangled together. He had me almost completely immobile, almost like he was using me as a body pillow. The heavy weight of his body on top of mine was a welcome prison I never wanted to escape. I could sleep like that forever, safe in the cocoon of his body.

Attempting to pull away from him I heard him groan as his hold on me tightened. Several more minutes passed before he released his hold on me and rolled to his other side. I crept out of bed, grabbing my sweats and a t-shirt as I headed downstairs. I had the day off and had a sudden craving for breakfast—a real breakfast—pancakes, eggs, the works.

The coffee was brewing and I was mixing pancake batter when I heard him moving around upstairs. Soon the shower was running and I was tempted to join him, but my growling stomach deterred me. I was placing various plates of food on the table when I heard him bounding down the stairs.

"She cooks!"

Turning to him with a smile, I found him leaning on the doorjamb watching me intently, his hair damp and circling his face. He wore a pin stripe suit, white shirt, and blue tie and he was gorgeous. I smirked at him and his remark before I went back to the kitchen.

"It smells delicious." Coming over to help me load the table with food, I shooed him away.

"No, my treat, sit down and enjoy."

Humoring me, he obliged. His chin was resting in his hands, that were propped up by his elbows, while watching me bustle through the kitchen.

"Coffee?"

I brought him a mug full of coffee and placed the few different flavored creamers I had on the table along with sugar. I noted that he didn't use any creamer but added at least two packets of sugar. I sat across from him, motioned for his plate and he held it out while I loaded it with pancakes, eggs, and sausage. I topped my plate with the same as he poured us some orange juice. He buttered his pancakes, topped them with syrup before digging in and I took a sip of my orange juice, watching him eat. He was busy chewing when he squinted at me. *He noticed.*

"Is that cinnamon in the pancakes?"

I smiled proudly, "I hope that's okay."

"It's great. I don't think I've ever had cinnamon pancakes." He continued eating, "You're hired."

Chuckling I retorted, "Don't get used to it!" Then I winked at him.

"So, what do you have planned today? Cecily gave you the day off, right?" I nodded. "The spa has openings today if you want to redeem those gift certificates from my parents."

I perked up at that, "Really, on such short notice?"

"Absolutely. Just say the word."

For half a second I contemplated it. "Yes! That would be amazing!"

Pulling out his cell and pushing a few buttons he made the call. "Hi, Ginger, it's James. I need to make some appointments for today. Yes. No. For Cassidy Charles, she has gift certificates for massage, facial, mani/pedi and a cut and color, though her color is perfect. Alright. Let me check." He pulled the phone away from his face, "Can you be there by ten?" I nodded enthusiastically. "That'll work. Thanks, Ginger." He ended the call and put his cell back in his breast pocket.

We finished our breakfast in almost complete silence, casting knowing smiles at each other. I was debating whether or not to bring up last night and decided that he should know I thoroughly enjoyed myself. After he'd untied me, we talked for a couple hours before he took me again. His libido was insane, not that I was complaining.

During our pillow talk we discussed things that your average new couple would discuss; a previous relationship, childhood memories, likes and dislikes and so on. There weren't any crazy revelations, though I suspected there was a lot he hadn't told me. We were getting to know more about one another other than our sexual appetites. It was refreshing.

"I really enjoyed myself last night."

He didn't say anything, just stared at me with those green eyes and that smirk that made me squirm in my seat.

"I have to go to work. Do you know where the spa is?"

"Oh, umm."

"It's in my office building across from the hotel, on the third floor. I'll let security know to expect you."

I stood to clear the dishes and he held his hand out to me. I accepted it and he pulled me to his lap, grasping my chin and pulling my lips to his. Quickly, the kiss moved from slow and sensual to heated and frenzied.

Breaking away between kisses I whispered, "If you're not careful, I'll take you again on the table."

He belly laughed which caused me to laugh; I loved this side of him.

"*I* do the taking, Cassidy, and don't you forget it!"

He kissed me hard and quick before placing me on my feet. Standing, he kissed my cheek before walking out the door. I peeked through the shades and watched him drive away.

I made it to the spa with time to spare and got comfortable in the reception area and was listening to my iPod when Ginger escorted me to a changing room.

"You'll get the massage first, followed by a facial. You can shower then, if you like, and then you can get your mani/pedi and then Scott will finish with your hair." Ginger was a little firecracker on five inch heels. I nodded as she handed me a robe and left me to disrobe.

They served me a light lunch after my shower and everyone was very professional through all of my appointments. I couldn't help but wonder if they treated all their customers like royalty or if it was because of James. I opted for a few highlights, at Scott's recommendation, and he also gave me a few long layers before cleaning up my ends. I felt like a million bucks when I was finished and headed out the door.

I got to the elevator and decided to pop up to see James. When I arrived at his floor Jennifer greeted me, but told me James hadn't been in the office all day. I couldn't stop the look that crossed my face as I got a sinking feeling.

"He's had meetings off site all day," she smiled sweetly and I took my leave.

Heading out of the elevator and into the lobby, I heard the shrill of a familiar voice. Walking hesitantly toward it, I saw Melissa Westin berating the security desk.

"Ma'am we have strict instructions that you're not allowed in the building when Mr. Benedict is gone."

Snickering to myself I snuck out of the building, pulling my coat tighter around me as I handed the valet my ticket and eagerly awaited the arrival of my car. November had officially arrived, evident by the chill in the air. I took a deep breath and enjoyed the cold that pierced my nostrils.

"Oh, it's you." I rolled my eyes, trying to ignore her. "I'm talking to you."

After taking a deep breath, I turned to her with raised brows. "Yes, can I help you?"

Putting on a fake smile, she said, "Have you thought about what I said?"

I was SO not in the mood for her and her bullshit. Looking her up and down, I took in her appearance. Did she always dress this way in thirty degree weather? Melissa was dressed in a short tight dress and her nipples looked ready to burst against the tight, shiny material as her coat hung open around her.

"Whatever it is you're trying to sell, I'm not interested." I waved at her and her lack of an outfit, dismissing her as I continued to scrutinize her with my eyes.

Her jaw dropped and I noticed her hand twitch. "Are you calling me a whore?"

My car arrived at that exact moment and I rushed forward with a tip in hand for the valet saying, "Thank you."

She shrieked over the hood of my car, "I asked you a question!"

"You said it, not me." I flippantly waved at her again before jumping in my car and driving off. I couldn't help but feel sorry for her and her desperate attempts to get James's attention. As I drove away I saw her yelling into her cell phone and wondered who she could possibly be calling.

I DECIDED TO take advantage of the free time and did some shopping before heading home. When I got home I was putting my purchases away when I got a text message.

> Have to work late.
> I'll be in touch tomorrow.
> Miss me.
> XO ~James

> Don't work too hard.
> Miss you already.
> XO ~Cass

I spent the rest of the day cleaning and enjoying my new movie streaming abilities thanks to James. I actually got to bed at a decent time feeling totally prepared for work the next morning. The next couple days passed and each day I got similar text messages from James, he was busy with work and would be in touch the next day. I was growing paranoid, wondering if something had changed and decided that if I hadn't heard from him by the end of the week I would call him out.

I got home from work late on Thursday. Work had kept me busy all week and I had been busy completing wedding arrangements for Dad and Lisa and preparing other holiday parties. The press hadn't been hounding me and I was grateful for that. Making a salad for dinner, I curled up on the couch with Chessa.

A bottle of wine later, I was wiping my eyes and missing Holly. One of her favorite movies was *Love Actually* and I couldn't resist the temptation to watch it while I got comfortable under a blanket.

I WOKE TO the sound of metal clicking and a hinge creaking. Cowering down on the couch while my eyes adjusted, Chessa jumped off to hide. *Traitor.* The TV was casting a blue hue throughout the living room but did nothing to give me away. I saw a tall shadow fall over the entryway between the living room and the foyer and my heart started hammering uncontrollably in my chest; I was having trouble maintaining steady breaths.

Looking for my cell phone, I felt around in my pockets and realized it was on the charger in the kitchen. Cal would never stop by this late and let himself in like this. Panicked, I started looking around the room trying to find something to protect myself with. Cal kept insisting that I get a gun and now I was wishing I would've listened. The shadow headed up the stairs and I made my move for my cell.

Reaching the counter as I heard the footsteps above my head, I ripped my phone off the charger, noticing missed calls and texts, but ignored them to call Cal. As the phone started ringing I prayed he answered, knowing he was working tonight.

"Cassidy, why are you calling so late?"

"Cal, someone's in the house. I don't know what to do." I was trying to whisper, looking for something to grab. I spotted my vase full of dying peonies, from a second bouquet James had sent, and dumped them in the sink and readied the vase in my hand.

"What?! Cassidy, are you sure?" I heard him mumbling something to his partner and then heard the distinct sound of sirens pierce my ear.

"Cal, yes, please hurry."

"Cassidy, where are you in the house and where's the intruder?"

"I'm in the kitchen, he's upstairs."

"Get out of the house."

I started to head for the front door when I heard the footsteps head down the stairs. I was stuck between the entryway and the living room and right on the other side was the bottom of the staircase. Cal was screaming on the end of the phone so I decided to throw my phone back toward the kitchen in hopes of creating a diversion.

The phone landed on the tiled floor with a crash and the shadowy figure circled around the wall just barely missing me. I held my breath, and when I thought there was enough space, I ran for the front door. I turned the knob, but it didn't budge. I was searching for the deadbolt when I heard thundering steps approaching me and I started sobbing. Realizing I was still armed with the vase, I increased my grip on it.

"Where are you going?"

Turning my head briefly, I shrieked as I threw the vase at my attacker. "The cops are on their way. Stay back."

~ JAMES ~

Missing her more than I thought possible, I realized that I hadn't seen her since Monday morning. When I wasn't dealing with business

I had been working with Annie and Smith trying to protect Cassidy. We did everything we could, legally, to keep her mom's story under wraps and to keep the reporters off her property. The details of the story were worse than I remembered and I couldn't imagine how she had dealt with this at such a vulnerable age.

Security had informed me that Melissa made an appearance on Monday, but not hearing anything else from Melissa, I let it go. Mom was doing well this week and Dad assured me she was getting enough rest. I had postponed the architects again regarding the country house because it was simply too much to deal with at the time. Looking at the clock, I realized it was almost midnight. I had tried calling and texting Cassidy earlier that night but got no response. She was probably ignoring me and I couldn't blame her, having neglected her for three days.

I packed up my belongings and headed to the parking garage, hopping in the Rover instead of making the walk across the street to the hotel. I hadn't slept for crap the previous three nights and I was beginning to believe that I slept better with Cassidy next to me. Having a key, being her landlord and all, I might as well use it, though I knew I was overstepping my bounds.

Pulling in behind her car, I noticed the place was dark, as it should be. I made my way up the steps, slipped my key into the lock and gently opened the door. The TV was casting a slight blue hue across the room. She must have gone to bed forgetting to turn the TV off. Quietly, I closed the door, turned the deadbolt and made my way up the stairs, spotting Chessa run up before me.

Entering her room, I made my way straight to the bathroom. Turning on the light after closing the door, I removed my jacket, shirt and shoes. I decided to peek on her sleeping image in bed, opened the bathroom door and realized her bed was empty. It dawned on me that with the TV still being on she was probably asleep on the couch.

When I reached the bottom of the stairs, I heard a loud clatter in the kitchen so I turned the corner to investigate. Everything seemed in place and at that moment I heard footsteps racing toward the door and someone yanking on the knob. Cassidy.

"Where are you going?"

As her image came into focus, I could see her desperately trying to open the front door. It dawned on me that she thought I was an intruder and before I could say anything more she turned and threw a vase at me. I raised my arm in defense just in time to stop the vase from slamming against my face.

"The cops are on their way. Stay back."

The vase hit the floor, broken to pieces against my arm. "Dammit, Cassidy, it's me."

"James?" Slipping to the floor, she hugged her knees to her chest. Her face came into view and I noticed tears slipping down her cheeks; she was shaking like a leaf.

"Cassidy, you're safe." Crouching down in front of her, I placed my hands on her knees. Her eyes were searching my face and when recognition reached them she threw her arms around my neck, apologizing. I sat down with her and scooped her into my lap, "I'm sorry, love. I didn't mean to scare you." We sat there for a few minutes, or maybe it was just seconds.

"I'm so sorry. The vase, are you hurt?" She pulled back to look at me and we heard sirens begin to pierce the air. "Oh, God."

The sound registered with us at the same time, "You called the cops? I thought it was a scare tactic."

"Of course I called them. I called Cal." Cassidy scrambled to her feet and turned on a few lights before opening the front door.

We stepped out onto the porch as the cop car pulled up in front.

Cal jumped out of the passenger seat with his hand on his pistol.

"Jesus Christ, Cassidy. Are you okay? What's going on?"

Making her way down the steps she said, "Everything is fine. I'm so sorry. James came over and I was asleep on the couch."

"It's my fault. She didn't know it was me." Standing behind Cassidy, I placed my hands on her shoulders and saw the relief wash over Cal's face as he examined her with his eyes to assure himself she was alright.

"You're lucky she figured it out before I got here. I could've shot you." Clipping his gun back in its holster, his partner got back in the car and on the radio, calling off the other squad cars.

"It didn't help that his hair was pulled back. I didn't recognize his shadow." Cassidy chuckled lightly, leaning her head back against my chest as I circled my arms around her shoulders.

"Dude, your arm is bleeding."

Cassidy bolted out of my arms, turning to examine my arm.

"Your sister has quite the arm. The vase she threw to fend me off must've cut my arm."

Examining my arm she said, "We need to clean this up. Hold it upright."

"It's just a scratch, I didn't even notice it." I went ahead and held my arm upright while trying to scope out the damage. "You're more dangerous than I would've thought." I winked at her as she swatted my shoulder.

"Alright, if you're both good here I should to get going."

We assured Cal that all was well and Cassidy and I headed back inside as he pulled away.

"I'm so sorry, James. I should've known it was you."

"It's alright. I tried calling and just assumed you'd be in bed. I just wanted to feel you next to me."

Tiptoeing around the broken vase, she headed to the kitchen and returned with a broom and dust pan.

"I fell asleep on the couch watching movies. I wasn't expecting to see you since I haven't seen you since Monday."

Her tone was dismal and I was immediately reminded of my error. She was busy sweeping up the glass as Chessa made her way over and I snatched her up to ensure she didn't step on any shards of glass.

"Work has been really hectic this week. I'm sorry if you thought I was avoiding you." She looked to me with a smile that didn't reach her eyes. "I wasn't."

"Hang onto her for another second, I think I got all the glass but I want to vacuum it real quick." Pulling out a vacuum from the closet, she quickly ran it over the floor and after a few swipes she put it away. "Let's go clean up that arm."

Carrying Chessa, I followed her up the stairs, into the bedroom, and dropped Chessa on the bed before heading to the bathroom where Cassidy was pulling out some first aid supplies. She turned on the water, wet a rag, and turned to me. She was staring at my chest and licked her lips, though I don't think she was aware she did it.

"Cassidy..." I said her name softly as my cock twitched.

Her eyes jumped to mine and she blushed, "Sorry. I don't think I'll ever tire of staring at you."

I smiled down at her as she took my forearm in her hand and began to wipe the blood away. After all the blood was gone and we were sure there was no glass in the cut, she placed some ointment and a bandage over it. It was a little worse than I thought, but I assured her I didn't need stitches. A massive yawn took over her face.

"You're exhausted. Let's get you to bed."

She didn't object and headed to the bedroom. I took the opportunity to take a piss, removed my pants and socks, and headed to bed in just my boxer briefs. Cassidy was already burrowed under the covers so I slid in behind her and adjusted the pillow under my head. As I did, she inched over so that she was tucked into me.

"You sneaky minx."

She was completely naked, having removed her sweats and t-shirt while I was in the bathroom. She quietly moaned, suppressing another yawn as I pulled her ass against my throbbing erection and buried my nose into her hair. I felt her breathing slow and willed myself to sleep.

"Cassidy?" She didn't respond and I kissed her hair, "I'm falling for you. Hard." Tightening my hold on her, I drifted to sleep.

twenty-four

Enigmas

~ JAMES ~

"Crap!" I woke to her bolting out of bed as sunlight filled the room. "I overslept. I forgot to set the alarm." She ran into the bathroom and I heard the shower turn on.

I lay there, waiting for her to emerge from the bathroom, not daring to join her since she was already late. She took what must've been the quickest shower in history and bolted over to the closet.

"Thank God for casual Friday!" She was throwing on some jeans over satin panties that matched her bra. "Don't you have to work?" She threw me a questioning glance.

Sitting up, I watched her scramble around the room getting ready for work. Shrugging my shoulders at her I explained, "I don't have any meetings until this afternoon."

She stuck her tongue out as she pulled the towel off her head and yanked on a tight fitting sweater. She tugged on some socks and headed back to the bathroom. I heard the sink running, decided to get up and found her brushing her teeth with one hand and combing her hair with the other. I stood in the doorway admiring her as she finished and she gave me a quick peck before scurrying out of the room yelling, "Call me!"

Listening to her run down the stairs, I made my way to the toilet. I was headed into the shower when I heard her scream my name. I leapt down the stairs and found her clenching a paper with the front door open.

"Cassidy, what's wrong?"

She was white as a ghost as I looked outside and didn't see any reporters. I pried the paper from her hands and my heart broke for her as my anger bubbled to the surface. A picture of her mom and the former mayor was covering the front page with some other smaller pictures of Cassidy, Calvin, and their father from years ago, presumably from the funeral.

"Fucking FUCK."

I threw the paper down and raked my hands through my hair. *How had that happened?* Annie and I had spent hours all week doing everything we could to bury this story forever. She ran past me to the kitchen, started dry heaving into the sink, and splashed cool water on her face when the heaving stopped. I made my way over to her as the sobs began unleashing.

Pulling her into my arms I whispered, "I'm so sorry, Cassidy. I'll find out who did this."

"I thought this was over. I, I can't, I... Oh God...the wedding... Dad." The sobs were racking her body so violently she could barely speak.

"Shh. Everything will be fine. I promise. I'll get to the bottom of this."

We spent the next thirty minutes arguing about her going to work. She called Lena to let her know she would be late while I called Smith and Annie. I found her upstairs putting on some makeup, trying to cover up the pain and anguish written all over her face, and I hopped in the shower before getting dressed.

Conceding to let me drive her to work, she was silent the entire drive. I told her to call me when she was ready to leave for the day and she agreed. I could only imagine how hard her life was after her mom died, especially with the scandal that surrounded it. Being thirteen at the time probably made it ten times worse and I wasn't sure I wanted to know what she was thinking about as I drove her to work.

When we pulled up to her office building, I grabbed her hand before she exited the Rover. "Cassidy, it's going to be alright. We'll get through this. Together." She nodded; I kissed her cheek and watched her walk into the building, slamming my hand on the steering wheel before driving away.

~ CASSIDY ~

AVOIDING EYE CONTACT with everyone, I walked into work making a beeline for my office and shut the door when I got there. I was attempting to massage my temples when there was a light knock on the door.

I took a deep breath, "Come in."

Cecily came in and shut the door behind her. She placed a coffee on my desk. "Do you have a moment?"

Her appearance in my office couldn't be good. "Of course. Everything okay?"

She eyed me suspiciously for a moment before she sat down across from me. "I won't beat around the bush, Cassidy. I saw the paper this morning and I can only imagine what you're going through."

Feeling myself pale, I grabbed the coffee she set down for me and took a sip, willing myself to keep it together. I thought this was all dead and buried and that I would never have to deal with the questions and judgmental looks again. I barely survived my teens because of this drama with my mother; I wasn't sure what to say to her.

"I…thank you."

"Cassidy, are you alright?"

Her words were kind and sincere and the tears began to well up in my eyes. *Don't cry, she's your boss!*

"I'm sorry. I'll be fine. I just wasn't prepared to deal with all of this again." I quickly swiped at a rogue tear.

"James has brought a whole new element to your world. You'll have to decide if this added spotlight on your life is worth the drama."

I tried not to flinch, knowing she was right. James was practically a celebrity around this town and that wasn't going to change any time soon. We had only been dating a couple weeks and already the skeletons in my closet were being hung out for all to see.

"I have big plans for you here at B & C. I'd hate for this romance to get in the way of that. I don't care who you date, I just don't want you to lose focus."

"Of course not. My job here is my number one priority, I assure you. My personal life won't get in the way."

"Alright then. Are you on track with everything; the wedding and the upcoming holiday parties?" I nodded and she stood. "Hang in there. I'll be heading out after lunch. Have a good weekend."

"You, too." She closed my door. Resting my forehead on the desk, I tapped it a few times against the hard surface before picking it back up. "Get it together, Cassidy."

I worked through lunch. And to my surprise, no one disturbed me. The only interaction I had with Lena was asking her to handle all my calls unless it was an utter emergency. *Crash into Me* started singing from my cell and I pulled it out of my purse and answered.

"Hey, I'm almost done here. I can get a cab home if it's a problem."

I heard him say, "It's almost seven p.m., Cassidy. I'm downstairs in the parking garage. I can wait."

I was shocked that it was so late, "Okay, I'm shutting down. I'll be down in a few minutes." Disconnecting the call, I smiled for the first time all day.

I left my office, noticing I was the last person there. The main office doors were locked and I dug in my purse for my keys so I could exit. After locking back up, I hopped into the elevator to the underground parking garage. I spotted him leaning against the back of the Rover. He looked up and his expression was composed, but he was flashing half a smile. Seeing him was an instant stress reliever. I picked up my pace, practically running, and threw my arms around his neck, burying my face in his neck.

He squeezed me tightly, "You okay?"

"Better now," I mumbled into his collar.

"Your brother called." Pulling back to examine his face he said, "He's worried about you. He said you've been ignoring his calls all day."

Dropping my head back to his chest I sighed, "Should I be concerned that you two are getting all chummy?" He pushed me to arm's length and rubbed his hands up and down my upper arms. "I'll call him when I get home."

"I already called him. He's picking up dinner and headed to your place. He's really worried about you. Is there something else going on I don't know about?"

Cal was over reacting, as usual, "No, there's nothing else going on.

He's overprotective that's all. I'm starving." I pulled away and walked to the passenger door, refusing to discuss it further.

He stopped me from opening the door and pressed me against the SUV. "You can trust me, Cassidy." He didn't give me a chance to respond and just pressed his lips to mine. The kiss soon got heated—like it always did with us—hands tugging and pulling on each other. He abruptly pulled away and opened the door. "Get in, we'll resume this later."

WE WERE GETTING OUT of the Rover when Cal pulled up. He was carrying a large carryout bag and I could see that Jane was with him. James and Cal shook hands and James took the bag of food from him. I opened the front door and ushered James and Jane inside. I was about to follow them in when Cal asked me to hang back.

"What's up?" I closed the door and waited for him to question me, knowing what was coming.

"Don't give me that. I saw the papers. Are you good?"

Cal stood at the bottom of the porch steps looking up at me as I shoved my hands in my back pockets. I shrugged my shoulders while rocking back and forth on my heels.

"Cassidy I know what all this did to you when we were teens. You're not alright."

I had avoided his eyes until that moment, "Cal, can we NOT do this? What do you want me to say? I'm angry, no, infuriated and sad. I want to crawl in a hole and never come out."

"Does he know?" He motioned his head inside, to James. "Does he know how badly you took it all before?"

"NO! And I'd like to keep it that way. I was a stupid kid crying out for help. I got the help. Leave. It. Alone."

"Cass…"

"Everything okay out here?" Jane poked her head out the front door.

"Yup, we're good." I seized the opportunity to walk inside, leaving her on the porch with Cal.

I heard her ask, "Cal, what's going on?"

A COUPLE HOURS later, Cal and Jane were heading out the door and Cal gave me a hug and whispered in my ear, "You should tell him." I glared at him when he pulled away and he took Jane's hand heading down the stairs.

"Night." I waved to both of them before shutting the door.

James was lounging on the couch with his arms outstretched to me when I walked back into the living room. I smiled and sat down between his legs, resting my back against his chest. He wrapped his arms around me as he kissed my temple. It was only ten p.m. on a Friday and I just wanted to go to bed. I couldn't suppress the yawn that followed.

"You alright?"

"I'll be fine when everyone stops asking me that." Remaining quiet, I immediately felt guilty for snapping at him. "I'm sorry. I didn't mean to snap at you. I just don't understand why this is being dragged through the papers again. What did I do?"

Sighing he said, "You did me, so to speak. This is my fault. If we weren't together this wouldn't have happened."

I repositioned myself so that I could see his face. "I don't understand. What's the fascination with my dead mother? Why can't this stay dead and buried?"

"I have a feeling whoever's behind this is out to deliberately hurt you or me."

That got my attention. "What? Why?"

"I have Annie and Smith working on it."

"Who's Annie?"

"She's my attorney." He looked at me like there was more, "The same attorney who helped me out when I was in college."

"Ok, wait, you mean the Domme?" I groaned, "This just gets better and better." I stood up and began pacing the floor.

"Cassidy, I don't want to fight with you. I just want to take you to bed and hold you. We need to talk about all this. The more details you can give me the more Annie, Smith, and I can help. Okay?"

Taking a moment to process everything he said and asked of me, my head began to spin. He was right; we should just go to bed. "I don't want to fight, either. We can talk about it later. Let's go to bed."

Once we were upstairs, I went to the bathroom to get ready for bed. When I reemerged, he was standing in front of me wearing a skin tight tank and boxer briefs. *Fucking hell.* He smirked at me and walked into the bathroom. *Had I just said that out loud?* I climbed into bed, naked, and flopped onto my stomach while hugging my pillow under my head.

He wasn't in the bathroom long before climbing in next to me. Propping his head up on his hand looking down at me he said, "You're exhausted." He started running his fingers through my hair as I closed my eyes and savored his touch. His hand started lazily caressing my back and then he started gently scratching my back.

"Mm," he stopped and I opened my eyes, "Don't stop, that feels wonderful."

He smiled, picking up where he left off. Soon he was lying down next to me and I turned my head away from him as he pulled me into my James cocoon that was fast becoming my happy place.

"Closer."

I heard him groan in response as he tucked me under him; the right side of his body covering my left. The weight of him on me was glorious. I was aware of his arousal as he wedged his leg between my two, drifting off as the warmth of his body became a fog around me.

I whispered, "This, this is my heaven."

I WAS AWARE of hot, large hands kneading the flesh of my thighs and ass. My eyes flickered open and it was almost entirely dark as I felt hot moisture gliding up my spine to my neck and then he started sucking on my neck. I turned slightly to give him better access and he bit down.

"Feels good." I was not coherent enough to speak properly, I could only feel. Oh God could I feel.

I was still on my stomach as he hovered over my back. His hands were positioned on both sides of my head, keeping his weight from pinning me entirely, and I realized that I *wanted* his entire weight pinning me. Reading my thoughts, he gently laid on top of me and I spread my legs, moaning at the feel of his hard cock pressed against my ass. He was not dressed anymore, wholly naked.

"I want you, Cassidy," he whispered in my ear and I shivered from head to toe.

"I need you, James." He growled in my ear before pulling my lobe between his teeth. "Please, I need to feel you and nothing else. Make it all go away."

He moved down lower between my legs and I lifted my hips to give him access. His hand traveled between my legs, moving down to cup my mound. He pressed his fingers to my pubic bone then ran them across my labia, easily slipping a finger inside.

"You're already wet for me." He pulled his hand away and a second later I felt his head at my entrance. I couldn't wait any longer.

"James!" It was a plea for him to take me.

He crashed into me at that moment and we were both left pulsing and panting before he began thrusting over and over again. I tossed my pillow to the side and grabbed the headboard in front of me. After several minutes of him hammering into me, he stilled and resumed biting and sucking on my shoulders. His hand moved over and down my side until it slid between me and the bed. Finding my clit, he started circling it.

"Cassidy..."

He started moving in and out again while applying pressure to my clit. "Please, James."

"What is it? Tell me what you want." He continued stroking me inside and out.

"Harder, I need you harder." Ramming into my backside over and over again I panted, "Oh, yes. Like that."

He placed his free hand between my shoulder blades and now I truly felt the weight of him on me. My breasts were pressed against the sheets, almost painfully so, and I couldn't move. My hips jumped and my clit pressed harder into his hand.

"You're so close, baby."

He was as out of breath as I felt. My knuckles were white as I gripped the headboard tighter and the spiral began. My toes were tingling and my belly was tensing.

I was aware that I was holding my breath when he bellowed, "Dammit, Cassidy, breathe!"

I took in a massive breath trying to get back under control, "James I'm going…"

"Me, too."

His thrusts become jerkier and soon I felt him shooting his seed into me as he changed direction against my clit. It was the final straw and my orgasm took over. My eyes saw white as the reverberations of my orgasm shot through my limbs, my grip on the headboard slackened and my hips relaxed.

He started to move out and off me when I begged, "Please stay. I want to feel you like this just a little longer." Dropping down onto his forearms, his breath was hot and heavy on my neck, and I smiled. "You, I just want to feel you."

"Anything for you, Blackbird."

I wasn't sure how much time had passed but I felt myself drifting off. "What time is it?"

"Who cares? Got somewhere to be?" We both chuckled as he rolled to his side and pulled me to his chest while kissing me. Kissing slowly and deeply for a long time, we explored each other's mouths before going back to sleep.

twenty-five
Wounds

~ CASSIDY ~

I WOKE IN THE MORNING TO THE familiar *whir thump whir thump* of the treadmill. I rolled over and grabbed his pillow, drowning my senses in his smell. I remembered our lovemaking from the middle of the night and smiled. I never thought sex could be so good and I loved what he did to me and with so little direction. I loved everything about him. I loved him.

I loved him?

No, it was too soon. I was crazy. It was just sex. Fucking hot, amazeballs sex. Nothing more. I knew *that* wasn't true. I *loved* him? I pondered that and recounted every single memory with him, the good and the bad. I struggled to process it all. I had only felt this way about one other person and that was so long ago.

"Morning, beautiful. What are you thinking about?"

My eyes darted to the doorway where he was standing—no, where he was posing. He was wiping his face with a towel only wearing his shorts and running shoes.

"You."

"What about me?" He crossed his arms and stared at me intently.

"That's for me to know and you to wonder." I got up on my elbows grinning from ear to ear. *I loved him. I did. Fucking hell.*

He sauntered over to the bed like only he could. He was considering his next move and so was I. He pounced first and started tickling me.

"You're going to tell me right now what you're thinking about, lady."

"James, agh. Stop." I was laughing uncontrollably, knowing I was a shit liar. "Please, I have to pee!"

Stopping his attack, he kissed my nose before releasing me. I scampered off the bed and he smacked my ass before I ran to the bathroom. After I was finished, I cranked on the shower as he walked in. I stepped into the shower once the water was warm enough and he followed behind me. He gathered my hair, pulling it over my shoulder and I felt him freeze. He spun me around to face him and started examining me.

"What are you doing?" He was touching a spot on my hip, and as I followed his gaze I noticed a faint bruise on my hip.

"Does it hurt?" I shook my head and he stood back up and turned me away from him again. "What about here?"

I felt his fingers caressing the spot on my upper back, where he held me down last night. "No." He kissed the spot before I turned to face him.

"I'm too rough with you."

"We've discussed this, I'm fine. I'll let you know if you're too rough." He smiled down at me. "I really enjoyed last night, especially when you were holding me down. I love the weight of your body on mine. Makes me feel safe, free, loved."

I realized what I had said and abruptly turned to grab the shampoo. I started lathering my hair as he did the same to his. "So, you like being immobile while I'm having my way with you?"

Blushing I confessed, "I do. Don't tell anyone, they might get the wrong idea."

"I don't kiss and tell, Miss Charles." He winked at me and we finished our shower.

We went down to the kitchen and I pulled out two cereal bowls and spoons. He was grinning from ear to ear with one eyebrow raised as I moved to the pantry and pulled out my favorite cereal.

"Cocoa Puffs? Really?"

I shrugged my shoulders. "Guilty pleasure. You want some or not?"

We finished our bowls of cereal and I put our dishes in the sink, and then sat back down at the table next to him.

"We need to talk." His tone was foreboding. "I have a meeting with Annie and Smith this afternoon if you'd like to come. I'd like to be honest with them about everything. I need you to fill in the gaps and what really happened." He reached across the table and took my hand in his.

I felt my throat getting tight, "I haven't talked about this in so long. Holly didn't even know the details." Pulling me to my feet, he guided me to the couch.

"What can I do to make it easier? I'm trying to protect you, but I need to know what I'm up against."

"I know. Umm, I'm not sure where to start."

"Wherever you want. Take your time."

"Alright."

With a deep breath and a heavy heart, I began my story.

"It was the summer before eighth grade. I was taller than most and awkward, so awkward. I played sports and had lots of friends or at least I thought I did. Mom wasn't around much that summer. We didn't know why back then, but we do now. It was a Saturday night and school was starting in just over a week. Dad, Cal, and I were sitting around the living room coffee table eating pizza and playing board games.

"Mom got home early that night. I should've known something was wrong because she was drunk. She started arguing with Dad, so Cal and I went to our rooms like we normally did. I fell asleep listening to my radio.

"Sometime in the middle of the night, I woke to voices. I opened my door and peered down the hall. Mom and Dad were screaming at each other, again. Normally I would've gone back to my room, but I'd had enough of my mother's drunken tirades.

"Mom was shouting at Dad about how she was done and she was leaving him for someone else. Cal was standing a few feet away looking shell shocked and Dad didn't seem to care. I think he knew their marriage was over long before we did. Something inside me broke. I grabbed the closest thing to me, an encyclopedia, and launched it at my mom.

"Before Cal and Dad could react, she lunged at me and started smacking and clawing at me repeatedly. She said cruel and hateful things to me while Dad pulled her off me and Cal was holding me back; I returned her fire.

"I started screaming at her, 'I hate you. I *want* you to leave. We don't need you. This is all *your* fault.' I was sobbing as I hurled my anger at her.

"Everything grew silent, and in the distance you could hear the sound of police sirens. Mom heard them before we did and she grabbed her keys and ran out the door. Cal started to go after her, but Dad stopped him.

"Two squad cars pulled up right after Mom pulled out. One car followed her while the officer in the first car came to the door. He said that one of the neighbors reported a disturbance. My dad gave him a rundown and then I noticed the cop looking at me.

'What happened to her?'

"Cal and Dad both looked at me and Dad rushed to me, pulled a handkerchief out of his pocket and dabbed at my face. I was unaware at the time, but I had a bloody nose, split lip and a few scratches on my chest and upper arms.

"The cop started questioning Dad about my cuts and Cal and I immediately told him that it was Mom, not Dad. They believed us. The cop returned outside where Dad and him talked some more. I went to the bathroom and tried to clean up my cuts with Cal's assistance.

"We were sitting on the couch almost an hour later when an officer came back into the house and motioned Dad over. Dad walked away from the officer and fell into a chair at the kitchen table and Cal grabbed my hand. Dad told us, with the assistance of the cop, that Mom's car went off the Reynolds Bridge.

"I broke the silence, 'Is she ok?' I didn't understand why we weren't heading to the hospital. The cop told us she was gone, that she didn't make it. I don't remember anything else from that night. I woke the next morning in my bed and soon realized it wasn't a nightmare."

~ JAMES ~

She was in a whole other world while the details fell off her tongue like she had told the story over and over again. I didn't dare interrupt in fear she might have shut down. We were sitting on the couch, her at one end and me in the middle, and she was revealing what had happened over the next couple days.

Cops, family, the funeral, reporters, the list went on and on. She mentioned that they found out her mother was having an affair with the Mayor, Brent Calhoun, and that apparently the affair had been going on all summer. The papers also made this information public knowledge since Mayor Calhoun was up for reelection and later lost.

"Oh, God. I remembered something else. No, that's not possible."

"What is it, Cassidy?" She started hyperventilating and I pulled her to me, trying to calm her down.

"Mom and Dad were arguing and I think I remember her saying something about a baby." Pulling back she looked to me, "Why would she be talking about a baby?"

This was horrendous. "Cassidy, was your mom pregnant?" She looked utterly confused and started shaking her head.

"There's no way, I mean, I don't know, she was drunk. Why would she drink if she was pregnant?" She bolted off the couch and grabbed her cell before I could stop her.

"Cal, was Mom pregnant?" She wasn't waiting long for her answer. She dropped the phone and sank to her knees. I was at her side in a second, picking up the phone.

"Cal, I'm here with her. Yes, I'll keep you posted. Alright, later."

Setting the phone down on the counter before pulling her into my arms, I carried her to the couch and didn't press her for any more details. She'd been through enough for one day, for one lifetime.

She was quiet for a long time, just sitting in my lap like a ragdoll. I began imagining how life must've been for her after her mother's death and the scandal surrounding it all. I wasn't sure how much time had passed when she got up and began doing mundane chores around the house.

"Cassidy?" I wasn't sure what to say or ask, but I knew she was pulling away from me and shutting herself down. She'd had a shock and needed to talk about it.

"Hmm?" She wouldn't look at me and started sorting laundry.

"Is there anything you need, anything I can do? Please don't shut me out."

"There's nothing to do. It doesn't change anything except maybe the image of my mother. I just wish it all had stayed dead and buried."

It was all my fault; if she hadn't been with *me* she wouldn't have been in the limelight like she was. I had to get to the bottom of it all, I owed her that much. "I have to run some errands. Are you going to be alright?"

"I'll be fine."

I walked to her and gave her a hug. She hugged me back, but her embrace lacked its usual vigor. Kissing her temple, I gathered my things and headed out the door.

I felt incredibly guilty leaving her and I stood at the bottom of the porch, pacing the short path for several minutes. My gut was telling me there were more details that dealt with Cassidy directly; Cal wouldn't be so concerned for her if there weren't. Maybe *he* was who I needed to talk to. She would kill me if she found out and I couldn't go behind her back like that.

My phone alerted me of a text. Smith and Annie were at my office waiting for me and I couldn't keep them waiting any longer. I hopped in the Rover and headed back downtown. The office appeared empty when I arrived, but I recognized the voices of Smith and Annie coming from my office. I closed the door for ultimate privacy.

Annie was looking over some files at the table and Smith was at the wet bar. I dropped my bag on the couch and removed my jacket before joining Annie at the table as Smith handed me a bottle of water before taking his seat.

"Did you have any luck finding out who provided the story to the paper?" I was looking at Smith.

He sighed, "I'm still looking into it. The editor isn't revealing his source."

I slammed my fist on the table.

"Dude, I'm not done. I've done a background check on all the employees. Turns out one of the copy editors had a kid in the same rehab facility with Dan over the summer."

"That's got to be it." Annie agreed and I thanked Smith. "That douche bag. What is the point of all of this?"

Annie and Smith both dug through their files and each pulled out folders. I set the other files aside as we started thumbing through Dan's files again. After a good hour or so we were about to go through the files for the third time when Annie gasped.

"Son of a bitch!" Annie started ripping some papers out of Smith's folder and comparing them to hers.

"What is it? What did you find?"

"Mayor Calhoun had a sister, Hilary Young, who was in rehab when he had the affair with Abigail Charles."

It only took me a second to register the connection, "Jesus Christ." I dropped my head in my hands and rubbed my scalp vigorously. "This is *beyond* fucked up."

Smith looked confused for a moment then asked, "Are you saying that Dan Young was Mayor Calhoun's nephew?"

Annie started to talk and I stopped her. "Mayor Calhoun was more than his uncle; he was his guardian and had been for years. Hilary was in and out of rehab programs, all paid for by Calhoun. After Abigail's death, Calhoun died a few months later by accidental overdose if I remember correctly. I remember Dan bragging about all the money he was getting, left to him by his uncle. Well, the joke was on him. Calhoun was in so much debt that his estate was worthless. There was only enough money left for Dan and his Mom to afford a tiny apartment on the other side of town. With Dan's mom back in the picture, he started using alongside her. I forgot about all this because Jason died a month later."

"Damn, that's messed up. But why torture Cassidy?" Smith asked what we all wanted to know.

Annie chimed in, "My guess is he wants to be paid off. He must have known you'd put it together. Or he's just cruel."

Annie might've been right. Maybe this was all about money, but I was worried that it was more than that. "Dan isn't logical and he has a nasty streak. Let's hope I can talk some reason into him."

"James, should we be looking into Calhoun's death? Accidental overdose sounds suspicious to me."

"Smith is right, James. We need to tread lightly. Her brother is a cop, right? Why don't you start there, maybe he can have some pull to get the case reopened."

I felt sick but agreed with them both. Cassidy wasn't going to handle this very well. There was no telling when Dan knew who Cassidy *really* was. Either way, she would feel like a fool. I would have to talk to Calvin to get his opinion before we made any moves on Dan. Though, I preferred to kill Dan. God help him if he was ever in my presence again. I pulled out my cell and called Cal.

"Cal, it's James. Are you free? I need to see you. No, my office would be best and the sooner the better. Thanks, man. See you soon." I set the phone on the table. "He's on his way. Smith, can you let security know he's coming?"

"No problem. Be right back."

Once Smith left the room, Annie placed her hand on mine and said, "You love her."

I turned to look at her. She was smiling broadly while studying me. I ignored her remark and started asking her some legal questions about restraining orders and such. We discussed those issues for quite a while.

"James, you love her."

"What is your problem?" *Why did everyone keep saying that?* I'd never been in love and probably wouldn't have known it if it had smacked me in the face.

"There's nothing wrong with it. She must be pretty spectacular if she's managed to tame the beast."

I sneered, remembering her nickname for me.

"Have you told her?"

"Annie, how do you know?"

"That you love her?" She waited for my nod. "Does she consume your thoughts, night and day? Would you walk on broken glass if she asked you to?"

"I'd kill for her, lay down my life if it meant she was safe."

"You love her." She patted my hand and smiled, "I'm so happy for you. You need to tell her."

There was a knock on the door and Cal walked in. He looked at Annie's hand on mine and raised his brows.

"That's my cue. I'll be in touch." She smiled at Cal before gathering her things and walked out the door.

Cal gave me a questioning look. "She's my attorney and a friend. Nothing to worry 'bout." I sat down on the couch and he did the same on the opposing one.

"Dude, what's going on? You've got me all suspicious." He was trying to smile while wringing his hands together.

I puffed out my cheeks as I exhaled. "I need you to think like a cop and not like a brother." He processed my words before nodding in understanding. "You've seen the papers." He nodded. "You know Dan."

"I know of him and his record of drug abuse. Of course I didn't find out until *after* the shooting. Cassidy wouldn't have been dating him had I known."

"I'm partly to blame there, too, man. Anyways. This is where it gets messy. Dan is the nephew of Brent Calhoun." I paused to give him a minute and I saw the change come over his face when he put it together. His jaw clenched as his eyes grew dark. "Calhoun had custody of Dan when this all went down fifteen years ago."

"Custody? Wouldn't Dan have been an adult?"

"I believe he was seventeen at the time, a year younger than me."

He got up and started pacing my office. I understood his frustration completely. "What the fuck? You're sure about this?" I confirmed. "Is this some revenge plot?"

"Not sure, but it seems that way. There's more." His shoulders sagged visibly. "I'm not sure if you know or not that Calhoun died a few months later." He said he knew. "Did you know his cause of death is listed as an accidental overdose?" That was news to him.

"Holy shit. You think he killed his uncle."

"*Suspect.* I've known Dan since we were kids. He's never sat well with me; there's always been something off about him. Calhoun gave Dan a life of prestige and privilege. I wouldn't doubt that if he felt threatened by your Mom…"

We both paled as my words resonated with us both. This just got worse and worse. Cal grabbed a bottle of water and started guzzling it down.

"Cal, I'm sorry. I didn't think this through."

"No. It's fine. You think he killed Calhoun *and* my mother?"

We sat in silence and I could see the cogs turning in his head.

"Cassidy needs to know. As much as I want to keep this from her, she has to know."

I began to object.

"Dude, you don't know everything."

Now I was the one chugging down some water. How could there possibly be more?

"How much did she tell you about Mom's death and what happened after?" I told him all the gory details as he dropped his head and tilted his neck from side to side eliciting a few pops and cracks.

"It broke her. She blamed herself for Mom's death for a long time. It was the most vulnerable time in any girl's life, but to have that guilt on her, too, destroyed her spirit. She was in therapy for years."

"Nothing wrong with therapy."

"Did you try to kill yourself?" I was speechless. "She swallowed half a bottle of pills, James. Dad found her just in time. Another ten minutes and she would've been gone."

"I had no idea. I never…"

"Don't hold it against her. She was so young and lost. She worked really hard for a long time to overcome those demons. If she finds out what we know now about Dan…well…I…she has to hear it from us sooner rather than later. The more prepared she is, the more proactive she can be in dealing with it."

"Okay, that makes sense. Shit, I wanted to keep this from her."

"I feel ya, dude. Is she home? I can follow you. Afterward, I'll call Dad to fill him in. God, this timing sucks; the wedding is less than three weeks away."

"She should be home."

"You need to be prepared for firestorm Cassidy. You got a glimpse last weekend, but she's got one hell of a temper."

"I'm sure it's not that bad."

He laughed, "Dude, I'm telling you. Prepare yourself."

I simply nodded before gathering my things.

twenty-six

Firestorm

~ CASSIDY ~

I WAS NUMB AND PISSED OFF. Mom was *pregnant?* I guess she really *was* planning on leaving Dad, *and* us. I didn't understand and I couldn't wrap my brain around it. I didn't think I wanted to understand. James must've thought I was a total basket case. After checking my cell phone and seeing I had no missed calls or texts, I decided to bake some brownies; chocolate would help. I cranked the stereo, grabbed my laptop and started browsing aimlessly while waiting for the brownies to finish.

The brownies were cooling on the stove when I heard the front door open. I watched as James walked in followed by Cal. *Lord help me.*

"Ever hear of knocking?" I looked back and forth between the two of them and they both looked guilty. "What the hell is going on? I know what this is and I'm not in the mood."

"Cass, we need to talk to you." Cal walked over to the couch, sat down on the end with his body turned toward me, and put his hand on my foot.

"About what?" Looking to James, who was being too quiet and eyeing me suspiciously, I grew nervous.

"I didn't want to tell you, but Cal said its best that you know and I'm starting to agree."

"You guys are scaring me. Just spit it out." I set my laptop down on the coffee table, placed my feet on the floor, and started ringing my hands in my lap.

They told me everything they knew about mom, Dan, and any other information they had at that moment. I was speechless.

Comatose.

After several minutes, all I heard was the gravely drone of their voices. James was kneeling in front of me with his hands on my calves. I stood up and his hands fell to the side as he let me pass. Cal grabbed my wrist as I tried to walk past him.

"Cassidy…"

"Don't." I jerked my wrist violently out of his hand and looked to James, "How long have you known this?" He looked to me and back to Cal. "HOW LONG?"

"I'm not sure what you're asking. We just put the pieces together today. If you're asking how long I've known Dan is bad news, the answer is since we were in high school together." He looked as distraught as he sounded.

"That's what you were trying to tell me that night wasn't it?" I started pacing between the living room and kitchen. "What did I do to deserve this, what did Holly do? I don't understand. If you had said something sooner maybe Holly would still be here."

"Cassidy, he had no way of knowing." Cal came to James's defense.

"Cassidy, you have to know that if I could change what happened that night I would."

Cal was right and I *knew* James would change it if he could, but I was unraveling, losing control. I was so goddamned mad at the universe, Dan and my mom. My blood was on fire and I could feel my body shaking as the anger took over.

~ JAMES ~

SHE WAS DEVASTATED, again, exactly what I didn't want. All of it was my fault. I couldn't bear to look her in the eyes, knowing the pain that would be on her beautiful face. Before Cal and I could take cover she started screaming and throwing everything and anything at us, the wall, and the floor. It was a hail of glass and knickknacks and throaty screams.

The shattering stopped as she walked toward the mantel and grabbed the beloved picture of her and Holly, examining it. Just when I thought she was about to throw it she put it back in its honorary spot. I looked to Cal and nodded. He seemed to understand.

"Cassidy, I'm going to go now. I love you. You're going to be alright." Looking back to me he said, "Please stay in touch. I'm not working tonight. I'm going to go see Dad and Lisa and fill them in."

Cal was gone and her shoulders were heaving as she tried to get her breathing under control. I walked toward her as glass crunched under my shoes. For the first time I noticed she was barefoot and there were spots of blood on the floor. I reached my arm out and gently took some strands of her hair between my fingers and she shuddered in response. Then, like a chain reaction, she started sobbing.

I cradled her to me before she sank to the glass covered floor; her sobs were so guttural that I was on the verge of begging her to stop. Her legs completely gave out so I lifted her in my arms. She was limp except for the sniffling and raspy breaths she let out between sobs. Her head was resting against my chest and her hands were lifeless in her lap. I turned to the stairs and started walking us to the bedroom and she began to quiet.

Setting her down on the end of the bed I said, "Stay here, I need to check your feet." I walked to the bathroom doorway and checked to see she hadn't moved. Rummaging through her cabinets I looked for bandages, ointment, and tweezers.

I sat down next to her with my supplies before placing her feet in my lap, examining them one at a time. Her left foot seemed to be fine. I ran my fingertips gingerly over the pads of her toes, the ball of her foot and the heel and didn't feel any slivers of glass and she didn't flinch. When I lifted her right foot, splotches of blood covered the bottom of it. I didn't even know where to start cleaning.

"Cassidy, I should clean this in the sink first." She was silent except for the small moan she released as I scooped her up.

I set her down on the counter and turned her to place her right foot in the sink. I turned the water to warm and let the water flow over her foot. The blood started to disappear from her foot and circled the drain. When the blood was all gone, I turned the water off before examining her foot again. I could see a glint of glass on the ball of her foot and I removed it easily with the tweezers. The bleeding seemed to have stopped, but I covered it with a bandage anyway.

She had another piece stuck in the pad of her big toe that I couldn't retrieve with the tweezers. I stuck her toe in my mouth and began sucking. That seemed to get her attention as she watched me with little emotion on her face. Eventually, I sucked the glass far enough out that I managed to grab it with the tweezers. It didn't bleed so I carried her back to the bed.

"I'm sorry." She wouldn't look at me, her voice was hoarse, but I was happy to hear her speak.

"You don't have to apologize. You have every right to be angry." We were lying down on the covers face to face, though she still wouldn't make eye contact. "I just want you safe and happy. I'm sorry it's so complicated."

"I don't deserve you." Her voice was cracking again.

"Shh, you're right, you deserve more." I pulled her to me as she clung to my shirt. I wrapped my arms and legs around her and soon I felt the calm coming over her, knowing she had to be utterly exhausted.

I went to get up to go clean the mess downstairs and she latched on to me tighter. I looked to her face, but her eyes were closed and I swore she was asleep.

She whispered, "No, please don't go. I need you, I love you, please don't leave me. Everybody leaves."

Her words were like a punch to the gut. "I'm not leaving you Cassidy...ever." I held her for quite some time before I drifted off to sleep with her, wondering if she knew she'd spoken the words to me out loud and not just in a dream.

I woke to find her curled in a ball on the other side of the bed. I noticed that it was dark and looked at my watch; it was past six p.m. I covered her with a blanket and headed downstairs, thinking about her whispered words 'I love you.'

I cleaned up all the glass and the mess. After searching her fridge, freezer, and pantry I began making dinner when I heard her gentle steps treading down the stairs. She poked her head around the corner like a child who had been recently scolded.

Realizing the mess was gone she said, "You didn't have to do that."

"Shut up, Cassidy." I raised my eyebrows at her, not sure if she was referring to the mess or to dinner. She looked lost in her own home, unsure of her next move. "Dinner's almost ready if you want to set the table."

She nodded, grabbed plates, silverware, and glasses and took them to the table. She sat down as I carried the food over. I scooped some pasta onto her plate, along with a chicken breast, before returning with sauce.

"It smells delicious."

Waiting for me to join her before taking a bite I said, "Your brother told me what happened to you after your mom died." The clank of the fork on her plate was deafening. "Cassidy, I don't want any more secrets. Cal told me out of concern."

Her face paled before it flushed and her spine went rigid. "Well *I* don't have any more secrets now, do I?" She placed her head in her hands and started rubbing her scalp.

"Cassidy, please talk to me."

"What is there left to say? You have your out. I'm the crazy girl who swallowed a bottle of pills. I understand if you want out. Go, go ahead. I'll survive. I always survive."

I pushed my chair out, standing abruptly, causing her to flinch. I squatted down in front of her and grabbed her chin from its hiding place, forcing her to look at me. "Listen closely. I'm not leaving you. We all have regrets, things we'd do differently. You're not going to do what you did again, are you?"

"I'm so embarrassed. Of course not! I was young and stupid. You have to know that." Her eyes were glassy and her chin was quivering.

"You truly are a phoenix, but you'll always be MY blackbird." I leaned in and kissed her gently. She hesitated for a moment before giving in. I pulled away leaving her breathless. "I want you to eat." I moved my plate and sat next to her, holding her hand while we finished our dinner.

~ CASSIDY ~

I PICKED AT my plate and ate as much as I could tolerate. After he cleared our plates, we curled up on the couch as James put a movie on. I couldn't even focus on it, and I tried. I even tried focusing on the sound of his heart as it beat below me, head resting on his chest.

"Cassidy?"

"Hmm?"

His hand moved over my back. Voice soft and concerned, he said, "Did you hear me?" I just shook my head. Sitting up and taking me with him, he pulled me to my feet. "Come on. Let's go to bed."

I didn't struggle knowing I was exhausted. Climbing into bed, I listened to him as he discarded his clothes. I knew it wasn't his fault, but I felt while he knew more than I wanted him to know about me, it threw up his huge wall between us. Curling up on my side of the bed, I felt his hand caress my shoulder.

"Cassidy, are you awake?"

Keeping my eyes shut tight, I remained quiet. I felt his lips on my shoulder before he rolled to his side of the bed. Soon his deep breathing notified me of his slumber. I lay in bed that night and struggled to sleep, to turn my brain off. James now knew a hell of a lot about me. More than I wanted him to know and probably more than I'd ever know about him.

Memories from those days, weeks, and months after my mother's death began to haunt me once again. The forgotten feelings and repressed memories were pulling me under to a place I didn't think I'd ever go back to. And I didn't know how to stop it. Everything felt like it was falling apart. The black hole was getting bigger beneath my feet and the pull was creeping up my body at a pace that terrified me. Soon it would swallow me up, making everything in my world black. My feelings, my vision, my thoughts, my heart, my soul... everything would once again become corrupt by the blackness of depression.

Somehow I managed to fall asleep because when I woke up he was gone. It didn't even really phase me. This was his M.O. most days. I rolled to my back and stretched my sore muscles. The dull throb in my foot reminded me of the damage I'd bestowed to my downstairs the day before. Embarrassed, I closed my eyes.

My phone chimed and when I picked it up from the end table, I saw a text from Cal waiting. I didn't even open it to read it. I knew I couldn't avoid him, he wouldn't let me, not for long anyway. But for now that's exactly what I was going to do. I was going to avoid them all. Call it shame, pride, anger, self-preservation, or something else. But I didn't care what anyone else thought. At least that's what I tried telling myself.

twenty-seven
Shattered

~ CASSIDY ~

I'D SENT JAMES A MESSAGE ASKING to be alone that night, and while he was hesitant, he finally agreed when I told him I was planning to hang with Cal. More texts from Cal came and I ignored them. Soon he'd either show up on my doorstep, or worse, involve Jane. I decided to text him quickly to appease him. I told him I was fine and that I was spending time with James. Yes, I lied. If Cal knew I was alone it would make things worse. And since Cal and James weren't really chummy, I figured I was safe from the lie.

I never dressed or showered that day. Walking around the house like a zombie, the darkness of my mood was almost welcome. I let the hopelessness sink in and take root. I couldn't walk anywhere in my townhouse without having memories of James. I wanted, no needed, to get out of there. It was already getting late. In the morning, I'd leave. To where, I wasn't sure.

I sent Cecily and Lena a message that I had a bad stomach bug and wouldn't be in to work. They both replied that it was no problem. Now how to deal with Cal and James. If I planned it right, I wouldn't have to deal with them. I'd be gone before either of them knew a thing. I packed a bag that night with everything I'd need, and then some.

After my shower in the morning I put the last of my toiletries in my bag and zipped it shut. The sound of the front door opening and closing caught me off guard. I heard his voice call my name and headed down the stairs. He couldn't know I was planning to leave, he'd never let it happen.

We nearly collided in the foyer and he smiled upon seeing me. He leaned in to kiss me and I recoiled. His green eyes narrowed on me and I avoided making eye contact. Gently, I pushed his arms off of me and walked around him toward the kitchen.

"Why are you here?"

The disdain in his voice was evident. "What do you mean why am I here?" I just ignored him and poured myself some juice. "Blackbird, what's wrong? Please tell me how I can help."

Sighing, I knew I had to hurt him, cut him deep for him to get the hint. "Don't call me that. I'm not your Blackbird." Hell, that's all I wanted to be. A blackbird could take flight and leave whenever it had the inclination to do so.

"Stop this right now!" His tone of voice wasn't lost on me.

Challenging him, "Stop what?" I glared at him. "Stop leaving before I wake in the morning! Or is that not a topic we can discuss?"

He ran his hands through those gorgeous milk chocolate locks and took a deep breath. "Why are you challenging me? This isn't about me. It's about you."

"Yes, I know. We can't ever talk about you. Only me. Well, you know everything there is to know now. Everything I didn't want you know." We just stared at each other. "Maybe you'd like to know how many men I've slept with, how many women..." His eyes got big. I'd said it to get a reaction. I'd never been with a woman before. "Maybe you want to know when I got my first period or the number of times my mother took her hands to me in anger."

"Cassidy, stop this."

"No, you stop it." I could tell he was battling with himself and how to respond. "I need you to leave. This isn't working." He flinched like I smacked him and took a step toward me. I circled around the dining table so that it was between us. The same table he'd fucked me on more than once.

"Come here!"

"I will not. Thanks to you I'm learning to let go of shit I don't need. I don't need you. I want you to leave." I still believe those words cut me deeper than they did him.

His face paled and I headed toward the door. I couldn't stand the pain on his face and thought I might throw up. I knew I needed him and that's what scared me. I hated my codependency and he was taking my new found independence from me and I had to stop it. Eyes downcast, I opened the door and motioned him toward it.

I was trembling when his body stood mere inches from mine. Watching as his hand moved, his thumb pushed my chin up until my eyes looked up at his. I tried avoiding eye contact and the only thing left to do was to close my eyes. But even I wasn't that childish.

"I'll give you space, but this isn't finished." My eyes searched his as the burn behind them became more evident. "We're not finished, Cassidy."

Jerking my chin out of his hold, I spit out, "We ARE finished. You need to leave."

He growled before he said what I wasn't expecting. "Ok, Blackbird. If this is really over then use your safe word."

Paralyzed, everything grew silent. Nothing but him and I in that moment. Say my safe word, that's all I had to do to truly end things with him? Panic seared through me. I just wanted to be alone for a few fucking days, run away and never come back. Shit! Even I didn't know what I wanted. I couldn't say that word and I wouldn't. I couldn't begin to fathom him ever doing anything so bad as to warrant me saying it.

Nodding, "Space it is."

Before I could stop it from happening, he cupped my face and kissed my forehead and then he was gone. That fucking forehead kiss broke me. Slamming the door, I pressed my face against the cool wood door and listened as he started his truck and drove away.

Barely able to breathe, I stumbled up the stairs and grabbed my bag. I put extra food in Chessa's dish and cleaned her litter box. She'd be good for a few days. Scribbling on a notepad, I left a note on the table in my foyer before walking out the door. I wasn't sure how long I was going to be gone, but wanted them to know I was ok, too. Them being Cal and yes, though I didn't want to admit it, James, too.

~ JAMES ~

SHE DIDN'T MEAN it. I knew that much. Had she meant it, she would've used her safe word. She knew the rules, my rules. Say *the* word and it would all end. I drove down the road away from her place and just couldn't let the unease go. Pulling over, I called Cal. Though I didn't want to admit it, there were some things he knew more about in regards to Cassidy.

"Hey, it's James." His next question threw me off.

"How was she last night?"

"What do mean last night? She told me she was with you last night."

His voice immediately became agitated as he grumbled, "Godammit Cass!"

Slamming on the gas, I turned my truck around and headed back to her place. "I'll call you back, Cal."

The light dusting of snow that we'd gotten the night before had already melted, my tire tracks already gone. Using my key, I rushed into the house and found it eerily quiet. She almost always has some kind of music playing. Now. Now it was utter silence.

I rushed up the stairs and found the bed disheveled, but nothing out of the ordinary. Striding into the bathroom, I took a close inventory of her toiletries. Her toothbrush was gone, as well as her brush and the shower caddy had a few items missing as well.

"Fuck!"

Yanking my cell out of my pocket, I dialed her number. It went straight to voicemail. I dropped my phone on her bed before I cracked the screen with my grip. Clenching my fists, I dropped down and slammed them on the wood floor.

Redialing Cal, I filled him in on what I'd found. As I made my way back down the stairs and to the foyer, that was when I saw the note. Dread filled me. My eyes scanned over it. There was no hint at all of where she may have gone.

"What does it say?"

I'd momentarily forgotten Cal was still on the phone with me.

Cal / James,
I need some time to be alone. Please respect that.
I'm ok, but I've never felt so lost, alone, and betrayed
in my life. While I know you're trying to protect me,
I'm not a little girl anymore. It's too much looking at
both of you right now. Please leave me be and let me
go just like I'm Letting Go.
~Cass

FUCK! Cal's thoughts were identical to mine and verbalized through the speaker so loudly that I pulled the phone away from my ear.

"I'm putting out an APB for her."

"Hold on Cal. Should we be that concerned? Maybe she really does just need space." I groaned. "And I may or may not have put a tracer on her car. I can find her, but we need to be smart about this. We both know if she finds out we're tracking her, she'll be infuriated."

"I don't care. Find her. She's good at covering and that's when I worry most about her. She's not ok. She'll deny it till she's blue in the face."

"Yeah, I'm starting to understand that. I'll find her."

I slid the phone back in my pocket and scanned the letter again. There was certainly shit we all needed to let go of, myself included. But she wasn't one of them. I crammed the note into my pocket and dialed Smith.

"I need you to trace her car."

epilogue

~ CASSIDY ~

Summer ~ Ten years earlier

CALVIN WAS HEADED HOME ON LEAVE. I hadn't seen him since my high school graduation the previous summer. He'd been overseas for several months and I had missed my big brother terribly. The couple of years with him gone had been really hard for me. I had become a recluse, for the most part, and focused on school and my part time job. I didn't have any real friends and that was ok with me. Friends, in my experience, came and went too easily for my taste.

I was parked in the short term parking lot, across the street from the baggage claim area exit. I watched as another slew of people started flooding out the doors. Squinting, I spotted two guys, in fatigues walking out the door together, with duffle bags over their shoulders. From this distance I couldn't tell them apart. They were about the same height and build, both blonde and tanned. *Cal brought a friend?*

When they crossed the street, and made it to the parking lot, I ran over to Cal and wrapped my arms around his neck. He dropped his bag and swung me in his arms as he croaked out, "You're choking me Cass."

"I am not!" He pried my arms off him and pushed me out to look me over.

"Look at you! Dad keeping his gun handy?"

"Shut up." I knew what he was referring to. I was a late bloomer, not really coming into my own until after high school. I wasn't gangly anymore, curves were beginning to take their shape on my body, a little too much so for my taste.

"I want you to meet my buddy, Paul. Paul, this is my baby sister Cassidy."

It was then that I really looked him over. He had a brilliant smile, was clean shaven and was sporting a buzz cut on top of his tall forehead. His eyes were striking. They were a deep blue, unlike mine which some called icy blue. My stomach flipped and I felt a twinge deep in my belly.

"Do I get a hug like that too?" I was dumbstruck and didn't know what to say to him.

"Back off dude. Baby sister." Cal elbowed him before picking up his bag and then headed for the bed of the truck.

I had brought dad's old Ford pickup, not expecting a third person. Not thinking, I willingly handed Cal the keys before he hopped up in the driver's seat. I got extremely nervous thinking about having to sit next to Paul. Who was I kidding? He was just being nice. No boy ever showed interest, and I was sure he'd be no different.

Playlist for Letting Go

White Houses by Vanessa Carlton
Shelf In The Room by Days Of The New
Bad Girlfriend by Theory Of A Deadman
Somewhere Out There by Our Lady Peace
I Stand Alone by Godsmack
Patience by Guns N' Roses
Music Of The Night by Andrew Lloyd Webber
Miracle by Foo Fighters
Crash Into Me by Dave Matthews Band
I Love It by Icona Pop
Stars by Grace Potter and the Nocturnals
Blackbird by Alter Bridge
It's Raining Men by The Weather Girls
Save A Horse by Big & Rich
Wild Horses by The Sundays
Wicked Game by Chris Isaak
Hey Baby by Pitbull, T-Pain
Blurred Lines by Robin Thicke
Sex On Fire by Kings Of Leon

More from J.M. Witt

The Anchored Hearts Series
Letting Go (Vol. 1)
Hiding Away (Vol. 1.5)
Letting Go of You (Vol. 2)
Fading Away (Vol. 2.5)
Letting Go of Us (Vol. 3)

The Blind Vows Series
Trust, Honor, Love: (Vol. 1)
Body, Heart, Soul: (Vol. 2)

Woodland Creek Series
Mina's Revenge

KinkyFodder Chronicles
My Secret Submission: (1)
My Secret Possession: (2)

About the Author

Residing in Metro Detroit, International Bestselling Erotic Author J. M. started writing poetry and short stories as a young girl. Rediscovering her love of reading, after having her fourth child, she started writing again. She also works full time as an Office Manager for a large landscaping company.

Letting Go, her first publication, was released in December 2013 and 10th novel was published in January 2017.

She enjoys music, time with friends, sarcasm, concerts, spending time with her children and husband, traveling, and getting lost in a good book.

And if you ask nicely, she might show you her flogger and let you sample it.

You can find her at
www.jmwittbooks.com
Twitter # wittymomauthor
www.facebook.com/jmwittbooks

Official playlist for Letting Go on Spotify

www.ingramcontent.com/pod-product-compliance
Lightning Source LLC
Chambersburg PA
CBHW030648260626
47157CB00007B/2542